"[A] well-plotted mystery . . . A must-read series to add to the ranks of culinary mysteries."   —*The Mystery Reader*

STATE OF THE ONION

"Pulse-pounding action, an appealing heroine, and the inner workings of the White House kitchen combine for a stellar adventure in Julie Hyzy's delightful *State of the Onion*."
—Carolyn Hart, author of *Dead by Midnight*

"Topical, timely, intriguing. Julie Hyzy simmers a unique setting, strong characters, sharp conflict, and snappy plotting into a peppery blend that packs an unusual wallop."
—Susan Wittig Albert, author of
The Darling Dahlias and the Confederate Rose

"From terrorists to truffles, mystery writer Julie Hyzy concocts a sumptuous, breathtaking thriller."
—Nancy Fairbanks, bestselling author of *Turkey Flambé*

"A compulsively readable whodunit full of juicy behind-the-Oval Office details, flavorful characters, and a satisfying side dish of red herrings—not to mention twenty pages of easy-to-cook recipes fit for the leader of the free world."
—*Publishers Weekly*

P9-CEU-852

Praise for the national bestselling
Manor House Mysteries

GRACE AMONG THIEVES

"Very believable and well researched . . . The characters are well drawn and believable . . . [A] reliable series with an interesting setting, a capable heroine, and interesting puzzle to work out." —*The Mystery Reader*

GRACE INTERRUPTED

"Hyzy has another hit on her hands." —*Lesa's Book Critiques*

"A most intriguing and engaging read."
—*Once Upon a Romance*

"Hyzy will keep you guessing until the end and never disappoints." —AnnArbor.com

GRACE UNDER PRESSURE

"Hyzy creates the well-researched and believable estate of Marshfield Manor, part mansion and part museum . . . Well-drawn characters like busybody secretary Frances, handsome landscape architect Jack, and stalking wannabe PI Ronny are supported by lively subplots, laying series groundwork to rival Marshfield Manor's own elaborate structure."
—*Publishers Weekly* (starred review)

"A strong, intelligent, and sensitive sleuth . . . Each page will bring a new surprise . . . A must-read for this summer!"
—*The Romance Readers Connection*

"Julie Hyzy's fans have grown to love Ollie Paras, the White House chef. They're going to be equally impressed with Grace Wheaton, a young, competent woman taking over a job she loves. Hyzy is skilled at creating unique series characters. Readers will love Grace." —*Chicago Sun-Times*

continued . . .

Praise for the *New York Times* bestselling
White House Chef Mysteries

AFFAIRS OF STEAK

"Hyzy shines in this volume. *Affairs of Steak* proves unequiv-
ocally that this series burns as bright as the sun during a sweltering D.C. summer." —*Seattle Post-Intelligencer*

"These are wonderful books, enjoyable to read, hard to put
down, and they make you really look forward to the next one
in the series." —*AnnArbor.com*

BUFFALO WEST WING

"[A] top-notch mystery writer. Adventure, intrigue, and a dash
of romance combine for a delicious cozy that is a delight to
read." —*Fresh Fiction*

"A captivating story from the very first page until the end . . .
Great job, Julie Hyzy. Another all-around great read!"
—*The Romance Readers Connection*

EGGSECUTIVE ORDERS

"The ever-burgeoning culinary mystery subgenre has a new
chef-sleuth . . . The backstage look at the White House proves
fascinating." —*Booklist*

"A quickly paced plot with a headstrong heroine and some
recipes featuring eggs all add up to a dependable mystery."
—*The Mystery Reader*

HAIL TO THE CHEF

"A gourmand's delight . . . Glimpses at the working class inside the White House . . . An engaging chef's cozy."
—*Midwest Book Review*

GRACE
TAKES OFF

JULIE HYZY

BERKLEY PRIME CRIME, NEW YORK

THE BERKLEY PUBLISHING GROUP
Published by the Penguin Group
Penguin Group (USA) Inc.
375 Hudson Street, New York, New York 10014, USA

USA | Canada | UK | Ireland | Australia | New Zealand | India | South Africa | China

Penguin Books Ltd., Registered Offices: 80 Strand, London WC2R 0RL, England
For more information about the Penguin Group, visit penguin.com.

GRACE TAKES OFF

A Berkley Prime Crime Book / published by arrangement with the author

Copyright © 2013 by Julie Hyzy.
All rights reserved. No part of this book may be reproduced, scanned, or distributed in any
printed or electronic form without permission. Please do not participate in or encourage piracy
of copyrighted materials in violation of the author's rights. Purchase only authorized editions.

Berkley Prime Crime Books are published by The Berkley Publishing Group.
BERKLEY® PRIME CRIME and the PRIME CRIME logo are
trademarks of Penguin Group (USA) Inc.

For information, address: The Berkley Publishing Group,
a division of Penguin Group (USA) Inc.,
375 Hudson Street, New York, New York 10014.

ISBN: 978-0-425-25966-5

PUBLISHING HISTORY
Berkley Prime Crime mass-market edition / July 2013

PRINTED IN THE UNITED STATES OF AMERICA

10 9 8 7 6 5 4 3 2 1

Cover illustration by Kimberly Schamber.
Cover design by Rita Frangie.
Interior text design by Laura K. Corless.

This is a work of fiction. Names, characters, places, and incidents either are the product
of the author's imagination or are used fictitiously, and any resemblance to actual persons,
living or dead, business establishments, events, or locales is entirely coincidental.
The publisher does not have any control over and does not assume any responsibility for
author or third-party websites or their content.

If you purchased this book without a cover, you should be aware that this book is
stolen property. It was reported as "unsold and destroyed" to the publisher, and neither
the author nor the publisher has received any payment for this "stripped book."

ALWAYS LEARNING   **PEARSON**

To my favorite English teacher,
Donna Wojtulewicz Sifling, who encouraged
my writing when I needed it most.

Acknowledgments

I adore visiting historic mansions—always have. Marshfield has become the manor house of my dreams, and although I'll never own anything like it in the physical sense, I'm delighted to be able to wander its rooms, and even better, to invite readers to join me in discovering its secrets.

So many friends have helped me get details just right for Grace's newest adventure. My good friends Hannah Dennison (Vicky Hill Exclusives Mysteries) and Betty Hechtman (Crochet Mysteries) provided lots of valuable information about charter airline travel. And major thanks to "The Poison Lady," Luci Zahray, for her pharmaceutical suggestion.

Thanks to my lovely eldest daughter, Robyn, who helped me out with art-related questions; my lovely middle daughter, Sara, for (as always) being the first to read and critique; and to my lovely youngest daughter, Biz, for copyediting suggestions as well as coming up with a fun title. We weren't able to use that one, but it gave us a chance to giggle. I love my girls!

Many thanks to my blog sisters, The Cozy Chicks (www.cozychicksblog.com), and my friends at CozyPromo. It's wonderful to be part of such helpful and supportive groups. Writing may be a solitary endeavor, but as friends we've become a team.

I am absolutely thrilled to be working with my wonderful editor, Michelle Vega, again. I'm grateful for, and delighted by, her ever-enthusiastic support. I owe a debt of gratitude to copyeditor Erica Rose at Berkley Prime Crime, who shows enormous patience with me despite my missteps with commas. And, as always, many thanks to my agent, Paige Wheeler, who negotiates contracts with cheerful aplomb.

To my family: Curt, Robyn, Sara, Biz, Paul, Mitch, Grandma, and Claudia—my deepest gratitude for your unwavering support. Love you!

Chapter I

HOT AND FRAGRANT, THE AROMA OF RIPENING
olives enveloped me the moment the limo door opened. I
boosted myself from the shadowed leather backseat, blinking against the sudden brightness of the lazy afternoon sun.
Our ride through Italy's Tuscan countryside had been
chilly, cushioned bliss, but the moment I crunched one foot
on the gravel outside, I was engulfed again by the day's
oppressive heat.

Bennett Marshfield, my boss and benefactor of this
whirlwind excursion, had come around from the other side
and now offered me his hand to help me alight. How he
managed to remain so cool and stately when beads of sweat
exploded at my hairline, I didn't know, but I accepted his
assistance as the chauffeur held the vehicle's door.

Bennett turned to him. "Will you be driving us to the
airport tomorrow?"

The elderly driver smiled. "It will be my great pleasure,"
he answered in heavily accented English. As he trotted to

the limo's trunk to retrieve our luggage, he added, "Signor Pezzati has arranged for me to be available whenever you have need."

Bennett thanked him as we made our way up the path to the grand villa before us. The patchwork of stones beneath our feet had been worn to a shiny, flat surface over the centuries, making me wonder about the warriors who had trod this path before us.

"Some place Nico's got here, eh?" Bennett said under his breath, though there was no one nearby to overhear.

Built in the fourteenth century and renovated countless times since, this former fortress was now home to one of Bennett's oldest friends, Nico Pezzati. Smaller than Marshfield Manor—though not by much—it sprawled atop this hillside like a cat sunning itself on the back of a lush outdoor sofa.

My pale pink blouse—the one a saleswoman claimed would "breathe" but rather saw fit to absorb moisture from the air and deliver it directly to my skin—clung for dear life against the front of my chest and between my shoulder blades. As Bennett and I took the uneven stone stairs up to the home's front doors, sweat rivulets raced down to pool at my waist. Another two minutes out here and I'd be drenched in my own perspiration. What a lovely way to meet Bennett's old school chum.

To my great relief, the moment we reached the top step, thick mahogany doors swung wide, and a delicious rush of cold air swirled around us.

A young man in a crisp, white shirt greeted us in enthusiastic Italian. "*Benvenuto,* signore *e* signorina." He flashed a smile that contrasted against his rich bronze complexion and switched to English. "Signor Pezzati anticipates eagerly your arrival."

"Thank you," I said as I stepped deeper into the oasis of cool. "We are very happy to have been invited."

I gestured toward the car, but before I could voice my question, the young man answered me. "Your belongings will be sent upstairs ahead of you."

"Thank you," I said again. "And you are?"

The young man pressed his fingers against his chest. "I am Marco," he said with a rousing, rumbling *R*. Sweeping his hand in front of us, he stepped backward, allowing us to pass. "*Prego*, please enter."

As we'd driven up, I'd been struck by the villa's austere appearance, tabby cat–colored bricks stretching outward and upward in bland, undulating monochrome. No doubt the structure had served well in its fortress days, but I'd had my doubts about how it would fare in its contemporary role as a Tuscan home for an elderly billionaire.

The moment I stepped inside the soaring foyer, however, I sucked in a breath of surprise. Yellow reflective walls, set ablaze by the sun streaming in from high skylights, made me believe the room was lined in gold. "Oh," I said. Words escaped me, and I realized by Marco's smile that he was used to such a reaction.

The floor, made of cobalt-blue tile, glimmered cool like a river. Marco urged us to follow it—and him—through a narrow walkway that led deeper into the home.

"Signor Pezzati wishes to visit with you on the terrazzo," Marco said as we traversed a shadowed room where draperies were shut against the day's relentless sunshine. The room featured painted wooden ceilings, thick green wall hangings, and a coat of arms displayed proudly above a fireplace that was almost as large as my entire kitchen. I knew Bennett to be an avid collector of antiques and priceless artwork, but what I could see in this room alone made me curious about how the Marshfield stash would stack up against Nico Pezzati's. Decorated to within an inch of its life, there was almost nowhere in this room for my eyes to rest as I took in the walls, the furniture, and the knickknacks. Every horizontal space was crowded with pieces, some of which, even from this distance, I recognized as extremely rare.

Bennett maintained small talk with Marco as we made our way toward the terrazzo. "How long have you worked with Nico?" he asked.

"I am here for one year," he said. "Signor Pezzati has been diligent in his teaching of me, and I have learned much of your language. You do not find I am difficult to comprehend?"

"Not at all," Bennett assured him.

Marco flashed a glance over his shoulder, silently seeking my opinion. I smiled at his eagerness to impress us. "You are far, far ahead of where I would be after only one year of Italian," I said. "You've made remarkable progress."

"I hope to visit America someday."

"Be sure to let us know when that day comes," Bennett said. "You will be most welcome at Marshfield."

We followed Marco along a circuitous path through several more rooms where the temptation to stop and examine the riches on display was overwhelming. I slowed my pace to be able to take in the plump furnishings, the gold-leaf walls, and the delicious, musty scent of history that permeated every inch of this home. I guessed that Villa Pezzati was about two-thirds the size of Marshfield Manor, but it easily housed three times the amount of treasures.

Marco noticed me lagging. "There will be time," he said with a knowing grin. "As our guests, you are to stay in this home as your own."

Marco stepped aside as we entered a wide, airy room obviously added on centuries after the fortress years. Decorated in buttery yellows and white, this room had a far more contemporary feel than had any of the others thus far. A wall of windows faced northwest, and I spotted our elderly host, his hunched back to us, reclining under a terra-cotta awning's shade. Two men hovered nearby. One stood, almost at attention, on the white-and-gray-patterned flagstone floor. The other looked as though he was having an argument with Pezzati. He paced and gesticulated, his raised voice coming through loud and clear. For all the good it did: Everything he shouted was in Italian.

"Prego," Marco said. He slid open one of the glass doors to allow us outside, silencing the pacing man's diatribe. Though he worked hard to arrange his face into a welcoming smile, the man fell short in quelling the blaze of his glare. I glanced to Bennett, who kept his expression neutral.

Bennett and Nico had been boys together at school and had maintained their friendship over many decades. The difference in the two men struck me as Nico struggled to his feet to greet us. The other man, who appeared to be a servant of some sort, reached forward to help the elderly gent.

I'd dreaded the idea of returning outdoors to the hotbox for this reunion, but I was pleasantly surprised. There was an awning above, and an outdoor air-conditioning system, the likes of which I'd never seen before, that wafted cool breezes across the luxurious patio. The view was spectacular. We were surrounded on all sides by wide-trunked trees, the captivating scent of sun-warmed soil, and the ever-present aroma of olive oil filtering through. "This is heaven," I said.

"Indeed," Bennett agreed. He crossed the terrazzo in three strides, preventing Pezzati from stepping away from his massive cushioned wicker chair, the back of which he clung to with bony fingers. "Nico," Bennett said warmly, reaching to grasp his friend's free hand. "It's been too long."

Bennett had provided a little background on our trip out here. Nico Pezzati had inherited his considerable wealth as a young man and had managed his many interests from a

New York City penthouse up until about fifteen years ago. Widowed young, and tired of the frenetic American pace, he'd relocated to Italy, near where his parents had been born. He had two grown children, a son he had disowned shortly after he'd moved here, and a daughter, whom Bennett barely remembered.

As he'd provided this history, Bennett had adopted a wistful, resigned look. "We lost touch over the years, Gracie. I think Nico was ashamed of his son. Having managed so much wealth so successfully himself, he expected no less from his progeny. His disappointment in Gerard's irresponsible behavior was too much for him."

"And they have no contact at all anymore?" I'd asked.

Bennett had given a thoughtful sigh. "I should be a better friend to Nico," he'd finally said. "We were so close so many years ago, and I'm beginning to grasp how little we've kept in touch." Turning to me again, he forced a smile. "Neither of us is getting any younger. Maybe this trip will allow us to reconnect."

I'd patted his arm. "I'm sure it will."

Now, as Bennett introduced me, Nico took my hand in both of his. He was probably my height, but seemed shorter due to his stooped posture. Behind his age-spotted, sun-scarred face, I could see the handsome man he'd once been. Deep smile lines and twinkling eyes led me to believe his spirit embraced a more youthful existence than his body allowed.

"Grace," Nico said, holding tight. He gave me a surreptitious once-over. "Your name suits you."

"It's my great pleasure to meet you," I replied. "Bennett has told me a lot about your adventures at school."

He chuckled. "I hope he hasn't told you *everything*," he said. "I have a reputation to uphold." Letting go of my hand, he turned to Bennett with a glimmer of understanding in his eye. "When you told me that you would be accompanied by an *assistant*, I confess I had entirely different expectations. You are still quite the active man, aren't you, my good friend?"

Bennett cleared his throat. "You misunderstand. Grace is my n—"

"Curator," I volunteered, realizing that by cutting Bennett off I was probably feeding directly into Nico's assumptions. I couldn't allow myself to be identified as Bennett's niece, though. Not yet, anyway. Not until we knew for certain, and we both understood that day might never come. "And estate manager," I continued. "I'm in charge of the artifacts, the tourism, and the grounds."

"Ah," Nico said in a gracious tone that made it clear he didn't believe a word I'd said, "my mistake. Allow me to present some of *my* assistants. They are nowhere near as lovely as you are, Grace, but I am in need of a different sort of comfort these days."

As though to emphasize his words, Nico lifted his free arm and the man who hadn't been arguing with him grabbed it and helped lower the elderly man back into his chair.

"Please, join me. Sit," Nico said. He gestured blithely to the other man. "That is Angelo, and this"—he pointed up toward the fellow who was now arranging pillows—"is Gianfranco. Neither man speaks any English, although I believe they've begun to catch on to a couple of words here and there."

At the sound of their names, both men made eye contact with us and gave a small nod of acknowledgment. As Bennett and I sat, forming a small *U*-shaped conversational area around a low, painted table, I studied the assistants. The larger of the two, Angelo, the one who had been arguing with Nico as we'd approached, stood about fifteen feet away from us, hands crossed in front of his waist, his pale face impassive, eyes staring straight ahead like a soldier who had just been told, "At ease."

Gianfranco, by contrast, was slightly built with a darker complexion. His glare bounced from us to Angelo, to Nico, to the house. His fingers were long and thin and in constant motion, much like his furtive glances. He attempted to re-fill Nico's wineglass, but when he lifted the yellow-and-blue pitcher to pour, nothing came out. Gianfranco barked an order at Marco, who disappeared back inside the house without a word of complaint.

Bennett and Nico faced one another, with me between them. I couldn't help but notice Nico's keen interest in my presence. "Your Marshfield Manor is doing well?" he asked Bennett, keeping his attention on me.

"Grace has been instrumental in boosting attendance," Bennett said. "She's been the best thing to happen to Marshfield in a long time."

"Yes, I can see that," Nico said. "And apparently the best thing that has happened to you, my friend."

Bennett sat forward. "I know you don't mean to offend, Nico, but you must stop this at once. Grace is my trusted assistant." He shot me an apologetic smile. He'd warned me that Nico was—in his words—*saltier* than most of his con-temporaries. "She is like a daughter to me." With a twinkle in his eye, he added, "Or a dear niece. Your innuendo is making us both uncomfortable, and I'm certain that is not your intent."

Nico listened, watching me with a shrewd expression. "I am deeply sorry," he said finally. "I am but a lonely old man in a broken-down body who lives vicariously through my friends' adventures. Please accept my apology."

"Of course," I replied. Without wanting to make too big a deal out of another pressing matter, I ran my hands down my skirt. "May I impose on you, Signor Pezzati?" I made a gesture toward the house. "Is there a place to freshen up?"

He smiled widely. "Again, I apologize. I was so eager to greet my good friend that I neglected to have Marco see to your needs." He waved to Gianfranco and spoke to him in Italian. The slim man smiled and beckoned me to follow.

When I returned a few minutes later, Nico regarded me with interest. I couldn't decipher his expression. But I didn't have long to wonder. Nico lifted a hand to summon Angelo. The brooding man was at his boss's side instantly. Speaking Italian, Nico pointed to the two of us and issued commands that I didn't understand. Angelo watched us both as he listened. The big man asked a question Nico didn't have an answer for, while staring at me with a glint of interest. After our host gave an elegant shrug and smile, Angelo nodded and left.

Nico explained. "I told him to have your luggage taken to a second guest room. Again, my apologies. When you arrived, my servants acted on an assumption and delivered all your belongings to a single room."

That would have been awkward. "Thank you for your understanding," I said. "May I trouble you to know what Angelo asked? I may not speak the language, but he seemed curious about something."

Nico smiled. "You are an astute observer," he said. "Angelo wanted to know if you are married. I told him I didn't know the answer to that. Are you?"

"What difference could that possibly make?"

"Angelo is not a man who hesitates," Nico said. "He moves quickly when he sees something he wants. Your wholesome American beauty has intrigued him, my dear. If you are not otherwise spoken for"—Nico chuckled—"or even if you are, Angelo would like to get to know you better."

"But . . ." I reminded him. "I don't speak Italian, and Angelo doesn't speak English."

"Who needs words when you communicate in the language of love?"

For the first time since we'd arrived in Europe, I wished we were on our way home.

Chapter 2

BENNETT MADE EYE CONTACT WITH HIS friend. "It would be best if Angelo kept his distance."

Nico nodded. "I will see to it that he does."

Angelo keeping his distance was as much as I could hope for. At the moment, I was doing my best to avoid thinking about the big man handling my luggage upstairs.

"He appears to have quite a temper," Bennett continued. "When we arrived, we obviously interrupted an argument. He seemed rather agitated with you."

"Bennett." Nico's face creased into a wide smile. "Like you, I was born and raised in the United States. I raised my family there as well. I understand your concern, but here in this gorgeous country we are less afraid to share our emotions. Angelo speaks loudly and with unrestrained gestures, yes, but he is kindhearted and loyal to me. He will do whatever I ask of him, even if he does not always agree. As will Gianfranco."

As though summoned, the slim man stepped forward.

Nico waved him back, and I was struck by the level of his servants' attentiveness. Back home, Bennett maintained a staff of personal assistants, but he'd never tolerate this amount of in-your-face responsiveness. Bennett preferred to do things on his own as much as possible, and I wondered if Nico's limited mobility now owed itself to years of dependence on others to complete simple tasks.

"I'm glad to hear it," Bennett said, but the concern in his expression didn't fade. Whatever we'd disrupted had been far more anger-filled than our host was letting on. Bennett kindly did not push the issue.

"Your trip up to my home was uneventful, I take it?" Nico asked as Marco returned bearing a tray with a pitcher of wine, fresh glasses, and a plate laden with cheeses and fruit.

"Thank you very much for picking us up," Bennett said. Marco poured wine all around and set out small plates on the low table before us. Surveying his work, he gave a quick, smiling bow, and returned inside. "This is a beautiful country. Grace and I have been enjoying ourselves immensely."

Bennett and I had been in Europe for two weeks and were set to depart for home tomorrow after spending the night here at Villa Pezzati. The first half of our trip had been devoted to touring France; the second week, Italy. The absence of responsibility, coupled with a change of scenery, had done wonders for my soul, but I found myself eager to be home again.

"My staff is at your service," Nico said. He grabbed a handful of grapes and sat back against his chair's plump cushion. He began tossing grapes into his mouth, one at a time. "Now, what can you tell me about our friends back home? There are not so many still living anymore, are there?" The question was rhetorical. He chewed his grapes thoughtfully, and mused, "You and I are getting old."

To me, Bennett wasn't old. Though in his seventies, Bennett kept fit and trim, and from the time I'd begun working for him at Marshfield Manor I'd been impressed with his sharp wit, his vigor, and his strength. I admired him, possibly even more than he realized.

"You remember Bill?" When Nico nodded, Bennett leaned forward to talk about an old school buddy who had recently relocated to Florida in order to launch a new hotel chain.

I let my mind wander as the two men caught up. We were surrounded by a vista of gorgeous green, rolling hills, and a scent that made me realize how hungry I'd gotten. I reached for a few morsels of cheese, took a sip of wine, and reminded myself to enjoy the moment. We would be going home soon, and this fabulous vacation—we'd spent more time playing hooky than working—would be over soon. As much as I missed Bootsie, my little kitten, and my room-mates, Scott and Bruce—who were no doubt spoiling her rotten—this getaway had provided me precious time to think. I'd contemplated my recent foolishness in matters of the heart, Jack's abrupt resignation, and what life in Embers-towne would be like now that Bennett's stepdaughter was moving in.

Hillary's announcement had been the proverbial straw. Rather than allowing me to crack, however, Bennett had whisked me away from the angst, and although it had been only two weeks, I felt as though we'd been gone for months. The weight of a recent tragedy and my role in it had pressed its angry bulk against my slim shoulders, nearly breaking me. Bennett had claimed he wanted to travel, but we both knew this trip was more for my well-being than anything else. For the first time in a long time, I'd been unburdened. I'd had no responsibilities for two whole weeks. We'd left my able assistant, Frances, in charge and she'd called us only once so far—to assure us that everything was going well and that she was running a tight ship. Of that I had no doubt.

Tomorrow, however, we'd fly back on the jet Bennett had chartered for this trip. I couldn't avoid reality forever, but I could enjoy the respite while it lasted. I took a deep sip of the dry white wine, and marveled again at the cool breeze that made this outdoor space a tiny bit of heaven.

"I do not care to speak of him," Nico said. My ears perked up and I tuned back into the conversation.

Bennett leaned forward along the arm of his wicker chair. "It's been how many years, Nico? He's your son. I remember when Gerard was just a—"

"Those days are gone. He betrayed the family and he must pay for his sins. He has not tried to contact me in fourteen years," Nico added. "I do not even think of him anymore. He is dead to me. My daughter, Irena, is my only living child now."

Bennett and I exchanged a glance. In his expression I read the same thought that had flashed through my brain: The fact that Nico had been specific enough to say "fourteen" rather than a vague "more than ten" or "almost fifteen" years since Gerard had contacted him led me to believe that his son's betrayal maintained a tighter grip on Nico's heart than he cared to admit.

"I'm sorry to hear that," Bennett said. "I remember him as a boy—"

Nico sliced the air with his hand as tears welled in his eyes. Blinking, he waved to Gianfranco, who leapt to attention. "More wine." Nico's voice was rusty, and no one needed a refill, but Gianfranco dribbled a little into each glass nonetheless.

"Tell me about Irena," Bennett said, gently changing the subject. "The last time I saw her, she was still very young."

Nico seemed lost in thoughts of his son. "Irena will be here momentarily. Angelo will fetch her on his way back.

She's eager to meet you both, but wanted to give us old men a chance to reconnect before she joined us."

To me, his words were a subtle chastisement, a reminder that I was not part of their long friendship. I shifted in my seat.

"I would be happy to stroll your beautiful property," I said, "to allow you to talk in private."

He opened his mouth to answer, but was interrupted by Angelo's return. The big man stepped aside to allow a woman—Irena, no doubt—to hurry over to Nico's side. She was curvy and tall with sun-kissed skin and blonde streaks in her dark hair. She leaned around the edge of his chair, placing her cheek against his weathered one. Though not beautiful in the traditional sense, a flirty combination of lush lips and sparkling eyes gave Irena the sort of playful, interesting face that makes men twist for a second look. She had to be at least forty years old, but with her skinny jeans, wedge sandals, and model-tousled hair, she appeared closer to my age.

"These must be your American guests," she said with a luminous smile and the barest hint of an Italian accent. "Signor Marshfield? It's been a very long time since I have seen you."

"It has," Bennett said as he and I stood to shake hands with our newcomer. "You were a very young girl last time we met."

"With braces on my teeth and pigtails in my hair," she added, placing a palm against her eyes in mock shame. "I look at pictures from those years and cringe." Everything about the woman was polished, from her nails to her cool, firm handshake. "I am so pleased to make your acquaintance," she said to me. To both of us, she added, "Father has talked about nothing else but your visit here, for weeks."

She joined us at the low table as we resumed our seats, and in moments, Gianfranco had poured her a glass of wine and again refreshed all of ours. He and Angelo retired to chairs that had been set off to the far side of the patio. Both men kept a close eye on our group.

Irena's arrival had spared me the discomfort of feeling as though I was infringing on Bennett and Nico's private time. She crossed her long legs and patted her father on the knee as she addressed us. "This patio is my father's favorite place in the entire villa. He shares it only with those he truly cares about."

"We are honored," Bennett said.

"Father says that you two have known each other since you were boys?" she asked, the lilt in her tone a clear request for tales about her dad's youth. "When we were little, he told stories. . . ." She caught herself, possibly at her inadvertent reference to her brother. Her cheeks grew pink and she flashed a worried look toward her father, who apparently didn't notice her slipup. "I remember begging him always to tell more about the extraordinary Marshfield. Is that where you live?"

Clearly pleased to be able to share, Bennett nodded. "Marshfield is a magnificent home," he said without conceit, "but for a child, it was wondrous. Nico—that is, your father—and I spent hours there exploring hidden passages and disappearing whenever we got into trouble."

I thought about those secret passages and wondered how many more there were that hadn't been revealed to me yet.

"Except for stories about his adventures with you, we . . . er, I . . . know so little about his childhood."

"Oh bosh," Nico said. "You know all you need to."

Irena's eyes sparkled, and she shifted to face Bennett. "Tell me, Signor Marshfield, is it true that my father was a scoundrel when he was young?"

"Who told you such a thing?" Nico demanded.

Gripping his fingers, she leaned toward him. "Father, I'm only teasing," she said quietly. With an apologetic look to us, she tried again. "I would love to hear all about my father's boyhood."

Unmoved by her explanation, Nico turned his head and stared off into the distance.

Irena let go of his hand, lacing her fingers across her knee. "As you know, I was born in America and lived much of my life there, but I have taken to this country"—at this, she opened her arms wide, as though to encompass Italy in its entirety—"with all my heart."

"You speak the language, then?" Bennett asked.

"Fluently. I studied in high school in New York, but there's nothing to compare with living among native Italians. This country has been very kind to me." She slid a sideways glance at Nico, who still seemed miles away. "As it has been for all of us."

Nico worked his jaw, then made as if ready to stand. At once Gianfranco and Angelo were at his side. "Signor?" Gianfranco asked.

Nico brushed him away. "I don't need your assistance to go to the washroom," he said. "Not yet, at least."

The two manservants looked to Irena, who directed them silently. Her request was pointed and unmistakable: *Keep an eye on him.*

Nico took several excruciating moments to unfold himself and get to his feet. Once there, he looked around in panic until Gianfranco rushed forward with a walker he'd hidden off to the side. Although his face was in profile, I read a combination of fear and fury on Nico's face: embarrassed to be seen needing help to get around, relief when his fingers finally wrapped around the apparatus's handle.

Irena watched them go, and the moment the glass door slid shut behind them, she sighed deeply and turned to us. "My father is a wonderful man, but he suffers. And often, he forgets to be polite. You are our first visitors in a long time, and I'd hoped he could stay cheerful at least while you were here." Her eyes closed, briefly. "I apologize if he's been difficult."

"Not difficult," Bennett said, "though I can't help but worry about him. How long has he had trouble getting around by himself?"

Irena wrinkled her nose. "It has been gradual," she said. The three of us were alone on the patio, but she lowered her voice anyway. "He could do more if he allowed himself to, but ever since Gerard—" She pulled her lips in, shot a wary glance at me, then continued, speaking primarily to Bennett. "My father doesn't like us to speak of Gerard, but he's my brother and I miss having him around." She paused, looking hopeful. "You've been my father's friend for longer than I've been alive. . . ."

Bennett breathed deeply, and sat back. "Nico shut me down when I wanted to talk about Gerard," he said. "And Grace and I are only here for the day. We return to the United States tomorrow."

Irena leaned forward to pat him gently on the knee. "I understand."

"If I'd known the situation, I could have planned to spend more time with your father. He may have come around. As it is," Bennett continued, "our charter leaves in the morning. If I weren't required to be at a board meeting the day after . . ." He shot me a look Irena wouldn't understand—Bennett had successfully steered a tricky buy-out of another company and this meeting was key to final negotiations. "If it weren't for that, I'd consider changing plans. I'm sorry."

"There is nothing to be sorry for," she said.

"Maybe," I piped up, "you could show me around the villa, Irena. That could give Bennett and your father a chance to talk in private. Perhaps he would be more open to discussing your brother if he felt safe?"

She gave a sad smile. "I will suggest it to him, but I

wouldn't be surprised if he refuses. He has made plans for your visit here, and my father is rather set in his ways. Deviation will be met with scorn. But if his strength holds out and he's still alert after dinner, then you and I"—her eyes lit up—"will find our own fun. As you can imagine, I have very little opportunity for girl talk among all these men."

Spending my last night in Italy with a relative stranger didn't appeal to me, but if it gave Bennett the opportunity to talk with his old friend . . . "That would be great," I said, hoping I sounded convincing.

Chapter 3

THE DOOR BEHIND US OPENED, SIGNALING Nico's return and preventing further discussion of Gerard. Bennett and I turned to see our host framed by the doorway and accompanied by Angelo and Gianfranco, who eased past their boss to stand attentively outside.

"Bennett," Nico called, beckoning with one gnarled hand as he held tightly to his walker with the other, "I have something of interest to show you." Almost as an afterthought, he added, "You girls may come, too."

Nico shuffled in place, turning his back to us as Gianfranco swooped in to tidy up our table. With an apologetic smile, he reached for our wineglasses, piling them and our untouched snacks onto a tray.

I thought I heard Bennett chuckle. "Looks like you have no choice."

"Come, come," Nico said as we crossed the threshold. Indoors, we were greeted by a dark-haired, mustachioed man. His prayerful hands tapped a quick rhythm close to his lips, and his glinting, deep-set eyes were harsh, conflicting with his obsequious smile. I disliked him on sight.

Behind me, Irena unsuccessfully muffled a groan. "I didn't realize you were visiting today, Cesare," she said as she came around me to embrace the short man, kissing him on both cheeks.

"So pleasant to see you again, my dear." Cesare's heavily accented English was luxurious and soft, in stark contrast to his firm grasp of Irena's upper arms.

With effort, she shook him off. "What a wonderful surprise."

Unfazed, his eyes glittered. "But I was certain your father told you I would be here to meet with his lovely guests." Before she could respond, he said, "No matter. You must have simply forgotten." He turned his attention to us and continued smoothly, "And you must be the venerable Bennett Marshfield." He gave a brisk bow. "I am honored. Cesare Sartori, at your service."

After Bennett introduced me, Cesare took my hand in his warm, pudgy one, and explained his presence. "My services have been engaged for this special evening." He bowed again and I realized who he reminded me of. The guy was a doppelgänger for the actor David Suchet, who so elegantly depicted Agatha Christie's Hercule Poirot on TV—except Cesare was much oilier.

From the back of the room, Angelo pulled out a wheelchair and helped Nico get settled into it, adjusting the older man's positioning and locking in place the metal footrests.

Through it all, Cesare kept talking. "I am the proprietor of a happily successful auction house not far from the Ponte Vecchio. From time to time, I am fortunate to acquire priceless items on behalf of Signor Pezzati. Most of what you will encounter here this evening has come from my acquisitions. Because my esteemed client no longer possesses the mobility, nor the vision, to do so, he has asked me for, and it will be my humble privilege to provide, commentary on some of the incomparable treasures you will see this evening."

As Cesare went on, Irena pulled Angelo off to the side to whisper in angry Italian, while Nico tried to get a word in edgewise, wagging a finger at them both from his low vantage point in the wheelchair. I wouldn't have been able to understand what they were saying even if I could make out the words, but none of them looked particularly happy. Cesare appeared unruffled by their lively discussion, expounding—with excessive animation—on how he dealt with only the most respected clients and vendors and how his name was accepted like gold throughout all of Tuscany.

I suspected he would continue with the self-admiration all night if Nico hadn't interrupted him, bellowing, "Just get on with it, man, before we sprout roots and are stuck here forever."

Cesare's mustache twitched ever so slightly. "Follow me." He clasped his fingers together in front of his chest and, with an odd forward-tilting posture, led us deeper into the massive home.

We returned to the dark room Bennett and I had passed through earlier. Marco had evidently been apprised of our impending arrival, because the draperies had been thrown open and sunshine filtered between dust motes that danced in its rays, bringing the cluttered, treasure-strewn room into sharp focus.

Cesare made his way first to the coat of arms hanging over the massive stone fireplace. He pointed upward, telling us the story of the origins of the Pezzati family and how experts from his "happily successful" auction establishment had been able to trace the lineage and reclaim heirlooms that had been lost or stolen over the centuries.

Next, Cesare talked about the tapestries that had been recovered, then more about how he'd overseen the authentication of each one and how his team of experts was among the most respected in the world. I stifled a yawn. At Marshfield, we had hundreds of tapestries and our own team of experts that we relied on to verify provenance, but I did my best to pay attention to the man. One never knew when there was a tidbit to be learned. Bennett was to my left, Nico to my right. Behind him was Angelo, ready to wheel his master to our next stop. Near Angelo, Irena noisily shifted her weight and let loose with impatient sighs timed, it seemed, to coincide with whenever Cesare took a breath.

The man was a font of information and his eyes grew wide and his brows expressive as he talked about the history of each piece he'd brought to Villa Pezzati. "This, as you can tell, is the signor's private room, the one where he keeps all family items. He will want me to show you his more expansive collection. Please, come along."

Clasping his fingers in front of his chest as before, Cesare again ducked his head and moved rapidly to an adjacent room. He held open a heavy wooden door, allowing us to pass into the area first, and the moment I did so, I felt a change in the temperature and humidity. "Oh," I said, my hand flying to cover my gasp of delight and surprise when I caught my first glimpse of the walls.

The size of a basketball court, this room had been added on to the old fortress, much the same way the porch leading to the terrazzo had been. Instead of a comfortable, modern room meant for relaxation, however, this addition clearly served one purpose.

Like the foyer, the room glowed. Strategically placed spotlights threw joyful explosions of illumination across the expanse. Ceiling-high windows, screened so as to prevent the sun's rays from falling directly upon any artwork, brightened the marble floor. The two-story walls were a comforting cappuccino brown, and four cushy, orange sofas lined the room's center. Two sofas faced north, two south. This was a gallery meant for long, lingering visits, for hours of art appreciation.

And what appreciation! I glanced over to Bennett, who was watching me with a bemused expression. I wanted to rush over to the Monet on the far right, but just then a Sophie Gengembre Anderson nymph caught my eye. I started, stopped, and tried to remember to breathe. There was so much to take in at once.

"You've far exceeded my expectations," Bennett said to Nico, who grinned up at his friend with unabashed glee.

"You like it, then?" Nico asked.

Bennett's answer was to stroll along the left wall, upon which hung a large John Singer Sargent masterpiece—an oil painting bringing all the pain and preparation of war to vivid, oversized life. "Where in heaven's name did you unearth this?" he asked, arms spread in conspicuous delight. "I've wanted this one for my collection, but I hadn't heard of it coming on the market for decades."

Nico curled and twisted his hand over his head, the way a magician might. But instead of producing a snowy dove, he pointed to Cesare. "There is my secret. Cesare brings beauty into my life. If it were not for this man's able assistance, my old villa would be nothing but a barren prison. With his help, it has become a museum—much like your Marshfield," he added with a wink up at Bennett, "where I can collect treasures and enjoy them during my last few years here on earth."

"Father, you mustn't talk like that," Irena chided. "You promised me you'd stay here, with me, for a very long time." She waited for him to look at her. "Remember?"

A look of understanding passed between them. He reached for her slim hand with his weathered one, and they gripped tight for a long moment. "Don't worry, child, I have no plans to escape this mortal coil. Not yet."

Bennett stood about ten feet beyond the Sargent painting, next to a waist-high, sleek metal pedestal upon which a bronze cast sculpture stared out from beneath its Plexiglas container. With his hands spread, almost as though he intended to embrace the clear box, Bennett grinned. "You still have it. After all these years?"

"Of course," Nico said, wiggling two fingers behind him. Angelo wheeled him forward. The rest of us followed in their wake until we surrounded the piece of art. I wasn't positive, but I would have guessed that this small masterpiece was a Picasso. I glanced to Bennett, who read my mind. He nodded.

"Wow," I said, coming around to get a closer look.

"Nico purchased this—oh, how long has it been?" Bennett asked.

"Too long," Nico answered with a snort. "We were but young boys."

Bennett seemed delighted to tell the story. "We were just out of school and hadn't found our footing in the business world yet," he said. "There was this wonderful gallery in Paris, right off the Champs- Élysées." To Nico: "You and I spent too much time there."

"We spent too much time in the bar across the street, you mean." Nico sat forward now, eager to be part of the telling.

High spots in Bennett's cheeks flushed pink, though he didn't seem displeased. "Thank goodness there's no law against being young and foolish."

Cesare gave an appreciative chuckle. Irena giggled. Angelo, not understanding, stared straight ahead.

To me, Nico said, "Your boss could have been quite the ladies' man. The women found him handsome, charming, and excruciatingly polite." He shrugged. "For an American."

Bennett was shaking his head. "I had Sally back home, waiting for me."

Nico shook a finger. "You weren't married yet."

"We were engaged."

Nico rolled his eyes. "She would never have found out."

Bennett sent his friend a warning look. "We were talking about the gallery."

"Which we visited almost daily."

"And one afternoon," Bennett said, his eyes taking on a dreamy cast, "there it was. On display—in the back of the shop, mind you—next to a few trinkets that had been gathering dust over the months we'd wandered through." Snapping out of his reverie, he said, "But you got to it first."

"That I did," Nico agreed.

"To my eternal chagrin."

Nico picked up the tale. "I purchased the skull immediately, using every franc I had on me, and even begging a few off of my good friend here. We knew there was a chance I'd been had, but there was an equal chance that the gallery's proprietor hadn't recognized the artist."

Bennett took a deep breath, staring off into some middle distance, as if the past was displayed there as clearly as if the events had taken place yesterday. "We raced to a reputable auction house"—at that he nodded acknowledgment to Cesare—"one that may very well, in its day, have been as respected as yours is, and we allowed their experts to take a look."

Nico grinned at Bennett. "And to think that on the trek to the auction house we were playing with it."

Bennett stretched out an arm, cupping his hand. "Alas, poor Yorick!"

"You didn't," I said.

"We did," they said in unison.

I was aghast. "With an original Picasso?"

Bennett's eyes crinkled with mirth. "Only on the way to the auction house. At that point, we still weren't sure if we'd picked up something valuable or a piece of junk."

Cesare had moved closer to the group, his dark gaze bouncing between the two men as they bantered. From the auctioneer's antsy body language, I got the impression that he wanted to join in the joviality but didn't quite know how.

Next to her dad, Irena smiled, keeping a protective hand on his shoulder because, caught up in the moment, Nico seemed ready to leap out of his chair. "Do you remember the look on the proprietor's face?"

Their laughter floated in the high gallery around us, filling the airy space with cheer and comfort. Bennett turned to me. "That's when we knew," he said. "The auction master called in one of his associates immediately and we were treated with the utmost respect. We discovered that Picasso had created this during the war, and even though bronze casting was forbidden at that time, a faction in the French Resistance kept the artist supplied."

Silence settled on us with strange immediacy, but the wistful looks on both men's faces made it a good moment rather than an awkward one. Eventually, Bennett turned to the Plexiglas container, resting his fingertips on the box's top edge. "Good memories," he said.

Nico inched forward in his seat. "You may take it out if you like."

Bennett's fingertips rose. "It isn't locked?"

"Why should it be? This is my home."

With an expression of pure excitement, Bennett made eye contact with me, practically asking aloud, *Can you believe this*? He gently gripped the Plexiglas and raised the container. Cesare was at his side immediately, nodding and offering to take the box from him. Almost without seeing the other man, Bennett handed it over, his attention riveted on the sculpture before him.

"Oh," he breathed, as he lifted the skull and hefted it in

both hands. "Heavier than I remember," he said, then added, "so long ago. So long ago."

"I never really understood your excitement until today," Irena said. "Until Mr. Marshfield was here to share in the telling."

Bennett nodded as he turned the skull from side to side, admiringly. Cesare looked like a man ready to have a heart attack. I think it was all he could do to not put the box aside and cup his hands beneath Bennett's to catch the treasure in case it dropped.

"Your father and I—" Bennett began with a smirk, then stopped himself mid-sentence. He'd twisted the piece every which way and was now scrutinizing a spot on the skull's right, just below where the earlobe would fall—if it'd had ears, that is.

When his face clouded, I asked, "What's wrong?"

Glancing up at the group, he shook it off. "Nothing," he answered. He was lying, though I couldn't figure out why. "I was just trying to remember," he continued with a forced smile, "didn't we both agree this looked like someone we knew?"

"Did we?" Nico seemed confused.

"Yes, I'm sure of it," Bennett said. I knew him well enough to know he was making it up as he went along. He lifted one hand from the skull to snap his fingers near his temple. "I can't come up with the name, and that bothers me." With an embarrassed glance to the group, he said, "You all caught me frowning at my frustration. I apologize; one of the problems of old age."

Now I knew he was fibbing. Bennett didn't try to hide his age, but he wasn't the type to blame a mistake on a "senior moment," either. He started to return the skull to its perch, but stopped. "Gracie," he said, handing it over, "I'd like you to feel the weight of this."

From the odd tone of his voice and his impatience motioning me forward, I knew there was something definitely amiss. Cesare was required to step back to allow me to stand next to Bennett.

"Are you sure you trust me?" I asked, trying to divine Bennett's thoughts.

He placed the skull in my hands. "I always trust you," he said, then added so softly that even Cesare probably couldn't hear, "Right there. Look."

He pointed to a spot on the skull that was immediately below where the right ear would have been.

I didn't see anything unusual where Bennett pointed. He avoided my eyes as he returned the skull to its perch and Cesare replaced the clear box.

"We have many more stories to share with these young ladies at dinner tonight, don't we, Bennett?" Nico said, apparently oblivious to his friend's discomposure. "Cesare, will you join us this evening?"

The dark eyes widened, and he placed his fingertips together, prayerfully again, but this time under his chin. "It would be my great honor," he said with a deferential bow. "I am delighted to accept."

"Until then, I beg my leave," Nico said. "I must rest." He extended his hands outward. "Please enjoy my treasures for as long as you like." To me and Bennett, he added, "Angelo or Marco will show you to your rooms if you care to revive yourselves before dinner. If you wish, I am certain that Irena will show you other areas you may care to explore. Please make this home your own."

With a beatific smile, he receded from our midst, stone-faced Angelo wheeling him away.

Chapter 4

I WANTED TO TALK WITH BENNETT ALONE, TO
find out what had bothered him when he'd examined the
Picasso skull, but we never got the chance. Our rooms,
much to my delight, were in one of the two central towers,
up several flights of stone stairs, making me especially
happy that we hadn't been required to haul our luggage all
the way up here ourselves. Marco accompanied us, preventing conversation. We left Bennett at his room on the second
floor, where he and I agreed to meet before we headed
down to dinner in an hour.

Marco led me up one more floor, where the tower narrowed slightly. "This way," he said, his voice echoing against
the stone walls. The effect would have been creepy if it
weren't for the waning sunshine trickling in from the corridor's narrow windows. From what I could tell, there were
only two rooms on this level. Before Marco opened the first
door to my right, I asked, "Do others stay in these rooms"—I
gestured farther down the hall—"or are we alone?"

When his brows came together, I realized he thought I was concerned about my own safety. "There will be no one to bother you, signorina. We do not allow strangers into the villa."

Rather than explain that I meant to ask whether the family and staff bedrooms were in this tower as well, I murmured my thanks. Gallantly, he turned the knob and pushed at the three-inch-thick wooden door. It slid open with barely a whisper, despite the fact that its heavy hinges had been in place longer than I'd been on the planet. Marco stayed in the hallway and I stepped past him, catching sight of my luggage in the far corner of this large room.

Before he left, I asked, *"Mi scusi, dove'è il bagno?"* one of the more important Italian phrases I'd mastered before we left home.

Curling his index finger, Marco had me follow him a little farther down the hall, just one door away from my room. I took a quick peek in and noted that the shower—darn it—was the handheld kind. The two things I missed from back home were fixed showerheads and full-width doors or curtains. Every single shower I'd taken in this country had resulted in puddles on the floor.

I thanked him, and as I made my way back to my room, he reminded me to feel free to call on him for anything I might need.

What I needed most, right now, I thought as I shut the door behind me, was to get myself ready for dinner quickly enough to allow time to talk with Bennett before we headed back downstairs. I needed to know what was troubling him.

I made way for my things, puzzled by the lack of décor in this room. If it wasn't used very often it made sense not to decorate the space, but compared to the rest of the house, where priceless items fairly sat on top of one another, this stark, barren room was a surprise. Other than the double bed, an insignificant dresser in serious need of refinishing, the foggy oval mirror that hung above it, and a couple of utilitarian lamps, the room was empty. There weren't even curtains on the two tall windows. At least the glass was clean. I peered out, over the lush landscape and at the neighboring tower. With the sun still bright enough, the rooms that mirrored mine were dark, and I couldn't see inside. I wondered if anyone stayed in them.

Didn't matter now. What I needed was to get myself out the door again.

I took take care of all necessary freshening, then pulled on a stretchy but forgiving black-and-white dress and sling-back low pumps. It occurred to me that there was no lock on my door, though, thankfully, someone had put a hook on the one for the bathroom. I took a final look at my reflection in the small mirror over the room's lone dresser, and headed downstairs to catch Bennett. We had at least a half hour before we were due at dinner.

Just as I made it to his room, I heard what sounded like an argument in Italian; one man's voice, one woman's. It wasn't Irena, of that I was certain. I wanted to creep closer and find out who was arguing, even though it was none of my business.

At that moment, Bennett's door opened, and he nearly jumped to see me standing there.

"I didn't mean to scare you," I said.

He glanced side to side down the corridor. "What's all that racket? Who's having a fight?"

"No idea," I said. "If you'd like me to find out, however . . ."

"I want nothing of the kind," he said. "You know what trouble you get into when you poke your nose into other people's business."

"I do," I said. "I'll stay out of it, but—" Ready to broach the topic I most wanted to ask about, I held off when the arguing abruptly stopped.

Bennett and I exchanged a silent, wary glance.

"I guess they've resolved their differences," I whispered.

Bennett frowned, keeping his voice low, too. "Either that, or they heard us talking and thought better of airing their grievances in front of guests."

"Speaking of which—" I began.

Just then, Angelo lumbered into view. Cheeks flushed, hands fisted, his face was a thundercloud of fury. That is, until he saw us. Eyebrows startled upward, he adopted a more passive expression. With a nod of greeting, he walked past at a quick clip and when he turned a corner, we heard a door slam.

"At least we know one of the combatants," Bennett said.

"I wonder what that was all about. And who he was arguing with."

"Grace." His voice was a warning. "Repeat after me, 'I will keep my nose clean this time.'" He held an index finger aloft, between us. "We have one more night here in Europe, and we've been safe thus far. Let's not take any chances."

"Yes, sir," I said, giving a mock salute.

"Shall we go down to dinner?" he asked. With a glance at his watch and a resigned shrug, he added, "We'll be early, of course, but I wanted to take another look at that gallery." His brow furrowed and his voice dropped another notch. "There's something not right—"

"About the skull?"

From the far end of the hall: "There you are!"

We both looked up to see Irena coming our way. "I was looking for you, Grace," she said, striding to join us. "Are you going down now? May I join you?"

"That sounds wonderful," I said.

I could tell from the look on Bennett's face that he preferred to hold off our discussion of the skull until we were alone. "I'll meet you there shortly," he said. "I have something I'd like to attend to first." He disappeared down the hall.

Irena fisted both hips as she assessed me. "Your last night in Europe," she said, her eyes glittering. "I can think of no better city to spend it in than here in *Firenze*. I have plans for us. This will be a night for you to remember when you return to the States."

"A quiet evening will be good enough—"

"Nonsense," she said, wrapping her hand around my arm and guiding me down the hall. "Tonight, my American friend, we will have fun."

I had the uncomfortable feeling that Irena's and my sense of fun were worlds apart.

DESPITE THE FACT THAT BENNETT AND I HAD made it our business to sample local cuisine at every opportunity on this trip, this night's dinner was—by far—the most incredible dining experience I had ever encountered. Each course was served to us by gloved butlers, and it was apparent from Nico's keen, delighted expression that he was eager to impress. He sat at the table's head, with Bennett to Nico's right and me next to Bennett. Irena sat across from us, and Cesare next to her. The rest of the long, sixteen-seat table remained empty.

I patted my lips with a napkin as our dinner plates were whisked away. Bennett sat back. "Nico, your chef is to be complimented. Where did you find this master?"

"I hired Antoinette as an assistant, but she quickly proved herself. She runs my kitchen now. Indeed, she believes she runs most of the household."

"A woman?" Cesare asked. The disbelief in his voice would have been laughable if the implication that a woman being unworthy of such a lofty position wasn't so offensive.

"You enjoyed your dinner, did you not?" Nico asked.

Cesare hurried to unruffle his host's feathers. "I am only surprised that you have not mentioned this woman before."

Lame, but Nico didn't call him out. Instead, he made a so-so motion with his hands and leaned forward, keeping his voice low. "Our chef is a bit temperamental at times, would you agree, Irena?"

His daughter sent a wary glance toward the kitchen. "If she weren't so talented, she'd have been sacked long ago."

"Bennett, my good friend," Nico said. "Take my advice. Two strong-willed women in one household may buy you many rewards." He shook his head solemnly even as a smile played at his lips. "But there is much risk, as well."

Cesare, ever eager to reclaim his standing in the conversation, laughed hard. Too hard.

"Grace has her hands full with her assistant, Frances," Bennett said. "But after a rocky start, I think they've found common ground."

Frances hadn't been first in my mind. It was Hillary I more worried about. With an uncomfortable pang, I realized that she would have moved into her new Emberstowne home by now. I wasn't looking forward to having her as a neighbor.

"Antoinette isn't so bad, Father." Irena's eye roll belied her words. "As long as she remembers her place."

Butlers set dessert in front of each of us. Even as I lifted my spoon to sample the gelato, I wondered how I'd fit another bite in my too-full stomach.

Irena leaned forward. "Angelo will drive us into town this evening," she said. "Father prefers that I be accompanied. Florence is full of students and I've never had a problem, but it makes him feel better to know that Angelo is watching out for me."

Oh great. Lovelorn Angelo assigned to accompany us on the town. "Will he stay with us the whole time?"

She laughed as though that was a funny question. "Of course not. How would we enjoy our girl talk if he did? No," she said with jovial finality, "he stays nearby and keeps an eye on me, but he doesn't actually join in the conversation."

"That seems unfair to Angelo."

Irena shrugged. "He doesn't mind."

For the first time since I'd encountered Angelo, I began to feel empathy for the big man. He, Marco, and Gianfranco were nowhere to be seen. I assumed they were taking their dinner in a less opulent spot in the house. I wondered what life must be like for Angelo—for all of them. To be on call for Nico all day and then for Irena all night. No wonder he asked about me. Other than the temperamental chef, Antoinette, I might very well be the only female he'd met in a long time.

"Speak of the devil," Irena said as Angelo strode into the room. She addressed him in Italian and he responded in the affirmative.

Dropping her spoon and making her apologies to her father and Bennett, she reached across the table to grab my hand. "Are you ready?" she asked. Behaving more like an enthusiastic twenty-year-old than a fortysomething woman, she sighed contentedly. "It's been so long since I've visited the United States. I can't tell you how much I'm looking forward to talking with you. I want to know everything about what goes on there."

I knew Bennett could read my mood. I also knew how much he appreciated the fact that I was allowing him this evening with Nico. I hoped that hard-smiling Cesare would take his leave sooner rather than later. Perhaps tomorrow, maybe even before we left, I'd find out more about the problem with the Picasso skull.

As I walked around the table, thanking Nico for a wonderful dinner and expressing my delight at spending the evening with Irena, I decided that while Bennett pumped Nico for information, there was nothing stopping me from digging into what Irena might know. I could do that. And maybe the evening wouldn't be such a waste after all.

"What are we waiting for?" I said. "Let's go."

Chapter 5

THE LAST TIME I WAS IN AN ESTABLISHMENT like this one, it was more than five years ago in New York City—and I'd left after ten minutes. Emberstowne didn't offer this sort of pulsating neon experience, but Troppo was Irena's destination of choice, and I'd resolved to be a good guest.

As I stepped from the cool, quiet evening into the stuffy, dark bar, the bass beat hit me full in the chest before the music reached my ears. "Wow," I said, but my voice was lost in the throbbing rhythm. Bodies gyrated—mostly in pairs—atop a blinking pink-and-purple dance floor. There was a rock band playing far across the room. They were pretty good, at least to my ear, and although I couldn't make out their lyrics, I could tell they were singing in English. That surprised me. I strove for a better look. Four men, leather clad and dark wigged, wore heavy eyeliner and studded dog collars around straining necks. I felt as though I'd stepped through a time warp. The music seemed familiar, but I couldn't put my finger on where I'd heard it before.

We wound our way through the crowds of drink-sipping non-dancers with me realizing, belatedly, that everyone there was at least ten years younger than I was. Which meant twenty years younger than Irena. I didn't bother trying to talk—she wouldn't have heard a word I said.

So much for quiet conversation.

She led the way through throngs of young people, some of whom glared at our intrusion, some of whom were too glassy-eyed and bland-faced to notice. Angelo followed us, and I got the impression that both he and Irena had a clear destination in mind. I hoped so. At this rate, there was no chance we'd find a table.

Through musky clouds of perfume, hot body odor, and the unmistakable, cloying scent of booze, we made our way through Troppo's immense gathering space. At a corner as far from the front doors as we could have gone, Irena pushed open a heavy, black glass door, taking us into a blissfully clear hallway that smelled of chlorinated water and sounded like someone had left a faucet running.

A stone waterfall along the right, bathed in spotlights, illuminated the dark passageway with dim patches of hot pink. The door shut behind Angelo, bringing welcome quiet. Only a hint of the vibrating backbeat made its way through the thick glass.

"This way," Irena said. Her words, coming so quickly after the booming bass, were overly loud, but I didn't mind that, or the sudden cool. I ran the side of my hand against my hairline to brush away lingering clamminess.

Irena didn't hesitate. She made straight for a stairway on the right and started up immediately, one long-fingered hand on its blue neon handrail. Turning, she said, "We'll be fine, Angelo. You can wait here."

The big man grunted, but continued to follow.

I closed the distance between me and Irena. "I thought Angelo didn't understand English."

"Yeah." She gave a soft, peppermint-infused laugh. "That's what he wants us to believe."

A maître d' met us at the top of the stairs, recognizing Irena immediately. They conversed genially in Italian for a moment before he led us into a cozy, candlelit room with warm-hued stone walls, deep-purple linens, and a view through a wall of glass of the busy dance floor below. We could see the band members working their instruments with pounding drive, but it was like watching high-energy, silent marionettes. Up here, the entertainment was provided by a quartet of musicians doing a fair rendition of a Beatles' ballad.

Our fellow patrons took advantage of the quiet. Most of them were deep in conversation, and all were dressed in what we Americans refer to as "business casual." I sighed with relieved pleasure as we made our way to one of the empty tables up against the wall window. This was a far cry from the noisy dance floor we'd just passed through.

The maître d' held the chair for Irena. Angelo, as though the thought hadn't occurred to him before, hurried to hold a chair out for me. My backside had barely touched the soft seat when he stepped away from the table, careful not to make eye contact. Nico Pezzati had obviously had that talk with him about leaving me alone.

"That will be all, Angelo," Irena said.

The big man tilted his head as though he didn't understand. She repeated it in Italian. He nodded and left, taking up a position at the shiny bar across the room, watching us.

"What's his story?" I asked. "Do his emotions ever range beyond bored and angry?"

Irena giggled, covering her mouth with her hand as though she didn't want Angelo to see her laughing. "You picked up on his personality pretty quickly, didn't you? I think Father keeps him around because he does what he's told without question." She flicked a glance sideways. He was still watching. He had to know we were talking about him. "Mostly."

Thinking about the argument Bennett and I had observed when we first walked in on Nico and Angelo, I had to ask, "Does he give your father a hard time?"

She gave a little hand flip-flop. "It's nothing. Angelo is just so—"

Irena didn't get to finish her thought. Her hand gesture must have looked like a signal to the waiter. The lanky older man sprang to our table, abandoning a young couple at the room's center where he'd been taking an order. The woman turned around to face us as the waiter left them, giving me a full view of her surprised frown. A moment later, she'd returned to her conversation with nothing more than a resigned shrug and shake of her curly head.

"And what would you prefer this evening, Signorina Pezzati?" the waiter asked in smooth English. Before she could respond, he began sizing me up. "We are honored to have a guest of our most favorite customer here with us tonight. You are American?"

How everyone in Europe always knew, I couldn't fathom. Bennett and I had been automatically handed menus printed in English just about everywhere we'd dined, here and in France, even before we'd spoken a word. "You're right," I said with polite admiration. "Excellent observation."

Chuffed by my compliment, his smile grew wide. "We are always pleased when Signorina Pezzati graces us with her delightful presence. And we are always especially pleased when she brings us a friend to meet."

I had begun to grow accustomed to charming speeches like our waiter's. The slower pace, the willingness of strangers to engage in conversation, and a general acceptance that

I hadn't anticipated had made this two-week excursion one I would never forget.

After he took our orders and left us alone again, I asked, "He refers to you as Signorina Pezzati. I take it you've never been married?"

"Ha." Her eyes flashed and her mouth twisted, not in anger, but in what I would characterize as amusement. "I was practically a child bride. Alas, my father did not like my first husband," she said, "so I found a new one."

Before I could ask if she was still married—something I couldn't help but doubt—the waiter returned with two glasses of wine and a small plate of antipasto he said was with his compliments.

When he left us again, I returned to the topic of her second husband. "Does your father like him?"

Elbows on the table, and holding her glass in both hands, she lifted a melancholy shoulder. "I wouldn't know," she said. "He didn't stay long enough for me to find out."

My expression must have given me away, because she patted me on the hand. "How strange that must sound to you. Don't be concerned, it all worked out in the end. We married quickly, divorced even faster." With a wistful look in her eye, she added, "He was, and is, a handsome, intelligent man." Dark brows arching over contemplative eyes, she took an absentminded sip and said, "Our marriage couldn't survive my father's wealth," as though that explained anything.

I didn't press her, guessing that Irena—like Bennett's stepdaughter, Hillary—had been taken in by a man more eager to share his wife's riches than willing to share her life. Irena was clearly better off without this man, but it was hardly my place to say so.

She leaned forward. "I went back to my maiden name because I prefer to put all my troubles behind me." Pressing a long finger against her lips, she swept the room with a self-conscious glance and whispered, "Besides, it is much easier finding future husbands when I am called signorina rather than signora."

We talked more, about her life here in Florence, about mine in the States, while gyrating bodies danced on the floor below to my right and Angelo maintained his watch on us to my left.

After another round of drinks, we'd gotten to that comfortable place in conversation where barriers begin to drop away. She'd invited me to return to Florence to stay at the villa whenever I wanted, and I'd reciprocated, offering my house with Scott and Bruce and Bootsie, or the Marshfield Inn. I knew Bennett would happily welcome her into his home, but that was for him to offer, not me.

It was finally time for me to bring up the subject I'd been wanting to ask about all evening. "Tell me about Gerard," I said.

Irena swirled her wine and stared at the luxuriant ruby legs inside the wide bowl. Irena's glass hadn't touched the table since we'd been served. It wasn't that she drank quickly or often; rather, it seemed her habit to keep the stemware suspended slightly above the table held in both hands, using her long fingers for emphasis. From time to time, she gave up one hand's grip when she gestured to make a point. She moved like a woman accustomed to being watched and liking it.

From my surreptitious glances around the room, I could tell her efforts were appreciated. With her dark, sparkling eyes, expressive brows, and this flirty way of holding her wineglass, she commanded attention. Many eyes were on her. Twice, as we'd been talking, men from other parts of the room made it clear they intended to join our conversation. Both times Angelo had interceded and we'd been left alone.

Even though she wasn't movie-star gorgeous, she had a

compelling aura. It was all in her confidence and her presentation.

She brought her wineglass up to almost eye height, staring at it the way an audience volunteer might stare at a hypnotist's watch. "Gerard," she finally said.

Our waiter was at our side in less than two beats. "Is there anything wrong?" he asked her, turning to me after the fact, as though suddenly remembering I was there. "Would Signorina Pezzati prefer something else? A different vintage, perhaps?"

She laid a hand on his arm. I wondered if she knew the little thrill she'd just given the man. Even in this dim room, I could see his cheeks brighten and his eyes light up. "No, I'm sorry. I'm simply in a thoughtful mood. Thank you."

Dismissed, he nodded and left us alone again.

"I know it's a difficult subject."

She wrinkled her nose. "Not for me," she said. "Gerard and I have never lost touch." Finally making eye contact, she shrugged. "He's my brother. I can't turn my back on him."

"But your father—"

"Father disowned him years ago. He doesn't understand that people can change. He won't give Gerard another chance."

"What did Gerard do?"

Her expression tightened. "My father forgave a lot. He's a kind man and he loves his family, but he couldn't forgive Gerard's deception. My brother stole one of our father's most cherished treasures. When confronted, he denied it. But we knew the truth."

For a woman who professed to keep in touch with her brother, she sounded angry. I asked her about that.

"Yes, of course I am upset," she said. "Our father is a generous man. He refuses me nothing. If only Gerard would have asked for what he needed instead of trying to take it." She stared out at the dancers below us. "Now it's too late. Our father has cut him out of all possibility of inheritance. He refuses to speak to his son."

"Your father said that Gerard hasn't tried to reach him for fourteen years."

"He said that? Today?"

When I nodded, she took a long sip of wine.

"I'm surprised. Father rarely speaks of the matter. They are both stubborn men. Gerard tried to make amends for a while. But now he is bitter. He knows the wealth our father has, and he's angry that he will never be part of that life anymore. I understand. Gerard lives in New York and claims he is too ashamed of his living conditions to allow me to visit. I send him what I can but"—she blinked away tears that had begun to shimmer in her eyes—"there is so little I can do." Setting her glass down on the table, she reached across and grabbed both my hands with hers. "I don't want to cry in public. Please, let's talk about something else. What did you think of Father's gallery?"

When she let go, I picked up my own glass. "Beautiful," I said, "though that hardly begins to describe it. I know Bennett was impressed. I wouldn't be surprised if he commissions a new spot on Marshfield property for something similar."

She laughed. "I must admit, I am a disappointment to my father in one respect. I have no knowledge of what he has in there." Lifting one hand, she waved it from side to side. "Of course, I hear names like Picasso and Monet and I understand that these are valuable, priceless, even, but I don't have the interest in collecting and buying and selling the way my father wishes I would." Grinning, she took a quick sip, then looked at me with new interest. "You, on the other hand, would be a great asset to my father. You not only understand what treasures he has amassed, you share his enthusiasm for it all."

"I do," I said. "I'd love to know more about that skull."

She nodded. "What a wonderful story they told. It makes me see them as young men."

"That was enjoyable," I said, warming to the subject. "Did you notice how Bennett seemed taken aback at one point?"

She tilted her head. "What do you mean?"

"When he held the skull. Remember?"

Blinking, she stared down at the tablecloth. "Yes . . ." she said slowly. "Now that you mention it, he did seem to hesitate a moment." She looked up expectantly. "Why? Do you know what troubled him?"

"No," I said, disappointed. "It seemed as though his re-action was off but I haven't had the opportunity to ask him about it. Something was odd. I thought maybe you'd have an idea of what that could be."

"I'm sorry," she said. "My father's been having difficulty remembering things lately, too. I didn't give that inci-dent a second thought."

Chapter 6

WE LEFT TROPPO IN THE WEE HOURS OF THE morning. It wasn't until the dancers below began to disperse that Irena and I realized we'd talked the entire night away. Our waiter had kept our glasses filled—I'd switched to water a few hours into our visit, thank goodness—and the snacks plentiful.

Angelo escorted us out into the damp morning air. He held the sedan's back doors open for us and took his position behind the wheel. Neither Irena nor I had been overserved, but we were relaxed from all the wine. The evening had turned out to be much nicer than I'd anticipated, and although it was far too late to confer with Bennett tonight—he'd have been asleep for hours by now—I knew we'd have the entire flight home to discuss the skull, my discoveries about Gerard, and whatever Bennett had learned from Nico.

I sank into the leather seats, which were so soft they practically wrapped around my tired body. "I need to be up and out the door in less than five hours," I said with a mock groan. "But this evening was worth it."

"I'm so glad you think so," Irena said with a happy pat on the seat between us. "But, five hours? What time is your flight?"

As we left the city proper and headed back to the villa, I could barely make out anything in the profound darkness. "Fortunately, we've chartered a plane and it won't leave without us." For Irena, chartered air travel was probably a regular occurrence. For me, it had been a singularly incredible experience. "We're supposed to be there no later than nine. Thank goodness we don't have to go through commercial flight security. We'd have to leave at least three hours earlier if we did."

"My father used to keep a jet at the airport," Irena said, dropping her head against the soft seat back and closing her eyes. "Unfortunately, he stopped traveling and gave it up." She raised her voice. "Remember, Angelo?"

The big man glanced up at the sound of his name, but didn't answer. Irena shrugged, turned to me, and opened one eye. "He understands," she whispered with a wry grin. Both eyes closed, she gave a sigh of pleasure then spoke again, a little louder this time. "Always the mystery man, aren't you? Someday I'll find the chink in your armor."

I caught Angelo's glance in the rearview mirror. He looked away immediately. I had no doubt that Irena was right and he'd understood every word we'd said. Maybe he'd hoped to overhear some juicy, private details. Poor boy. He would be disappointed tonight.

I dozed on the ride back, waking when the big sedan slowed to a stop. Angelo was out almost immediately, coming around to open our doors. "Thank you for driving us tonight," I said as he handed me out of the car.

He responded in Italian but when I turned to ask Irena what he'd said, she was already halfway to the front door.

"Good night, Angelo," I said as the big guy made his way back to the car.

He nodded. *"Buona note e sogni d'oro."*

I hoped that didn't mean "Go sleep with the fishes."

"GRACIE, ARE YOU IN THERE?" BENNETT knocked on my door, dragging me from a wild and wacky dream where I'd been slow dancing at Troppo's on its flashy dance floor, trying, without success, to figure out who I was dancing with.

I peeled open my bleary eyes wide enough to notice that it was still dark outside. "Grace," Bennett called again, "we've got a problem."

The digital readout on my cell phone told me it was five fifteen in the morning. "Just a second," I croaked, swinging my legs off the bed. I slipped on my travel socks and stumbled to the door. Once there, I groaned with frustration, having forgotten that I'd wedged my big suitcase against it. When I'd finally been ready to sleep, I'd discovered that I couldn't relax knowing that nothing stood between me and angry Angelo except a lockless door with hinges that barely whispered. I hadn't been crazy about the idea of anyone being able to walk in on me unannounced, so before I went to bed, I'd taken the precaution of jamming the luggage up under the knob.

"Hang on." My voice was rusty, and my vision was blurred. I cleared my throat as my fingers found the suitcase's handle and tugged at it, with considerable effort. "I did a much better job than I thought I did," I muttered when it finally came free.

Awake now, I scampered back into the main part of my room. "Come on in," I called as I pulled the bedspread off the bed and wrapped it around myself. I generally wore shorts and a T-shirt to bed—nothing revealing or particularly skimpy—but I still felt weird letting anyone see me in my sleepwear. I ran my fingers through my hair, working through the gentle knots, trying to make myself look alert and presentable. Fat chance of that, but Bennett didn't seem to take even the slightest notice of my disarray.

"Nico's man took a phone call about an hour ago from our charter," he said.

Why is it when we're swimming up to the surface of wakefulness, we must repeat things in order to track conversation? I heard myself say, "Our charter?"

"Yes, our flight," Bennett said, "it's—" For the first time since he strode in, he seemed to actually see me. Frown lines between his brows softened and one corner of his mouth turned up. "You look like you're about twelve years old."

I clutched the covers around me with one hand and rubbed my eyes with the other. "Right now I feel more like a hundred and twelve."

"Late night?" Bennett said with more mirth than I felt like dealing with at the moment. "I hope you had fun, at least."

"I learned a lot." My mind finally engaged, I asked, "What kind of problem is there with our flight?"

"It's been canceled."

I sat on the bed. "And you have that board meeting tomorrow, don't you? I know you can't miss it."

He grew pensive. "Makes me wonder . . ."

"What's on your mind?"

With a reluctant shrug, he continued. "I've told you a little about the company we're acquiring, WizzyWig. What I haven't mentioned before was how much one of its vice presidents, Vandeen Deinhart, would prefer I disappear from the planet. Vandeen claims he's afraid that he'll lose his prestigious position with the company."

"You think he would interfere with our return trip to keep this deal from materializing?"

"If I don't show up at the meeting, the sale won't go through. We've signed a preliminary agreement, but that agreement expires at this meeting. I have the option to renew, but only if I do so in person. Once that's signed, we're supposed to set the official date for closing the deal. Deinhart has effectively delayed this again and again. There are no delays left. I know he's done this in the hopes that the deal will fall through."

"Why didn't you mention him before?"

"I didn't want to worry you or hamper your enjoyment on this trip in any way," he said with a sheepish grin. "But I'm being silly. I don't believe Deinhart would stoop so low. It's beneath his dignity."

"You think he may be embezzling from WizzyWig?"

He scrunched his face. "Nothing quite so crass. He's a wily one, that Deinhart. My guess is that he'd be careful to keep his own hands clean. I do, however, suspect he may benefit from his position in the company in ways that— though not illegal—could be construed as inappropriate."

"For instance?"

He gave me the "No more discussion" face. "I'm certain he's not behind this. Forget I said anything."

I swallowed my impatience. Bennett wasn't giving me the full story and I got the impression there was more menace to this Deinhart character than he was letting on. I'd learned, however, that Bennett wouldn't share information until he was ready to do so. Even with me. Resigned, I returned to the issue at hand. "The charter company should be able to find us a replacement flight, shouldn't they?"

"They're working on it," he said, "but they warned that the fleet is stretched pretty thin right now. They'll do their best to get us in the air by this evening."

I wanted to ask why Bennett had felt the need to wake me up if the end result meant I could sleep later, but he looked so concerned about the situation that I knew there must be more.

"What aren't you telling me?" I asked.

"There's nothing wrong with the plane," he said, "but the pilot is another story. He was arrested last night. For assault."

"The same guy who flew us out here?"

Bennett nodded.

"No way. We talked with him," I said, my voice taking on a "this is ridiculous" tone. "That guy is a milquetoast."

Bennett snickered. "There's a word I haven't heard in a long time."

"The guy had zero personality. When we came aboard and he greeted us, I wondered how he'd ever made it through a job interview in the first place. He was about as passionate as . . . as . . ."—I looked around the room and, coming up without a fitting example, I kicked the nearest thing I could find—"this footstool."

"I'm only reporting what I was told."

I rubbed my eyes again, wondering if, perhaps, I was still dreaming. "Sorry for the outburst," I said, chuckling to myself. "But I can't imagine our pilot assaulting anyone. You'd find his face in the dictionary under 'mild-mannered.' The kind of man who would apologize to the rock he tripped over."

"It's always the quiet ones who surprise you."

"True enough." I slid a longing glance toward my pillow and wondered how hard it would be to fall back asleep. "How long before we need to be out the door? And is there anything we need to be doing?"

"As a matter of fact, there is. Nico's assistant is working on finding us another flight."

"But if our charter company promised—"

"They warned that there's no guarantee they can have a

new pilot here in time. If Nico can arrange for our transportation sooner, we'll take him up on it. That's why I came pounding at your door. We need to be ready to go at a moment's notice." Bennett fixed me with a meaningful stare. "Even worse, we may have to share the flight back."

"Share?" I repeated, annoying myself by doing so. "With whom?"

"That depends upon the luck of the draw," Bennett said. "I've done this sort of thing before and although I'm not fond of sharing flights with strangers, it could be my only hope of making the meeting on time. It's infinitely better than flying on a commercial vehicle, even first class."

So much for crawling back to bed. "Thanks for letting me know."

"Nico is taking care of everything for us. His driver will be ready whenever we need to leave, and he's having the chef prepare breakfast now so that we won't have to travel on empty stomachs."

"That's very kind of him."

Bennett turned to leave. "I'll meet you down there."

"Wait," I said. "I wanted to talk with you about that Picasso skull."

Bennett raised a finger to his lips. "Later," he whispered.

BREAKFAST AT VILLA PEZZATI WAS AN EVENT I'd tell my grandchildren about—if I ever had grandchildren. I couldn't imagine how much effort it must have taken to have gotten such a fabulous meal together so splendidly on such an abbreviated timetable.

The chef had done her very best to include a number of American offerings along with traditional Italian breakfast fare. The food was wonderful, but it was the presentation and the service that stirred me most of all. I felt as though we'd been transported back in time. At dinner last night, we'd had butlers at the ready, but this morning, they were doubly attentive, presenting breads, cooked and cold meats, cheeses, eggs, fruits, and delicious pastries for us to sample, until I had to push myself from the table, knowing that otherwise I might burst.

With my coffee—an Americanized version because I hadn't quite gotten used to Italian coffee over the past week—replenished yet again, Bennett, Nico, and I sat back to discuss the flight situation.

As we did, a butler came in to hand Nico a linen note. The elderly man groped his shirt pocket for reading glasses, which another butler hurriedly nabbed from a nearby table to present to him. Nico read the note slowly, eyebrows up, mouth turned down. When he finished, he looked at us. "Good news, to some degree," he said. "There appears to be a flight leaving for the United States this afternoon at two o'clock." He handed the note back to the butler who'd first presented it and spoke to the man. "Let them know we need more details."

"Do you know where the flight is scheduled to land?" Bennett asked. "Or who we would be traveling with?"

Nico signaled for more Italian coffee for himself and Bennett. As it was poured, he shook his head. "You know as much as I do at the moment, my friend. My assistant is moving forward to attempt to secure your passage on this particular flight."

I wondered if that "assistant" was Angelo. I hadn't seen the big man all morning.

Nico took a slurpy sip of his hot brew. "The good news is, however, that if this works out, you'll have a more relaxing morning than we'd anticipated."

After we'd enjoyed our fill, Bennett asked if it would be all right to have Chef Antoinette come out of the kitchen so that we could thank her personally. Nico smiled as though he thought the request quaint, but indulged us just the same.

One of the butlers brought her out. No more than five feet tall, she had black-rooted, dishwater-blonde hair and was wearing a strawberry-stained white apron that barely made it around her girth. With a darting glance at Nico, she nodded as she mumbled, *"Buongiorno."*

Bennett spoke to her in broken Italian with Nico helping whenever he stumbled on a word, but I caught enough of the conversation to understand Bennett's effusive compliments and humble gratitude.

Antoinette's eyes grew wide and glassy. She listened, swallowing visibly. Her mouth went tight as her cheeks flushed red. When Bennett finished, she flashed an inquiring glance toward Nico. Then, as though throwing caution to the wind, she rushed forward, grasping Bennett's hands in both of her ruddy ones, thanking him in overjoyed Italian and, if I understood her correctly, wishing him a long life, much prosperity, and all the graces God could offer.

She bobbed low, and as she made her way out again, thanking Bennett, thanking Nico, and thanking me, I was moved by the woman's heartfelt gratitude. We all want to be appreciated, I mused. Here was a perfect reminder of why I should always make a point of thanking people and letting them know that their efforts were valued. I wasn't bad at that, but I could be better. I decided I would be, starting now.

Barely had the door swung shut behind her when one of the butlers returned, bearing another linen note. Nico read it, again slowly, nodding as he did so. He folded it and placed it on the table. "Your passage on the two o'clock flight is confirmed. My assistant is finalizing the details as we speak. The aircraft is a privately owned jet. There will be about six other people on board. They, too, have an important engagement tomorrow, but they will be happy to take you along."

"That's wonderful news," Bennett said, "Do you know who we're riding with?"

Nico pulled the note and reread it. "SlickBlade," he said.

Bennett leaned forward. "Come again?"

Nico repeated the name, as Bennett sat back, baffled. "Never heard of them. They must be a razor company. Maybe a division of a bigger firm."

The name seemed familiar to me, but I wasn't sure where I'd heard it before.

It was clear Nico didn't have a clue, nor was he concerned about it. He struggled to stand. "You have several hours before you must leave. Let us retire to the terrazzo until you must bring me sadness by leaving my beautiful home."

Chapter 7

ANGELO DROVE US TO THE AIRPORT. WHEN he'd first taken his seat behind the wheel, Bennett tapped him on the shoulder. "What happened to the man who drove us here originally? I thought he would be driving us back."

Angelo turned his considerable bulk in the front seat and held up both hands, telling Bennett in Italian that he didn't understand.

Angelo turned forward again and started the engine. "I guess it doesn't matter, does it?" Bennett said.

I glanced in the rearview mirror to catch Angelo looking at me. "I guess not," I mumbled.

Once we'd passed through the front gate Bennett cleared his throat. "It was good to see Nico again. Good to reconnect. I'm glad you were able to spend time with Irena. I have a sense that the two of you hit it off pretty well."

I didn't want to talk in front of Angelo, but I wasn't quite sure how to communicate that to Bennett. "She's great," I said. "The place she took me was perfect for conversation, although it didn't seem as though it would be when we first walked in."

"Were you able to ask her about her brother, Gerard?"

I pointed out Bennett's window. "Aren't olive trees lovely? I never get tired of them."

He gave the passing landscape a cursory glance. "Yes, but—"

"I imagine it would be wonderful to come out here during harvest."

He opened his mouth, but I kept talking. "Or harvesting grapes. That would be something to see, wouldn't it?"

I watched concern work across Bennett's face. "I take it you'd like to come back again someday."

"There's an incredible amount of history here. So much to see." I didn't know how much longer I could keep up inane conversation, but Bennett seemed to get the idea. Or at least I thought he did when he sat back and folded his arms.

A moment later, however, he asked, "So, you don't want to share what you know about Gerard, is that it?"

"I think it might be better for us to wait awhile," I said with what I hoped was a facial expression that communicated my reluctance to talk in front of Angelo. To my dismay, the big man's body language suggested he was fully tuned in to this conversation. "Let's talk on the plane, okay? It will be interesting to see who we're flying back with."

Bennett waved a hand in the air. "Nothing to be nervous about. I've encountered my share of corporate types before. They tend to fall into two groups—the workers and the partiers. The first group never stops talking the whole flight, but they're so worried about anyone overhearing that they keep their voices down. The second drinks for the first three hours then, sleeps the rest of the way. Either way, we should be in for a mostly quiet flight."

"I hope you're right," I said.

"SlickBlade," Bennett said absentmindedly. "I wonder where the company is headquartered."

At the airport, an efficient young woman wearing a trim blue uniform and a wide crimson smile met us at the car. "You are Mr. Marshfield?" she asked in heavily accented English. "And Miss Wheaton?"

As she explained that she would be escorting us to our plane, Angelo and a skycap—I wasn't sure what they were called in Italy—unloaded our luggage onto a wheeled cart and the skycap rolled it away.

When Bennett and I turned to thank Angelo, the big man nodded acknowledgment, then surprised me by grasping my forearms. The rumble in his voice was low as he said, "Safe travels," in English.

He pivoted, easing back behind the wheel in barely the blink of an eye. He roared away from the airport as the cheery young woman with the bright red lips urged us forward. "Come along, please, we are nearing time to leave."

The plane was a little bigger than the one that had brought us to Europe. Because we weren't flying commercial, there were no security lines to navigate and no boarding passes to obtain. The chipper young woman's responsibility apparently ended at the tarmac where, under the afternoon sun, she handed us over to another blue-uniformed woman, who introduced herself as Evelyn.

About forty years old, with dark hair pulled back in a tight bun and the hint of a New England accent, Evelyn came across like a self-assured corporate executive: bright-eyed, capable, and all business. I wondered if she was employed by the charter company or by SlickBlade.

"I'll be your flight attendant today," Evelyn said. "Welcome. Your pilots will come to say hello before we take off, but for now please rest assured that your luggage is being taken care of, and all you need worry about now is relaxing on your flight home."

"Are the other passengers—those from SlickBlade—already here?" Bennett asked as she escorted us up the airstairs.

"They have arrived," she said, gesturing vaguely in the direction the plane was facing. "It seems they decided to add another passenger at the last minute."

She stepped into the fuselage, turning to face us as we crossed into the passenger seating area. "Wow," Bennett said in an unusual expression of appreciation. "SlickBlade must do well for itself."

He wasn't kidding. If I hadn't known better I would have thought I'd stepped into someone's living room instead of onto a plane. Soft music drifted around us as I took in the cream-colored cushy seats, teakwood tables, and curvy blue neon lights running along the plane's center. A flat-screen TV took up one side wall, with a built-in cream colored sofa opposite.

"Oh, you mean because of all this." Evelyn circled a hand in the air. She winked at us. "It's more like they have friends in high places."

Bennett and I exchanged a puzzled look as we made our way through the elegant space. Evelyn ran a hand along the back of one puffy leather headrest. "You'll notice how far apart these are spaced?" She grabbed the top of the seat with both hands and swiveled it right then left. "Each goes all the way around and reclines fully so that passengers may sleep if they like—any direction they like. Here. . . ." She pointed to the control panel on the armrest. "Push a button and the lights dim, push another and I'll come over to get you whatever it is you need, whether it be a pillow or to have your drink refreshed. My galleys are at the front and back." She pointed. "All meals have been prepared by local chefs here in town, and I can guarantee they'll be delicious."

"Sounds heavenly," I said. "Do we choose where we want to sit, or are we assigned?"

"I suggest you choose two together in the front, or if you prefer, the very back. That way you don't split the group up. They tend to make use of the sofa and television, though I'm certain you'd be welcome to join them. Either way, there's no doubt it will get cozy in here."

My preference would have been to take the back seats, but Bennett pointed to the two up front, on either side of the cabin. "These will do," he said, lowering himself into one.

I sat in the other. "So much for having a quiet conversation," I said gesturing to the expanse between our seats. "We'll have to shout to hear each other."

Evelyn brightened. "Oh no, this is an incredibly quiet plane," she said. "Not only that, but look. . . ." She pulled at a recessed handle built into a wall directly in front of Bennett that separated the seating area from the front entrance. With a smooth, almost inaudible *whisk*, she pulled another seat out from the wall. It wasn't as soft and cushy as the reclining models, but it would serve its purpose if Bennett and I chose to have a private conversation en route.

Just as she folded the seat back into the wall, we heard a ruckus coming from outside. Men were shouting, or more accurately, shouting insults at one another, each voice trying to outblast the others, it seemed. I stood to see what was going on, but Evelyn waved me back. "Sounds like Slick-Blade is here." She started for the door to welcome them, but before she disappeared around the corner, she turned and winked. "Buckle up."

Chapter 8

BENNETT'S FROWN MATCHED MY CONCERN. I whispered, "I hope they don't plan to carry on like that for the whole flight," but he couldn't hear me over the din of the approaching argument. From what I could tell, it was mostly good-natured, but there was no disputing that it was loud.

"I think Evelyn sold us a bill of goods," Bennett said. "They haven't been inside arranging passage for one of their group, they've been drinking. Heavily, too, from the sound of it."

At that, a man stumbled through the doorway, grasping both sides of the wall that separated the passenger cabin from the front of the plane. "Hey," he slurred, leaning forward, "who are you?"

The guy was younger than I'd expected, twenty-five, tops. Tall, wearing a midnight-black wig that skimmed his shoulders, he had to be sweltering hot in his black leather pants, black T-shirt, and matching leather jacket, rife with chrome zippers. He didn't wait for us to identify ourselves. He raised his head, apparently focusing on the seat behind me, and I could tell he was trying to gauge how hard it would be to reach his goal. Clearly, it took all his effort just to remain upright.

A set of male hands clapped his shoulders from behind. "Easy there, Jeff. We'll get you settled."

The guy behind Jeff poked his head around. "Hello," he said. All I could think was that these two patronized the same wigmaker. Their faces were completely different, but their hair was identical. "Don't mind my friend here. He'll be asleep inside of five minutes." To Jeff, he said, "Easy does it, buddy. One foot in front of the other. Yeah, there you go."

I watched the two men navigate an unsteady path between us, and found it curious that the helpful friend had a pair of drumsticks poking out of his back pocket.

Bennett leaned forward, sending me a look that communicated his intense displeasure. I held up both hands in supplication. What could we do? We were the guests in this situation. If Bennett didn't have a commitment for the next day, we could have begged off and tried to secure alternate transportation. But that was not an option.

The next through the door was a giant of a man. Tall and muscular, with a creased, pockmarked face, he was at least thirty-five years old, maybe more. He had sweat-flattened dark hair that curled at the nape of his neck and a vaguely familiar face. He wore expensive jeans and carried his black wig down by his side like a briefcase. The glittering diamond stud in his ear had to be at least two carats. He was flanked by two women, who were having a discussion between themselves, chatting and gesticulating in front of him as though he weren't there. The women were dressed more appropriately for the weather in skimpy pastel tops, pale capris, and high, strappy sandals.

The passage wasn't wide enough for them to come

through as a threesome, so the big fellow allowed the two women to enter first. They gave us a passing glance, but didn't miss a beat in their conversation.

Their companion smiled at me, then at Bennett. "Hi, I'm Adam. But most people call me Slick." He reached to shake Bennett's hand.

"I'm Grace," I said as he shook my hand. The light was beginning to dawn. "You were playing at Troppo last night, weren't you?"

His craggy face broke into a smile. "You caught the show? Awesome." He looked up to where Jeff was being tucked into the seat behind me. "You hear that? This lady here was at the dance club last night." To me, he asked, "What did you think? You like our sound?"

In my peripheral vision, I could see Bennett's confusion. "To be honest, I spent most of the evening upstairs." Adam's face fell, so I quickly added, "But for the time I was down on the main floor I thought you were great." It was the truth. I'd almost said as much to Irena last night. "You had quite a crowd there," I said. "Lots of dancing."

Adam looked as though he wanted to say more, but the last of the group jostled in behind him, led by a gorgeous collie that pranced onto the plane, straining against its collar. At the other end of the leash was yet another black-wigged man. Older than the two young men behind me, closer in age to Adam, he called to his eager pooch, urging the dog to heel. Clamped to the man's arm was a tightly packed woman who wore too much eyeliner and too little blouse. The narrow walkway didn't allow the three to walk abreast, so when the dog finally did heed its master, the woman was required to step back to allow the duo to proceed first.

The man stopped to coo softly to his dog, patting its side, saying, "There's a good girl. We're here now. Time to relax."

He couldn't see the daggers of resentment the woman shot the dog, who was behaving exactly as one might expect, pawing the ground, panting, glancing around at her new surroundings with happy, doggie expectation.

The man greeted us with a big smile. "That's right," he said, pointing at Bennett, "we've got guests on this leg. Millie, say hello."

Judging from the look on Bennett's face, he thought the woman's name was Millie, but as became apparent a split second later, the guy had been talking to his dog. Millie frisked forward, her gorgeous coat practically sparkling in the light, and placed a long white paw on Bennett's lap.

Grinning at the pooch's friendly demeanor, Bennett took the paw in his hand and said, "Hello, Millie."

The man introduced himself as Matthew, and the woman who'd boarded with him watched this little interplay with what could only be described as hot, molten loathing.

"Beautiful, isn't she?" Matthew asked in a proud papa voice. Before Bennett could answer, Matthew turned to me, almost shyly. "Hello." He introduced himself and his dog, and seemed surprised when his companion elbowed into the small space between us.

"I'm Pinky." Her smile didn't reach her eyes and her name didn't match her face. She had the brand of sass I'd expect to see in a dive bar: beer in one hand and a cigar in the other, hurling insults at the young guys playing pool all the while hoping one might ask her to join them.

She had a weathered, puffy look about her, and I got the impression that she was biting the insides of her cheeks. Her anger wasn't directed at me but at the poor dog, whose eyes were considerably more friendly than Pinky's. "We're the last to board because she"—Pinky flung her hand in Millie's direction—"needed to make a stop, if you know what I mean."

Not knowing what else to say, I shrugged. "Better out there than in here."

Matthew smiled. "See, that's the kind of attitude I like," he said to Pinky before moving deeper into the cabin and tossing another comment over his shoulder. "I think maybe you made a mistake joining us. Get with the program, Pinkster, or you'll never make it in this group."

She mouthed, "Pinkster?" and tightened her lips, but didn't say a word. I swore her cheek biting intensified.

Evelyn took a position at the front of the cabin and clapped her hands to get our attention. "Now that everyone is aboard, I'd like to go over a few guidelines before we take—"

She stopped mid-sentence as a man appeared behind her. Dressed in a navy-blue jacket with matching slacks and the sort of buttons and pockets you'd find on a uniform, he carried a duffel bag over one shoulder and took in the limited surroundings. I guessed him to be about forty-five years old, handsome, with a full head of dark hair and a dazzling smile that he used to his full advantage. "I am sorry to interrupt," he said in a deep Italian-accented voice as he extended his hand to Evelyn. "I am Rudolfo." I didn't think it possible, but his smile widened. "You may call me Rudy."

Evelyn was a full head shorter than our newest arrival, but that didn't stop her from adopting an authoritative voice. "You must have the wrong airplane," she said, gripping his upper-arm sleeve with one hand as she tried politely to navigate him back out the door. "This flight is full."

He didn't budge. "You misunderstand. I am here for service."

"Excuse me?" Evelyn said with a skeptical lilt. "Service for what?"

Her efforts to escort him out hadn't done much good, and he stepped into the widest part of the cabin, where we could all see him and hear every word of the conversation. "I have been contracted to accompany you. To assist."

Evelyn blinked a couple of times as she processed this. Her head tilted. "There's been a misunderstanding," she said. "Obviously."

"No misunderstanding." He held a finger in the air as though suddenly remembering something. He dug into the pocket of his uniform jacket and pulled out a folded set of papers. "Here are my orders."

Evelyn's body language was like that of a feral cat's facing an adversary. She puffed herself up to her greatest height, clearly wary of this stranger, yet poised to strike if he continued to threaten her authority. She took the pages out of his hands and scanned them quickly. As her shoulders relaxed, she began to frown. "Well," she said briskly, "it seems as though your story checks out. You'll understand if I call the office and verify." She didn't phrase it as a question as she moved for the phone.

Rudy appeared momentarily perplexed, though not the least bit put out. "You wish me to begin preparation for takeoff?"

Wound tight already, Evelyn didn't like being interrupted from her call. She held up a finger and spoke through clenched teeth. "Just. Stay. Right. There."

Rudy faced us, smiling. "Hello," he said while Evelyn completed her call. "You are going home?" He barely waited for our acknowledgment before continuing, "This airplane visits your North Carolina and also New York, yes?"

I exchanged a glance with Bennett as we both shrugged. Up to this point we hadn't known the plane's ultimate destination. "We're getting off at the first stop," I said. "Charlotte."

Evelyn returned to tap Rudy on the shoulder. I could tell from the consternation in her eyes and the tight set to her smile lines that she was following orders she didn't agree with. "Welcome aboard, Rudy," she said. "I didn't realize that you and I were going to be a team." She pointed to the rear of the plane. "Why don't you get yourself settled in the crew area in the back galley, and I'll be with you just as soon as I finish going over safety protocols."

Rudy's wide smile was back. "It will be my pleasure."

Evelyn caught my eye. "The more the merrier, I suppose," she muttered.

I watched Rudy make his way to the rear of the plane, wondering what was up with that.

Chapter 9

AFTER THE PILOT AND CO-PILOT CAME through to say hello and to assure us of a safe flight home, we were off. The guy with the drumsticks had pulled them out and maintained a constant, albeit quiet, rhythm on his thigh, nearby pillows, whatever he had handy. Bennett tuned him out, and I was surprised to find the patter rather soothing. Drunken Jeff managed to remain sound asleep—as evidenced by his cabin-shattering snores—but only until we reached an altitude where seat belts could be undone.

Awakened by the pilot's announcement, he gripped the back of my seat to pull himself up to standing. I turned to see his florid face hovering over my headrest. "Where are we?"

His warbling cry and yellowed, bloodshot eyes told me he hadn't actually sobered up yet.

"Sit down," Adam called from farther back. "And be quiet. I'm trying to read." I twisted to look. Adam leaned back in his oversized chair, one arm braced behind his head, his free hand holding a fat hardcover, reading glasses perched on his nose. If I didn't know he was the leader of a rock band, I would have taken him for a dad on vacation, or a college professor enjoying a little downtime.

Rudy hurried over to Jeff, easing the bewildered man back into his seat as his companions laughed among themselves then resumed whatever quiet conversations they'd been enjoying before the interruption.

Evelyn came around behind Rudy to talk to me and Bennett. "We're serving dinner on this flight, as you know." She handed us each a printed menu card from a small stack she held close to her chest. "We have a wonderful menu, and all I'll need is for you to make your preferences known."

She started to move to address the next row of travelers, including Jeff, but held up a finger as though suddenly remembering. "I have food allergy information on file for most of the group, but I don't have that information handy for either of you." She wagged her finger at us. "Be sure to let me know soon."

Bennett was way ahead of her. He tapped the menu. "I can tell you already that I don't want asparagus." Continuing to tap, he added, "I think I'll enjoy this pasta primavera, but without the asparagus."

"Got it," Evelyn said, jotting down a note. "Anything else?" She looked to me then back to Bennett, who had relaxed again.

"That's it," he said. "I'll eat almost anything else." One brow arched. "Almost. But asparagus?" He shook his head, frowning. "Won't touch the stuff."

"Millie won't eat asparagus, either," Matthew chimed in. Hearing her name, the collie regarded Matthew with devoted dark eyes. He and most of the others had taken spots on the long sofa. Matthew stroked the dog's back with obvious affection, talking about her the way parents often brag about their kids' antics. "You should see her pick the pieces out and drop them next to her food bowl." He laughed. "It's hilarious."

Pinky had separated herself from the group by taking a seat beyond the sofa. Although I could tell that she had been listening in on the conversation, she stared out the plane window with an expression so forlorn that it was obvious she wanted to be anywhere but here.

Matthew rubbed Millie's face. "You know exactly what you want, don't you, girl?"

Millie barked in happy response. Pinky sent the dog a scathing look of contempt before resuming her lonely gaze.

"You feed her table food then?" Bennett twisted his chair all the way around. "Is that healthy for a dog?"

"Yeah," Matthew assured him. "Only the best for my girl here. Organically grown, pesticide-free. I want to keep her around for a good, long time."

I could have sworn Pinky snorted at that. Matthew must have heard it, too, because he turned to her briefly before returning to our conversation. "So what do you do back in North Carolina?" Matthew asked us. "Are you two, uh, together?"

Bennett told Matthew all about Marshfield Manor and how I'd been hired as assistant curator just over a year ago. He left out any mention of the murder that saw me promoted from assistant to full curator and estate manager, but he gave a succinct overview of our tourist business and hinted about the treasures we shared with visitors.

"I've heard of Marshfield," Matthew said. "Been meaning to visit there, but haven't gotten around to it."

Matthew told us that SlickBlade had been contracted to open for a big-name group at an upcoming concert but declined to mention the group's name.

"You're not into heavy metal, are you?" he asked.

"Not especially. I'm more classic rock. Some heavy metal is okay—"

He smiled. "Don't worry. That's why there are so many varieties of music out there. Not everything appeals to everyone. You'd probably be surprised to find out that I enjoy operettas, wouldn't you?"

I was.

"Gilbert and Sullivan," Matthew said. "Can't get enough of them."

Delighted to discover a fellow fan, Bennett jumped into the conversation and soon the two men were discussing their favorite productions and even occasionally singing a lyric or two. I listened, joining their animated conversation from time to time. Behind us, Adam read, Jeff tried to go back to sleep, Pinky fumed, and the other travelers chit-chatted among themselves. Through all of this, Evelyn made sure our drinks were refreshed and that we had all the snacks we needed. She went out of her way to see to everyone's needs, quietly reminding Rudy that he was on board to work, not to socialize.

The cheerful cabin steward had been finding plenty of opportunity to stop by and talk with the two women who'd come on board. Although I hadn't learned their names, I knew that they were part of the band's crowd. They weren't cruel, but it was clear they had no interest in befriending Pinky, who had apparently latched onto soft-touch Matthew at the very last minute. Once aboard, however, her interest in the musician had dwindled, as had the group's interest in her. Maybe she'd seen this as an opportunity for a cheap ride home. I couldn't decide what her story was, and truth be told, I didn't care.

"May I get you another?" Evelyn asked Bennett with a wide smile as she pointed to his nearly empty glass. "We still have a long ride ahead of us."

Bennett picked up what was left of his Manhattan, drained it, and handed the glass to her. "One more," he said. "It'll help me sleep. After dinner I'll be dead to the world."

I winced, hoping no one noticed. Referring to death so lightly always sent a zing up the back of my neck. Personal quirk.

Evelyn winked. "You've got it." She turned to me. "Another lemonade?"

"I'm fine," I said. "Thanks."

Pinky spoke up. "I could use another drink."

I didn't make it a habit to monitor another's alcohol intake, but I was pretty certain Pinky had downed her third, and was now requesting a fourth. Maybe she'd been thirsty and had been enjoying lemonade, too, but the woman's glassy eyes made me doubt that. Evelyn plucked the proffered glass from her chubby hand and asked, "Death in the Afternoon, right?"

Before I could stop myself, I blurted, "That's the name of the drink?"

Pinky glared. "Don't get so high and mighty. I'll have you know that Ernest Hemingway invented it. He named it after one of his books."

"Oh," was the best I could manage. "And is it any good?"

"It's powerful," she said, "and doesn't make my brain foggy the way whiskey does."

"Good to know," I said politely, but she had already returned to staring out the window. I shot Bennett a "Whoops!" expression, which Matthew also caught. He waved a hand as though to dismiss my concerns. For two people who'd arrived together, they hardly behaved like a couple.

Delicious scents wafted our way from the rear of the plane—dinner would be served in less than an hour—and Matthew decided that it would be a good opportunity to allow Millie to visit the area of the plane that had been identified for her special needs in flight. He excused himself. Pinky watched them go, readjusting herself in her seat, looking as though she might need to use the human facilities herself.

I crossed the aisle and pulled the hidden jump seat out from the wall in front of Bennett. Evelyn dropped off his fresh Manhattan. Finally alone, he and I would be able to talk privately—relatively speaking—for the first time since we had arrived at Villa Pezzati. Without hesitation, I pounced on the big question that had been troubling me since our visit to his friend's in-house gallery the day before.

I kept my voice low but found it impossible to keep my anticipation level down. "What was up with that Picasso skull?"

Bennett glanced around the plane's cabin. Though luxurious and comfortably sized, it was still close quarters. He inched forward in his seat, then leaned toward me, elbows on his knees, drink in both hands. "It's a fake."

I'd expected him to tell me he had doubts about the piece's authenticity. I hadn't expected an unequivocal declaration. "Are you sure?"

He swirled his drink, sending a nonchalant glance around to ensure no one was listening. "Right here"—he tapped a spot just behind his right ear, where he'd indicated for me to look when I'd held it—"the real skull has a scratch." He took a deep sip of his drink, then amended, "More like a chink, actually. A deep one, roughly in the shape of a *P*. When Nico first acquired it, we discussed—at length—whether it had been left there intentionally or if the skull had suffered some damage in its travels. I'm sure you noticed that the skull at Nico's home had no such mark."

"Could it have—?"

Bennett anticipated my question. "The indentation was too deep to have been buffed out." He gave a vehement head shake. "That's beside the point, though. Nico would never have changed it. Never."

The enormity of what he was saying took a moment to sink in. "Have you said anything to Nico?"

"How could I? We were never alone long enough for me

to bring up the subject. And when I asked to visit the gallery again, I was accompanied by Gianfranco and Cesare. I couldn't spend any additional time with the skull because I thought my curiosity might look suspicious and I didn't know who to trust. I used my time there to take a closer look at some of the other pieces on display."

"And?" I was afraid of what he might say next.

The ice in Bennett's drink made soft clinking sounds against the glass as he swirled it again. "There is at least one more counterfeit piece in there. I'm sure of it. My guess is that there are more that have been replaced by forgeries. More than can be identified via my quick cursory examination. If it hadn't been for the skull—an item with which I'm intimately familiar—I never would have even thought to look."

"This is terrible news for Nico," I said. "Someone close to him is stealing."

Bennett gave a solemn nod. "Whoever switched it took great pains to make a copy—a too-perfect copy. It's a huge endeavor and I would bet my entire fortune that whoever did this didn't act alone and didn't act without power. You saw Angelo. He could snap either one of us in half if he had a mind to it."

"You think Angelo's behind it?"

"I don't know what to think." Bennett set his drink down, staring at me with intense concentration. "All I can say for certain is that Nico trusts too blithely. There are far too many individuals with access to his treasures. Cesare could easily have made the substitution during one of his visits. There's too much to consider."

"What should we do?"

He lowered his voice even further, despite the fact that no one paid us any attention. *"We,"* he said, emphasizing the word, "aren't going to do anything. You have a knack for getting into dangerous situations. I don't intend to let anything happen to you this time. I'll handle it."

I didn't like the sound of that. "Bennett, please. We'll be home soon and far away from scary Angelo or slimy Cesare. I can help without endangering myself."

"I've had time to think about this. I can't move forward, can't make any allegations without proof to back them up."

"Do you have proof?"

Matthew and Millie returned, interrupting us. Matthew took in a deep, appreciative breath. "Smell that, girl," he said to Millie, who stared up at him, pink tongue hanging out, and dark eyes full of love. "Dinner smells like it's almost ready."

Millie scooted around Matthew's legs just as Pinky grabbed her purse and got to her feet, apparently deciding to use the facilities after all. Despite the plane's extra personal width, the quarters were compact. As Matthew reclaimed his seat, we hit an unexpected moment of turbulence. Millie let out a high-pitched yelp of pain. Pinky jumped back.

Millie lifted one white paw and whimpered.

"Watch out," Matthew said, bending down to check her.

Pinky blinked. "Not my fault. What do you expect on a plane like this? It's built for people, not animals."

As though she understood, Millie whimpered again, nuzzling Matthew's hand.

Propelled by anger, embarrassment, and probably one too many Death in the Afternoons, Pinky slung her purse over an indignant shoulder. "Stupid dog. She should be riding in the cargo hold."

"What is wrong with you?" Matthew asked.

Evelyn came by at that moment with a treat for Millie. "Here you go, girl," she said before turning to Pinky. "We do have a few extra seats in back, if you'd prefer to sit there."

Pinky turned her back to Matthew, Millie, and the rest of us and marched to one of the open seats. Evelyn leaned forward to pet Millie, making eye contact with Matthew as she did so. "Where did you pick that one up?" she asked quietly.

Matthew scowled. "I'm too old to be falling for this sort of thing, but . . ." He sent a venomous glare toward the back of the plane. "She latched on to me last night and made me feel like I was being some knight in shining armor by getting her back to the States. I'm an idiot."

I dropped my voice. "You don't think she's on the run? I mean, from the authorities?"

He scratched the back of his neck. "Nah. The attendant back at the airport ran a quick check on her. Adam insisted on it." He jerked a thumb toward his reading friend. "When Pinky's in a good mood, she seems okay. Too bad she hasn't been in a good mood since she came on board."

Bennett asked a question about Millie's lineage and the two men began discussing dogs they'd had as pets. Evelyn took her leave, explaining that she needed to get back to preparing dinner. I participated in the conversation for a while then excused myself as a thought took hold. Evelyn had been incredible thus far. It couldn't be easy to keep a drunk man, two indifferent women, a dog owner and his dog-hating girlfriend, two eye-rolling friends, and two strangers happy. But from the moment we'd arrived, she'd worked tirelessly to ensure everyone's comfort, even that of her unwelcome assistant.

I thought about how much Antoinette, Nico Pezzati's chef, had appreciated our kind words about breakfast, and I decided to make an effort to thank Evelyn when I had a chance to catch her alone.

Rudy had taken a position in the business area at the front of the plane, but I'd lost sight of Evelyn. I assumed she was at work in the other galley. This was as good a time as any, I thought and started back. I passed the two chattering women, who didn't pay any attention, and Jeff, who had turned on his side and was again fast asleep. Across the aisle from him, the man who had helped him aboard, whose name I'd discovered was Carl, wore headphones. He kept up a beat with those never-ceasing drumsticks and didn't look up as I passed.

Adam did, glancing up from his book to make eye contact. His dark brows raised and he smiled slightly. I nodded a return greeting.

A set of cubicle-type walls separated the cabin of the plane from the rear area, with the side of the lavatory on my right and a floor-to-ceiling storage cabinet configuration on my left. They served as a clear separation between the two sections. I made a sharp right into the galley area, which was a lot more spacious than I'd expected. There wasn't a door, or any other sort of barrier to stop me from entering the work space, but as I drew closer, I could see that the lighting was different, as was the floor. No soft carpeting, no fancy fixtures; this section was purely utilitarian.

The smell of dinner was strong here. Garlic, tomatoes, and a hint of basil floated around the *L*-shaped space. I moved along next to the stainless steel countertop and heard Evelyn working around the tight corner to the left.

"Evelyn—" I began as I reached far side, then: "You're not Evelyn."

My brain took a full three seconds to process what was going on.

Pinky stood in front of four dinner plates, all of them heaped with steaming pasta primavera. I noticed several things at once. Her eyes were wide, her hands were filled, and all the color slid from her face as her bottom lip dropped open.

I took a step closer. "What are you doing?"

Evelyn came up behind me. There wasn't enough room for her to navigate around us, but she was close enough for me to feel her breath when she demanded answers of her own. "What are you two doing back here? I looked up and

saw Grace wander in. And you're here, too?" she said to
Pinky. Then to both of us: "This area is off-limits to
passengers."

I didn't wait for Pinky to reply. I stepped forward and
grabbed what was clearly a bubble sheet of medicine from
her hand. The almost empty ten-tablet foiled blister pack
reminded me of the dispenser for the medication I occasionally used when my cat allergies kicked up. But these
weren't tiny antihistamine tablets. These were bigger, and
orange. "What is this?" I asked, shaking the packet in her
face, noticing at the same moment that she had crushed
several of the tablets and sprinkled them into the food on
one of the dinner plates. She hadn't, however, crushed them
well enough—I could still see tiny flecks of bright orange
coating that hadn't yet been mixed into the sauced entrée.

"What are you putting into the food?" My pitch rose
with biting anger. "Are you drugging all of us?"

It took only a moment for me to comprehend the scene
more clearly. She'd targeted only one entrée. When I realized whose, my knees went weak.

She'd added the drug to the only plate that didn't have
asparagus.

Bennett's meal.

My entire body reacted. Adrenaline and fury narrowed
my field of vision. I saw her as though through a telescope.
Her face was pale, her eyes panicked and wide. Sweat bubbled through her thick makeup.

I stepped in, closing off any chance for her to escape.
"What. Are. You. Doing?"

Behind me, Evelyn's voice rose in her own version of
alarm. "What is that? Poison?" Her voice grew ever more
panicked as she cried, "Who are you?"

Face flushed, Pinky tried to shove past me. Where she
thought she'd be able to go on a plane this size, I had no idea.
I was taller and younger, and I hadn't had four heavy-duty

drinks to weigh down my brain. I spun her around, banging her against the plane's fiberglass wall as I did so. Holding her arms shoved against her squirming back, I called for help.

There was no need. By this time, just about everyone had made their way into the cramped galley. I heard Bennett's voice above the others' exclamations. "Gracie, are you all right?"

"I'm fine," I managed through clenched teeth. Pinky was trying to fight her way out of my grasp. "I need someone to hold this woman down. She's got some serious explaining to do."

Chapter 10

PINKY FOUGHT, BUT WITH ADAM'S AND RUDY'S assistance, we managed to get her back into the passenger cabin, where the two men pushed her into a seat. I'd kept the blister pack tight in my hand and had the presence of mind to grab the tainted food as well. I studied the serving platter: Rectangular-shaped and as delicate as fine china, it nonetheless bore tall edges to prevent spillage. High-end airplane dinnerware. Who knew there was such a thing?

For her part, Pinky looked ready to leap out the nearest door, parachute or no. Rudy held her in place with a grip on her bare upper arm, squeezing so tightly it looked as though he might break the skin. She winced as she wriggled against his grasp. Tiny tears formed at the corners of her eyes. "Stop," she said, "you're hurting me."

He pulled her upward, making her cry out. "Why were you attempting to harm these passengers? What is your reasoning?" Rudy's free arm came up as though he planned to backhand her across her jaw. Without thinking, I dropped the blister pack and grabbed his hand.

"Easy," I said. "We don't want to knock her unconscious."

Reluctantly, Rudy lowered his arm and released his hold on her bare skin. His fingernails had left deep indentations in her soft flesh. Balancing the dinner plate, I bent down to retrieve the blister pack, ignoring the chatter going on around me. The band members and the two girls had turned on Matthew, chastising him for bringing her on board.

Evelyn was beside herself. "I should never have left the food unattended. I didn't expect to be gone more than a minute." She sat, fingers massaging her temples. "My fault. My fault. But no one ever goes back there. I never thought . . ."

I tuned them out. All I cared about was why Pinky had targeted Bennett and exactly what it was she'd been attempting to do. I read the foil covering over the medication, my anger at a new high. "Thorazine?" I exclaimed.

Pinky looked away.

The noisy conversation around me stopped dead. "Thorazine?" Adam repeated, taking the blister pack from my hand. "That's an anti-psychotic medication." He sent Matthew another disdainful glare. "Did you know *anything* about this woman before you decided to invite her along?"

Matthew worked his jaw. "She said she needed my help."

"Your help to kill one of us, that is." Adam examined the blister pack. Eight tablets were missing. "All of us have been drinking. You mix alcohol with this much Thorazine and it's good night, sleep tight. Permanently."

"It was Bennett's dinner," I said. "She'd broken up the tablets into his food."

Evelyn gasped. Bennett met my eyes. His gaze was alarmed, but steady.

"How do you know?" Adam asked.

"Asparagus." I offered the savory dish for examination. "There's none on this plate, the one she was working on when I caught her. And Bennett was the only one of us—that I know of—who requested no asparagus."

Adam turned to Pinky. "What were you doing?" he asked. "Spit it out. Or I swear even though we're miles above the ocean we'll toss you out of the plane right now."

He was bluffing and Pinky knew it. She made eye contact long enough for me to see contempt simmering there, then squared her shoulders and looked away.

Adam tried again. "What's your real name?"

She didn't acknowledge him.

"How do you know Bennett?" I asked.

That got her attention. She glared up at me. "I don't."

"Then why—"

Matthew interrupted. "Millie," he said, his voice cracking with emotion. "Millie won't eat asparagus either and you knew it." He shook a finger at Pinky. "You don't like her. Admit it."

He faced the group to explain, "Thorazine is sometimes used to sedate dogs for air travel. I wouldn't ever let anyone give that stuff to Millie, but it's clear Pinky was jealous."

Next to him, as always, Millie nuzzled Matthew's leg.

But I'd been watching Pinky as he talked. Her demeanor had shifted the minute Matthew mentioned sedating the dog. Though it was subtle, I caught the change in her expression. Relief. Matthew had just given her an out. She jumped on it.

"Okay, fine," she said, rolling her eyes. "You're right. I was upset that you spent more time with your dog than you wanted to with me. I didn't think a little sedation would hurt her, though." She lifted a shoulder as though absolving herself. "I didn't mean any harm."

"No," I insisted, my words coming out fast and hot.

"Those drugs were meant for Bennett. If he would have eaten what was on the plate, he wouldn't have made it home. I want to know why you want him dead."

"I told you," she said, gripping her armrests with both hands, "I meant it for the dog. Can I get up now?"

"Absolutely not," I said, pushing her back when she'd almost risen to her feet. "I don't believe you."

Adam crossed his arms. "I'm inclined to not believe you, either. Last night at the club, you wouldn't have known that the dog was coming with us. Yet you brought the drugs. Why?"

Her mouth opened, bottom lip quivering. I'd put money on it being an act. "But . . . I did know. He . . . he talked about the dog. That's all he talks about, right?"

Adam turned to Matthew. "Well?"

He blew out a breath. "I don't remember if I mentioned Millie. Last night's kind of a blur. I don't even remember inviting Pinky. Not specifically. She sort of invited herself along."

Adam looked to me, but I didn't know where else to take this until we landed. "Should we notify the pilot?" I asked. "Aren't there protocols for this sort of thing?"

Rudy cleared his throat. "She is American. As is everyone here, I believe, except for me. I do not think that becoming involved in foreign politics is a good maneuver. Especially," he added, "if all she had hoped was to quiet the dog."

"Fine," Adam said, as though we'd come to a consensus. "We'll wait until we're in US airspace then ask the pilot to radio ahead. We'll turn her over to the authorities then."

"No!" Pinky shouted. "You can't. Seriously. Please. I didn't mean anything. I can't be arrested. Please."

The sullen, angry woman was gone. Perched at the edge of her seat now, she stared up at us with pleading eyes. "Listen, you can't do that. I'm not going to cause any more trouble. I swear."

Adam turned to me again. "What do you think?"

Bennett and I exchanged a glance and I knew we were both in agreement. "There's no way for us to know what she had planned, but it's entirely possible she was trying to harm Bennett," I said. "We can't discount that. We can't pretend that isn't a possibility. I say we turn her over to the police the minute we touch down."

Murmurs from those surrounding us probably helped Adam to make up his mind. "Makes sense," he said. He turned to Evelyn as he consulted his watch. "We'll still be in the air for a long time. We should take turns keeping an eye on her. I don't trust her. Not one little bit."

I exhaled, relieved that I wouldn't have to go up against Adam on this one. Although I understood that he was the leader of the band, the one everyone else looked to for direction, if he'd disagreed with my reasoning, I would have fought him every remaining minute of our flight. Fortunately, we seemed to be on the same page.

Evelyn piped up. "I don't know about serving dinner," she said uneasily. "I can't be certain that she didn't gain access to our entire food supply."

"I didn't touch anything," she said. "Except for the dog's food."

One of the two women who'd kept up the relentless chatter, and whose names I still didn't know, said, "If she was only working on the dog's food, then I don't see why *we* can't eat."

Adam beat me to answering. "Do you really want to take that chance?"

The woman looked at her friend for support. She squirmed. "I guess not."

I turned to Evelyn. "Do you have any prepackaged snacks on board? That might be enough to get us through."

Awakened by the ruckus, Jeff stumbled to his feet. His black T-shirt had ridden up and half his hairy belly was exposed. "Something smells good," he said, sniffing the air. "I'm hungry. What do we got?"

Evelyn said she would check in a minute.

Jeff noticed that were all standing in a crowd around Pinky's seat. "What's going on?" he asked. "She get airsick or something?"

"Or something," his friend Carl said, leading Jeff back to his chair. "I'll tell you about it."

Adam settled himself next to Pinky. "I'll take the first watch. We've got a long ride ahead of us."

"Count me in," I said. "I'll take over after you."

Rudy patted him on the shoulder. "I will help, too," he said with a glance toward Evelyn. "If you can spare my assistance."

She gave a terse nod, her expression at once analytical and relieved. "I've never encountered a situation like this before," she said to me. "This is highly irregular. I'm not sure I approve of keeping the pilot in the dark."

In a low voice, I agreed with her. "I'm hoping I'm able to get some answers out of Pinky when it's my turn to babysit."

Bennett joined us. "I'm not sure you will," he said. "Look at her. There's more going on behind those eyes than she wants us to realize." He gripped my shoulder. "Be careful, Gracie."

Chapter II

ADAM HAD HIS HANDS FULL WITH PINKY. SHE fidgeted in her seat, stood and stretched every few minutes, and wandered up and down the aisle, complaining that her legs were aching from lack of circulation. If her grievances had come after a couple of hours, I may have felt more charitable, but she got up to move after less than fifteen minutes and she was blasé about her detention and our scrutiny. I sensed she was up to something.

As a group, we discussed the food situation. Jeff was all for eating whatever food had been prepared, despite the risks involved. The rest of the passengers, including Bennett and me, decided to make do with whatever sealed snacks Evelyn was able to scrounge up.

"I'm hungry," Pinky said. "I'll eat the food. Give me whatever plate you want. You guys are all being paranoid."

With good reason, I thought. Her announcement, however, lent credence to her claim that she hadn't bothered any of the other dinners. The group changed. "What the heck?" Matthew said. "I'm starved."

Evelyn told me that she intended to personally inspect every bit of food before serving it, adding in a whisper, "The rest was waiting in a warming tray that I don't think Pinky even knew existed. I'll use that"—she wrinkled her nose—"and make it stretch. We'll be okay."

After everyone was satiated, more or less, a few passengers turned off their personal lights and decided to sleep the rest of the ride home.

All the excitement kept me from being able to relax. I decided it was my turn with our prisoner. "Adam." I tapped him on the shoulder. "Let me take over for a while." I pointed out the windows, where the daylight was beginning to wane. "We've still got a long way to go."

He shot me a look of gratitude. "If you insist . . ."

Doing my best to battle my jitters, I took his seat, aware of Pinky's glower of animosity. Despite her declarations to the contrary, I knew she'd targeted Bennett, and I wanted answers.

"Pinky's not your real name, is it?" I asked, keeping my tone even.

"Back off. I'm not your friend."

I scooched forward to the edge of my seat, hot anger rising up the back of my throat, my entire body tingling with the urge to grab this woman by the neck and take her down. "I'm not trying to be your girlfriend." Lowering my voice I fairly growled at her. "You tried to harm Bennett. That makes you my enemy."

"I told you. I wanted to sedate the dog." She came almost nose to nose with me. "But you are my enemy. I won't forget what you did to me."

I nearly launched out of my seat. "What *I* did to *you*?" About to remind her that it was *she* who'd been caught in an act of sabotage, I clamped my mouth shut and counted to three. Arguing with this nutcase wouldn't get me anywhere. Not where I wanted to go, at least. "Oh, no, sweetheart," I said, reveling in my burst of snippiness, "you got *yourself* into this mess."

Her eyes flashed. "You and your sugar daddy are in a world of hurt—you just don't know it yet."

I pounced. "I knew you were targeting Bennett."

At that she faced the window. "I'm tired. Leave me alone."

"Not until you tell me why you did it."

Still staring out the window, she remained silent, working hard to keep her expression blank, but there was no mistaking the fury rippling its way across her features.

I tried again. "I've never met you before. Bennett doesn't know you, either. I suggest you tell me what this is about before we turn you over to the police."

She took a quick breath.

"Oh, so that bothers you, does it?"

Making eye contact now, she rolled her eyes. "As if."

But there was something there. A twist of fear behind her unsteady frown.

"You have a record," I said as realization dawned. "Back in the States, I mean. I'll bet you weren't supposed to leave the country, were you?"

She didn't answer.

"Were you?"

If she could, she'd have bitten my head off. "Mind your own business, *sweetheart*." Leaning forward, she tossed my word back at me with a chilly smile. "Sticking your nose into things is what gets you into trouble all the time, isn't it?"

"Is she bothering you, miss?" Rudy asked me.

I could have decked him for interrupting. The pent-up anger Pinky was harboring had been ready to blow. I'd felt it. The fact that she knew enough about me—about us—to make a statement about meddling in other peoples' business told me I was onto something big.

"Everything is fine," I said, tersely. "Thank you."

But it was too late—the light of rage snuffed right out of Pinky's eyes. The disruption had allowed the angry woman space enough to calm herself.

Rudy placed his hand on my shoulder and spoke softly. "I can sit with the lady for a while if you like to walk around and talk to others."

"No—" I started to say.

"I have to use the bathroom," Pinky said. She boosted herself up and spoke in a clear, loud voice. "Did you hear me? I have to go to the bathroom. The potty. Are you going to let me go like a civilized person, or will you make me hold it for the whole rest of the ride?"

Adam and Matthew exchanged uneasy glances. The two women kept their heads together and shot looks of disdain Pinky's way. "Don't ask me to go with her," one of them said to the group. "I never signed up for that job."

I wasn't keen on accompanying another adult to the washroom, either. Evelyn spoke up. "There's barely room in there for one person so I don't recommend two trying to squeeze in. Besides, there's only soap, water, and paper products in there. We don't stock anything that could even be remotely considered dangerous."

Rudy watched all this through narrowed eyes. He worked his mouth then shook his head. "No."

Evelyn asked, "What do you mean?"

"She must stay in sight." He folded his arms and lifted his chin as though daring any of us to argue.

Evelyn shot me a look that spoke of exasperation. "I'll tell you what, Rudy. Why don't you go into the lavatory and see for yourself. If there's anything in there that gives you concern, we'll remove it." She spoke to him as though talking to a stubborn toddler. "Does that sound fair?"

He continued making pursing movements with his lips.

"Please," Pinky said. "I really need to go."

Rudy didn't answer. I knew from the look on Evelyn's face she wanted to ask, "Who put you in charge here, buddy?" but she was doing her best to achieve her goal without pulling rank. The entire cabin had gone silent as though waiting for some god on high to make a solemn pronouncement.

"You Americans," he finally said. Whatever that was supposed to mean. He strode toward the rear of the plane. Over his shoulder, he said, "I will do as you suggest."

Pinky made little huffing noises as though severely put out by our lack of courtesy. I couldn't imagine what kind of trouble a visit to the lavatory might cause, but I wasn't in the mood to be granting her any favors, either.

As Rudy moved off to inspect the washroom, Evelyn took a deep breath, surveying the cabin with a practiced smile. "Can I get anyone anything?"

It was hard to ignore the banging and bumping noises coming from the lavatory. From the sound of it, Rudy must have been ensuring that the wall and ceiling panels were solid despite the fact that there weren't very many places to escape, not when flying thirty thousand feet in the air. He emerged a few minutes later.

Pinky griped, "It's about time." Without waiting for any of us to give her a verbal okay, she stood and started away from us, purse slung over her shoulder.

"Hey," I said, going after her. "Leave your purse here."

She spun, giving me a withering look. "You're going to make me leave my purse?" Her laugh was ugly. "Give me a break. What do you think I have in here, anyway?"

Before I could answer, she unzipped her bag and thrust it at me. "Go ahead. You want to know what I'm carrying, look. Knock yourself out."

All eyes were on me, standing mid-aisle with this

oversized shoulder bag gaping up at me. "Anybody else want to check it?"

No takers.

I pawed through, grateful for the fact that the bag wasn't stuffed. I pulled items out one at a time and dropped them on her vacated seat. Wallet, makeup, cell phone . . .

"Hurry up, would you? And you can leave a few things in there, if you know what I mean."

I saw what she was talking about. A collection of female necessities. I reached around them, finding little else. There were no hidden pockets, no unexplained weight. Not even any more medications. I thought that was odd. Empty now, the purse had contained nothing more frightening than a brush, comb, and massive wad of cash.

"This is a lot of money to be carrying around," I said, holding it up.

She snatched it from my hand and stuffed it back in, along with the other items I'd found. "Yeah, well, I don't like using plastic. Last I heard, it wasn't a crime. Or are you going to have me locked up for that, too?"

Turning away from us, she marched around the back of the plane and slammed—inasmuch as one can slam something so lightweight—the lavatory door. It wasn't until we heard the "Occupied" lock turn that we all breathed easier again.

Evelyn approached Rudy. "You and I should remain in the galley until she returns to her seat. I don't want her accessing anything we might have in storage back there."

Rudy nodded.

"Evelyn," I said quietly, mostly so that Pinky wouldn't hear through the door, "When I caught her drugging the food, I'd come back to talk to you."

"Oh?"

"I'd intended to thank you for all your help, and for all you've done for of us." I smiled. "I still do want to thank you, but right about now I'd have to say you've gone far above and beyond the call of duty."

"That's very kind of you."

"We're all very grateful for your calm influence on this situation."

"I wasn't feeling very calm when we confronted her and saw those pills." Evelyn kept her voice low. "I've handled many in-flight emergencies in the past, but nothing like this. I confess, I'm rattled." She waved air near her face. "More than a little."

"Thanks just the same," I said.

Rudy watched our interchange with wide, dark eyes, looking for all the world like a puppy who hasn't gotten an expected pat on the head.

"You too, Rudy," I said. "I don't know what we'd do without you here."

His chest puffed. "It is my honor to be of value."

I returned to my original seat. Bennett was settling himself. Before he got too comfortable, I wanted to revisit the topic that had been on my mind before all the excitement threw us into a tizzy.

"So," I began, "until Pinky returns, why don't you tell me about Nico's fake skull? What kind of proof do you have?"

Chapter 12

BENNETT GESTURED FOR ME TO TAKE THE jump seat near his. I pulled it out from the wall again, and lowered myself onto it, making sure no one would eavesdrop. I needn't have worried. Matt and Adam were deep in discussion and over the quiet drone of the plane's engines, I couldn't make out any of their conversation.

One of their female companions made herself heard. "I'm not watching the troublemaker. We came on this trip for fun." Shaking a finger, she said, "Having anything to do with that mess is about as un-fun as you can get." With that, she turned back to talk with the other woman.

I couldn't figure out what role these two played in the band members' lives. Maybe they were in charge of business issues. Although that didn't seem likely.

As soon as my backside hit the seat, Bennett leaned close. "I think we're in deeper trouble than we thought, Gracie," he said with a furtive glance around. "I didn't really pay her any attention, but with all the fuss . . ."

He was speaking slowly and quietly. When he let the thought hang, my impatience made me feel as though teeny bugs were trying to escape from under my skin. "Yes? What?"

His gaze darted around the cabin before he answered me. "While you were going through her purse, I had a chance to really look at her."

"Do you know her?" I couldn't help rushing him. If he recognized her that would give us another clue as to why he'd been targeted. "Do you?"

He made a "Quiet, please" gesture with his hands. "Her expression changed while you were going through her purse. She made a face and it struck me that I'd seen her before."

"Where?"

He stroked his left temple, and I could see how hard he was concentrating. "I know how ridiculous this is going to sound, but I'm almost certain that she's the woman who was arguing with Angelo the other day. Remember when we heard them?"

"But . . ." Now I struggled to remember. "We didn't see who he was arguing with. I know we were curious, but I thought we'd just shrugged the moment off. Unless . . ." Light began to dawn and I found myself getting caught up in the possibility. "When Irena came to escort us downstairs to dinner, you went off on your own, didn't you? Did you see this woman? This Pinky?"

"You know how context often influences one's impressions? If this is the same woman, she was in a maid's uniform. Her hair was tied back." He gave an uncertain shrug. "And there's always the chance I may be mistaken about her. She might not be the woman I followed after all."

"You followed her? Why didn't you tell me?" This revelation was huge, and my words came out rather sharp.

"I had no reason to, young lady," he said in a tone a father might use when his daughter got snippy. "Until now, that is. After Angelo stormed by, I decided to find out if I could determine who he was fighting with."

I softened my next admonishment. "Didn't you tell me that we should keep our noses clean this time?"

"I said that you should. I never said a word about myself."

I was about to retort, but he continued, "I didn't get a good look at her and perhaps I'm making a lot out of nothing. But I'm fairly certain this is the same woman. She tried to open a door that was locked. When she turned around, she scowled—exactly as she did when you were rummaging through her purse."

"Did she see you?"

"She did not," he said with more than a little pride. "I've been around you long enough to know how to operate in stealth."

My jaw dropped in mock indignation. I tried not to laugh as I said, "Operate in stealth? You make it sound as though—"

The lavatory door banged open and even though it came from across the plane, the noise made me jump. "All right," Pinky said, hands in the air. "Whose turn is it to sit with me this time?"

No one volunteered. I didn't want to give up my chance to talk with Bennett now that we'd finally found a few free moments with no one else around, but the two female groupie-esque women ignored Pinky. Adam and Matt gave each other resigned glances, both looking as though they hoped the other would volunteer first. Jeff and Carl ignored us.

Bennett frowned, then made ready to stand—I assumed he meant to take a turn—but I beat him to it. "I'll do another shift." I worked up a smile and shot it at Pinky as I made my way toward her. "It'll give us more chance to catch up."

Evelyn interceded. "Listen, this flight was supposed to be relaxing. Thus far it's been anything but." To me, she said, "Let me take a shift, okay? It's the least I can do on behalf of the company to make your trip more comfortable."

"That's not your responsibility."

She placed a cool hand on my forearm. "Technicalities don't matter. I feel responsible, and that's what counts. Go on back to your seat and let me do this for all of you. We've gotten through dinner and there's not much for me to do for the next several hours." With a wink, she added, "This is usually the time passengers fall asleep; I'd rather have something meaningful to do instead of being so bored I start counting snores."

Having paid attention to our interchange, Pinky marched past, causing us both to take a step back. "Check this out," Pinky said loudly as she flopped into her seat. "I hit the jackpot. I get the stewardess all to myself." She made sure everyone aboard was looking her way when she added, "Eat your hearts out."

Evelyn took a deep breath and assumed the seat nearest Pinky's.

"You got a deck of cards?" Pinky asked, looking innocent and subservient now. "We could play gin rummy."

"Rudy," Evelyn called to her colleague. "We keep a few decks up front in the top cabinet. Would you mind?"

He nodded. A moment later, cards in hand, Pinky began looking around for a suitable playing spot. "We'd do better if you sat closer," she said, eyeing the front seat Bennett occupied. She pointed to the jump seat I'd abandoned. "If we pulled out the tray table on that first chair, it could work."

Bennett didn't need to be asked twice. "Be my guest," he said, standing. He and Pinky exchanged seats. Evelyn settled herself in the jump seat and made ready to pull the tray table out. Pinky held up a finger. "Hang on," she said. "I need to get comfortable."

She demanded a blanket and pillow, which Rudy hurried to produce. I lost interest in her peeves and pleas, turning my attention instead to Bennett. His new spot, smack in the center of the sideways sofa, made continuing our private conversation impossible.

"I'll be fine here, Gracie," he said, reading my mind or maybe my expression. "Why don't you and I use what's left of the trip to sleep? We will have plenty enough to deal with when we land."

I knew he was referring to the Picasso, and I could barely contain my impatience to find out how he planned to prove his claim that the item was fake. Swallowing my aggravation over Pinky's interruption, I made my way to the front of the plane and lowered myself in my cushy seat once again. Tense and out of sorts, I tried to focus on relaxation, but all I could think about was the fact that Bennett may have seen Pinky at Villa Pezzati. The ramifications—if indeed she was the same woman—were huge.

The more I thought about it, the more anxiety built. I clenched my fists, staring out the window in a futile attempt to clear my brain. I pieced together what we knew for sure: Pinky was a last-minute addition to the flight, and despite her claims about the dog, the fact was she had attempted to slip a potent tranquilizer into Bennett's meal. Not only that, but it seemed she had more information about Bennett and me than she should. Who was this woman?

I worked to steady my breathing, which was beginning to come in short bursts. My heart pumped furious blood up into my face and out to my extremities, making my head pound and my legs and arms tingle with terrific anger.

What if I hadn't chosen that particular moment to visit the back of the plane? What if the food Pinky had sabotaged been served to Bennett? What if?

The plane's expansive cabin became claustrophobic. Rage worked its way through my body, scratching closer to the surface of my skin, itching to break free. I wanted to take Pinky down. I wanted to hold her there, threaten her, make her talk. Make her explain why she'd targeted this gentle, kind man.

Though healthy and in great shape, Bennett was in his seventies, for crying out loud. I didn't know much about drugs, but the amount she'd added to his meal was certainly more than a single dose. The fact that Bennett had consumed a couple of alcoholic beverages beforehand made me weak with fear. Although I was certain Rudy and Evelyn had basic emergency training, there was no one aboard—there was no equipment aboard—to handle the sort of trauma we would have faced. Bennett could have died.

And if Pinky was, indeed, part of Signor Pezzati's staff, then this was no mistake.

I fidgeted with restive energy at the very possibility. Trying to focus my nerves, I dragged one leg under me and stared out the window at the empty sky. The plane's engines maintained their monotonous background noise, drowning out small talk and quiet movement. Any other time the white noise might have put me to sleep, but not today. Forcing myself to concentrate on the tops of the puffy clouds surrounding us, I thrummed my fingers on the armrest and bit the insides of my cheeks until I tasted blood. I despised being inactive.

Like it or not, however, I had no authority here, and precious little experience interrogating suspects. Hard as it was for me to wait, I knew this matter was better left to the authorities. We would hand her over the minute we landed and then, boy, I'd arm the police with as much ammunition as I could.

I didn't agree with the consensus to keep the pilots in the dark about the alleged criminal on board, but I couldn't come up with much of an argument for informing them.

Their job was to fly the plane. As we got closer, we'd ask them to have the police meet us at the gate. Beyond that, there wasn't much they could do, anyway.

Pinky and Evelyn had settled in around the small tray. The flight attendant's back was to me as she shuffled. For someone so determined to play gin rummy, Pinky's attention wandered from the cards. She seemed to be studying the other passengers, looking for something. I couldn't imagine what thoughts lurked behind those shifty eyes, but I didn't trust her as far as I could throw her.

Watching her surreptitiously, I pulled out a book and pretended to read. Evelyn alternated leaning forward and back as she dealt. Pinky stretched her neck slightly, angling to see something at the plane's very back, but I couldn't turn to look without making it obvious I was mimicking her movement.

Rubbing her chubby lips together, like someone who's recently applied lip balm, she cast her gaze around the area. I averted mine just as it was about to alight upon me. I thought I heard her snort, but it could have simply been plane noises.

Finished dealing, Evelyn sat back in the jump seat. She waved a hand in the direction of the draw pile between them. "Go ahead."

Pinky hadn't even picked up her cards. "I need something," she said, eyeing the floor.

Evelyn tilted her head, mildly impatient. "What now?"

And at that moment, I knew.

When people claim that incidents unfold in slow motion, they aren't exaggerating. Brains race thousands of times faster than events can develop and when catastrophe hits, when disaster strikes, or when one person is about to make a devastating move against another, the brain shifts into hyper speed. In that instant of realization, the brain decides on fight or flight. With accelerating fear and anticipation, tied up with calculations of outcomes and trajectories, all bound together with enough adrenaline to launch a person skyward, the mind moves faster than the speed of light.

By comparison, all surrounding activity crawls.

Pinky's body language was too tense as she reached for her purse, her choreographed movement too nonchalant. Her purse was too weighty. Even as I rose to my feet—no matter how fast a mind can race, the body can't possibly keep up—I caught the sag at the sack's center. When I'd pawed through it earlier there had been nothing in the purse that could have caused that deep of a drop, that solid of a *thunk* onto her lap.

"Evelyn." My mouth felt heavy and uncooperative. Syllables took their sweet time to roll off my tongue. Standing now, I reached out, a mere step away from Evelyn's side. She turned at the sound of her name, her eyes widening in a mixture of curiosity and confusion as I grasped for her shoulder.

But Pinky was ahead of me. Her arm up to the elbow inside her cavernous purse, she was on her feet before my voice squeaked with warning. Disregarded, her purse dropped softly to the floor as a vicious black gun materialized in front of Evelyn's face. Pinky didn't waste movement. Closer to the flight attendant than I was, and clearly not suffering from the element of surprise, she lunged into action.

Pinky's free left hand grasped Evelyn by the top of her head, grabbing tight fistfuls of hair. Evelyn dropped to her knees with a whimper.

Time and action all caught up now, Pinky pointed the gun at me. "Don't move."

Chapter 13

WHIPPING AROUND TO FACE THE REST OF THE passengers, Pinky shouted, "Don't anybody move."

I froze in place, weight on my forward foot, one hand still outstretched, so close, yet not close enough to Evelyn to drag her out of harm's way. As I eased to straighten, I became aware that Bennett had gotten to his feet. Matt and Adam jumped up right behind him.

"Stay back," Pinky shrieked, her eyes wild, her grip tightening in Evelyn's dark tresses. The woman on the floor cried out again, clearly in pain.

"What is wrong with you?" I asked. "Put that gun away."

Pinky backed into the corner, pulling the other woman, squirming, beside her. "No one moves unless I tell you to. Do you understand?"

I sent a fearful glance around the cabin. Wide, panicked eyes met mine. Even the two chatty women had silenced themselves. Everyone stared at Pinky. At Evelyn. At me.

"What do think you're doing with a gun on a plane?

Don't you realize how dangerous that is?" She seemed un-moved by my high-pitched rant. "For you, too," I shouted. "If we lose cabin pressure, we're all dead."

Pinky took a shaky breath. "One bullet hole in the fuse-lage won't make a difference," she said. "Not unless I blow out a window." She waved the semi-automatic. "Trust me, you don't want that."

"Listen, Pinky," I began, realizing how little I knew about this woman. I didn't even know her first name; I'd venture to guess that no one on this plane did. "You don't want to threaten—"

"Don't tell me what I want and what I don't want," she said through clenched teeth. "If you hadn't butted your nose into my business, we wouldn't be here right now."

"You tried to kill Bennett." My voice was high and wild, my rage raw and uncontained. I nearly leapt across the aisle to attack.

It was only hearing Bennett's low, "Gracie, no," that stopped me.

"Yeah, and if it weren't for you, he would be dead by now." She lifted her chin toward Bennett. "And we'd all be better off." Evelyn clenched her eyes and lips shut as Pinky twisted her hair. The captive woman trembled with fear.

"So you admit it—"

"I admit nothing. I'm not going down without a fight." Her eyes were flat, dark, and dead. This was a different woman than we'd seen earlier. Terror was making her ruth-less. "You can either let me go when we land, or you all die." She hefted the gun. "This holds seventeen rounds, and I'm a crack shot. Do the math. Nobody goes home unless I go free."

The plane erupted with loud confusion. Above the din of the two women screaming, Adam and the other band members shouting, I heard Bennett. "Why?" he asked.

No one listened.

"Pinky," I said, keeping my own voice low. I took a hesitant step forward.

She leveled the gun, eye height. "Go ahead, take one more step. I dare you. You'll never take another. Don't push me, honey. I can place my shot where it will do the most damage: jammed into the back of your thick skull."

I sucked in a breath.

"I don't want to hurt anyone," she said. "Not because I'm a nice guy, but because that will only complicate my departure."

I didn't doubt it. There wasn't even a glint of compassion in that expression.

"Now," she said, raising her voice, "everybody listen up."

The group fell silent. Once comforting, the solid roar of the engines reminded us that we were tens of thousands of feet in the air. Vulnerable.

"You will all sit down," she began. Pointing the gun at Rudy, who had inched toward the rear of the plane, she added, "You, too. I want to be able to see all of you. See what you're doing."

Slowly, everyone began reclaiming their seats. "That's better."

Millie barked her displeasure.

Pinky glowered at the dog. "Shut that mongrel up," she said.

Matthew pulled Millie closer, stroking her fur and murmuring softly. "Don't shoot my dog," he said.

Pinky looked away. "I don't hurt animals."

"But people are fair game?" I asked.

"Just the ones who get in my way."

Bennett had remained standing. "Why?" he asked again.

Pinky didn't answer. She aimed.

Bennett didn't flinch. "Why do you want to kill me?"

"Bennett." My voice came out raspy. "Don't goad her. Please don't."

"You have no idea how bad I want to get this over with," she said. I was the only one close enough to see her other hand, in Evelyn's hair, spasm as though pulling a trigger. I winced.

"No—" I cried.

"It's a simple question," Bennett said, stepping out into the aisle. All that did was give Pinky an easier target.

I swallowed. "No," I tried again, hardly able to manage more than a pleading whisper. "Bennett."

Clasping one of the leather seat backs in a strong grip, he didn't pay me any attention, but affected an air of curiosity. "I assume you're not acting alone, Pinky—or whatever your name is. You've been assigned to get rid of me, and I want to know why." He waited a beat then curled up one corner of his mouth. "That's presuming you even know the reason."

"Of course I know," she snapped.

The plane dipped slightly in several quick bursts of turbulence, making Pinky stumble. Evelyn yelped as tufts of her hair were yanked out. The dark tresses floated to the floor as Pinky shifted to regain her footing.

Bennett never lost his grip of the headrest. "Then by all means"—he held out his free hand, encompassing the group—"enlighten us."

Indecision danced in the back of her eyes for a fleeting moment. She ran her top teeth over her bottom lip then said, "Can't."

Bennett didn't break eye contact. When he took another step forward, I sucked in a terrified breath. "What is it you want from me?" he asked. "There must be some way to settle this."

Again, she wavered. "Back off, old man," she finally said. "You got lucky this time, but you won't again. If I didn't need to get off this plane, you'd be dead on the floor right now."

Harsh words, steady gun. This woman wasn't messing around. She blinked hard, twice, the way drivers sometimes do to stay awake. I got the impression she was desperately fighting for the best answer to this mess. "What I want," she continued, "is safe passage off the plane when we land." She worked her mouth. "You all get that? Easy stuff. You keep your mouths shut until I'm out of here, and nobody gets hurt."

"Except me, you mean," Bennett said. He took a step closer to her.

"Don't!" This time I shouted, my word a strangled cry.

He held a hand up to me to warn that he knew what he was doing.

"I told you," Pinky said, looking around as though seeking a way off the airplane, "all I want is to get away. We land; I go. You keep your mouths shut about all this. You breathe a single word, and I'll hunt you all down and kill you one at a time."

"I don't think so," Bennett said.

Pinky watched him.

"Why do I get the impression that your deal doesn't include me?" Bennett asked with conversational nonchalance. "Why do I get the sense that someone—you perhaps, maybe a colleague—has plans for my demise whether you go free after this debacle or not?"

Her eyebrows jumped; it was an involuntary affirmation, which twisted my stomach. "Just let me go," she said avoiding his question. "Make it easy on yourselves."

"Young lady," he said, "you're brandishing a firearm on an airplane. You've taken a hostage. There is no chance whatsoever you're leaving this plane in anything but handcuffs. If you tell us who's really behind this, it could go easier for you."

Pinky yanked on Evelyn's hair, pulling her to her feet. The woman stumbled upward, tears of pain in her eyes, but she didn't cry out. Facing Bennett, Pinky spoke low, her voice menacing. "You take one more step, she dies. And then I'll have nothing to lose, will I? Right now, you let me walk away and she lives."

She let go of Evelyn's hair, but held her tight by the upper arm. For her part, the flight attendant looked as though she'd drop to the floor if Pinky let go.

"Everybody sit down," Pinky said. She waved the gun at Bennett. "That means you, too."

He glanced over at me. We were the only two who had remained standing. With an expression of vexed resignation, he nodded acknowledgment and retreated. As we both sat, Pinky shoved Evelyn into her own vacated chair, not the jump seat, and trained the gun's barrel at her forehead.

"That's better. Let's all just stay calm for the rest of the flight. No one moves. Not an inch, do you all understand?" She waited for murmured acquiescence as she worked her mouth. "How much longer do we have before we land?"

Evelyn stared up at her captor, eyes blank.

We all turned as Rudy spoke up. "Six hours," he said. "That is a long time to hold us in our seats."

Pinky scrunched up her nose. "And a long time for me to stand. I want to sit." Contemplating her options as the rest of us anticipated her next move, she began to make puffing noises through pursed lips. Her leg bounced. This was not a woman with a plan; this was a woman who couldn't figure out what to do next. What scared me most of all was that she expressed no remorse for what she'd done so far, and only the barest hesitation to escalate the situation.

"Here's what's going to happen," she said, raising her voice, though the cabin was as silent as a small plane compartment could possibly be. "I'm going to sit. This woman here"—Pinky pointed at Evelyn with the gun—"will sit in that little side chair." She indicated the jump seat. Looking around at all of us staring back, she pointed the gun again. "You, the other flight attendant. What's your name again?"

He raised his chin and his voice. "I am Rudy."

"Well, Rudy, I'm putting you in charge. You make sure that nobody moves. Got that? And nobody leaves the plane until I get away." She stopped, considering this. "For at least a half hour." She waited for him to nod before adding, "Don't worry. You'll survive." With a smirk, she added, "As long as you behave."

Rudy cleared his throat and half rose from his seat. Pinky's eyes narrowed. "Evelyn is the primary flight attendant," he said. "There are important things she must do before we land. If she doesn't, there will be questions."

Pinky scratched her chin with the back of her wrist, fingers wrapped around the gun's grip. I took consolation in the fact that at least her index finger wasn't on the trigger.

Perhaps sensing the woman's indecision, Rudy spoke up again. "These tasks are imperative," he said. "There is no changing that."

Pinky looked over to me, as though gauging whether to have me and Evelyn change places. Before I could even consider what I'd do if she proposed a switch, Pinky shook her head at Rudy. "You do them."

Almost completely to his feet now, Rudy said, "But then I must have free access to the front." He pointed past us to underscore his meaning. "You will allow me?"

"When do you need to do these 'tasks'?" she asked.

He stared at the back of Evelyn's seat as though he was hoping the woman would turn around and give him guidance. "An hour before we land," he said. "Or maybe one half of one hour."

Pinky's jaw pulsed, but she relented. "You will not move without my permission. And when you're up here"—she gestured toward the front of the plane with her head—"I will be watching you. Is that clear?"

Rudy blinked. "Clear. Yes."

"Now, sit." She nudged Evelyn up and into the jump seat with the barrel of the gun. As Pinky resumed the front seat, she swiveled so that she could keep us all in her sights. Turning to me with cold resentment on her face, she glanced down at her gun then back up at me. "I actually hope you try something stupid. I really do."

Chapter 14

I DIDN'T KNOW HOW MUCH TIME TICKED BY. I rarely wore a watch and couldn't consult my cell phone, which was, in any case, turned off and stowed in my purse. What felt like an hour was probably no more than ten minutes, but I felt every inch of every second, doing my best to quell heart-in-my-throat fear.

We'd come to as much as of a truce as we could have, given the circumstances. Other than Millie's occasional barks and nuzzling whimpers, not one of us made a sound.

Matthew tried for some leniency. "She has to go," he said, petting Millie's head. "Her designated spot is up front. It won't take more than a minute or two."

"No," Pinky said.

She didn't elaborate, and no one pushed her. The smoke-screen card game long forgotten, Pinky was ensconced in the soft leather chair, Evelyn on the edge of the hard temporary seat. No one spoke.

We waited for one thing: to land. For this nightmare to

be over. For all of us to depart with no one getting harmed. We hadn't discussed Pinky's planned escape among ourselves at all. What choice did we have? Pinky seemed all too willing to influence us with her seventeen-round weapon. She was going to get away with this.

And yet . . .

I craned my neck to check on Bennett. He sat far back, on the opposite side of the aisle, staring out the windows, probably thinking exactly what I was: There had to be some way to stop her. There had to be a way to find out who wanted Bennett dead.

"Turn around," Pinky said to me.

I sighed for effect, but complied. "How do you expect to get away?" I asked her. "I don't understand."

"You don't need to worry about that, do you?"

I faced the window.

A short while later, metal scraped against metal: a lock turning. I sat up. Evelyn spun toward the sound. Pinky faced her seat forward and stashed her gun next to her leg as the cockpit door opened.

The co-pilot held up a hand. "Everybody still awake, eh?" Tall and muscular, he had short, curly red hair and what would have been an infectious grin in another life. "Most folks are dead to the world right about now." He laughed at his own joke. No one joined him.

Confused, he took in our silent, immobile group. "Everything okay back here?" He placed one sturdy hand on the back of my seat, the other on Pinky's. "You all aren't worried about that bit of turbulence, are you? It's going to get worse before it gets better, but there's nothing dangerous."

"That's great," Pinky said with a tight smile. "Good to know."

Encouraged by this minimal response, he grinned at the rest of us. "Think of it like a fun roller coaster. A few dips and rises here and there, but everyone gets off the ride in one piece at the end."

"Let's hope you're right," I said.

He gave me a puzzled look. "So you are nervous, huh?"

I ignored Pinky's glare. "More than you realize."

"Seriously?" He leaned in closer, patently concerned for my well-being. "There's nothing to be afraid of. I've been flying for years and been through much more tense situations than we're in now."

Because he faced me, he didn't see Pinky raise the gun just enough to remind me it was there. Yeah, like I could have forgotten. She pointed it at the back of his head and shot me a look that warned me to shut up.

I nodded. "Thanks," I said. "That helps."

He wasn't about to be dismissed so quickly, and I berated myself for engaging him in conversation. I'd put his life at risk. "You fly chartered jets often?"

It came across like a bad pickup line. "Nuh . . . no, this is only my second time on a charter."

Behind him, Pinky's eyes widened. An unambiguous signal to cut this conversation short.

"Well," he said, straightening and stretching his long arms out on either side of his body. "Smaller planes are my favorite way to fly. There's nothing else in the world like it. It's like—I don't know—like being strapped to a bird." Chin up, arms out, his face took on a look of pure rapture. He stayed that way for less than five seconds, but it felt like a thousand years.

"Thanks," I said, breaking his spell.

"You get used to the motion of the plane. You start realizing it's normal." He tilted his head, dropped his arms, and regarded me. "Start thinking of it like that and you'll never be afraid again."

"I would like to not be afraid."

"It's easy." The grin was back. "My name's Robert, by the way. But I like Bobby better." He looked ready to settle in for a chat with an eye toward more. Maybe that *had* been a pickup line.

When Pinky aimed, with a menacing appraisal of the back of Bobby's head, I practically screamed at him to leave. I forced myself to adopt a haughty air of disinterest. "That's great, thanks," I said, and turned to face the window.

He made a sound like *"Humph,"* and waited a few beats as though hoping I'd return my attention to him. When I continued ignoring his presence, he shrugged and continued to the back of the plane, where we heard him enter and lock the lavatory.

"What kind of smart-aleck are you?" Pinky shout-whispered.

I pulled my lips in and fought the bile rising in the back of my throat.

Moments later, the washroom door opened, and I studiously avoided making eye contact with co-pilot Bobby. He loped up the aisle to the front of the plane, slowing as he passed my seat. I pretended to sleep and a moment later he was back inside the cockpit; I could practically feel the collective breath of relief we all took when we heard the door latch.

"Don't try anything like that again," Pinky said.

I didn't even try to disguise the peevishness in my tone. "I'm tired of your antics. You've got control now. Why don't you just shut up?"

I knew I shouldn't egg her on, but the tension in the plane, the encroaching claustrophobia, and the very real fear that the co-pilot could have been shot—which would have been my fault for talking with him—sent my nerves spinning.

Rather than react, however, she settled back into her seat, leaning her head against the cushy back, watching

Evelyn as though she expected the other woman to leap up and wrestle her for the gun. Evelyn kept her face averted and I thought I noticed small chunks of hair missing from her scalp. I could only imagine how much pain she was in.

Not wanting to cause more, I sighed and looked away. I knew we all fervently wished that we'd land in Charlotte in a hurry.

Over the next hour or so, the turbulence continued, and just as Bobby had predicted, we became accustomed to the bumps and jostles. There were far fewer dips than there had been and, despite the circumstances, despite the rush of adrenaline that zipped up whenever I thought of how close Bennett had come to ingesting the killer drugs, my body craved rest. I'd been up since early this morning, and I knew that hours in this gently rocking plane could easily lull me to sleep.

Behind me, others had already begun to doze. Soft snores came from both sides of the aisle. I turned to see Adam, Rudy, and Bennett still awake but everyone else in various stages of slumber. I felt a prickle of annoyance but realized that when the body is pushed to its limits, something has to give. We'd all been stressed to the max, wreaking havoc on our energy levels. The threat of imminent danger was gone, and so our bodies did what was required to recharge.

I fought the urge to close my eyes, adjusting myself in my chair, blinking and pinching the skin on my forearms and legs to create quick bursts of pain that I hoped could keep me alert. Never again would I criticize a movie or a book where the captives fell asleep. I was discovering, much to my frustration, how difficult it was to remain conscious.

Evelyn stared at me, her eyes wide and her fingers gripping her knees as though to keep them from knocking or her hands from shaking. We knew better than to speak, but I tried my best to communicate support.

Pinky, it seemed, was having difficulty staying awake as well. As her eyes fluttered, her chin lowered, and her jaw began to drop. After as many alcoholic beverages as she'd had, I wasn't surprised. With a start, she sat up. I turned back to the window before she realized I'd noticed.

Pinky had the gun tucked next to her beside the armrest, where I couldn't see it. I wasn't able to tell if she had a finger on the trigger or if she'd let her grip relax. Attempting to disarm her would be a risk—a big one—but what other choices did we have?

I bit my bottom lip. We could let her go, I thought. Give in to her demands and pretend that she'd never threatened any of us.

I didn't like it.

Pinky's chin dropped again. This time, however, instead of snorting herself awake, her head lolled to one side, and she began breathing evenly. I watched her for a slow count of ten, then fifteen. Her lips, slack and open, moved as though she were trying to mouth, "Weh weh weh."

Evelyn watched me intently as I pantomimed sticking a gun at my side and then silently asking her if she could see it.

Her dark eyes were full of terror and determination as she leaned forward ever so slightly to get a better angle. The jump seat creaked and we both froze, but Pinky's body had relaxed. She was out.

Evelyn pointed to where the gun was, then lifted her hand and extended her fingers in a clear message: Pinky had let go.

Careful not to make a sound, I twisted around to see Adam, Rudy, and Bennett all watching with rapt attention, Rudy on the edge of his seat. He lifted a finger to his lips and shook his head. It was at that moment that I realized the next move was up to me.

I don't know what I'd hoped—that when the coast was clear one of them would step forward to disarm Pinky? Doing so would cause commotion, wake her up. Evelyn was closer, but her jump seat made too much noise.

I breathed as slowly as I could manage, keeping my mouth open to quiet the sound. Without grasping the armrests—in case they squeaked—I slipped my feet out of my shoes and noiselessly maneuvered myself to a crouching stand.

I would have one shot at the gun. One.

My fist came up to my mouth as I fought down my rising panic. It didn't help to note how badly I was shaking. Freedom could be two steps away. All I needed to do was cross the aisle, reach down, and grab the gun. Could I do it smoothly enough? What if it was jammed too tightly against her leg?

Three steps, I decided. I'd take three. That would put me that much closer. Give me better leverage from above. I might be able to slip it out without her noticing.

My breaths came shallow and fast.

Evelyn shook her head, her eyes wide. I didn't know what she was trying to communicate, but her fear was palpable. I pointed to her then spread my hands, asking an inaudible question, "Do you want to get the gun?"

She shook her head, violently. Put her hands up, as though begging me to sit down again.

I turned to the three men watching me. Matthew was awake now, too. Millie had gotten to her feet and was prancing and panting, clearly hoping someone would finally let her relieve herself. I held up a hand, hoping that would keep the girl quiet, but the alert look in those dark brown eyes told me she was ready to bark.

Now or never.

One.

I took a step forward. The quiet hum of the plane masked

the sound of my movement. Pinky's breathing deepened, slipping into soft snores.

Two. Another step forward. I could see the gun. I glanced back at Matthew, who was furiously petting Millie, rubbing her face and nuzzling her snout, doing his best to keep her quiet.

This was it. I took a deep breath and froze as Evelyn let out a gurgle of fear. Her face crumpled, and her hands came up next to her head. She clenched her eyes and let out a low moan. I stopped in my tracks, holding my breath. Pinky didn't move, but Evelyn stared up at me with wild eyes. It was clear the tension had taken her to the breaking point. She wasn't going to last another second at this rate. She was going to explode. I had to act.

The minute I leaned into Pinky's chair to reach for the gun, Evelyn screamed and leapt to her feet, smacking me backward. I landed, double-*thump*, hitting the side of my chair before ending up on the floor.

"I can't take it! I can't take it!" With me out of her way now, Evelyn grabbed for the gun.

Pinky, almost forgotten in the sudden frenzy, woke up with a shriek, becoming immediately aware of Evelyn's attack. Evelyn had gotten to the firearm first and the two women struggled, grappling and fighting for control.

I scrambled to my feet, aware of the men doing the same. Just as I got both hands around Pinky's upper arm, she twisted the gun's barrel downward, into Evelyn's face. In panic, or the sudden comprehension of the situation, Evelyn went rigid. Her eyes wide, she let go of the weapon, both hands flying up in surrender.

Evelyn's abdication was lost on Pinky. Hot in the throes of the battle, she thrust herself backward. In the space of two heartbeats, I watched the knuckles on her gun hand go white. Her arm extended, her face contorted, and she squeezed.

The blast knocked me sideways. All my senses dulled at once. I knew I'd fallen against the chair's armrest, knew I'd clenched my eyes. With hands wrapped around my head, I realized I couldn't hear.

My hip had bounced against the floor and my head smacked the side of my seat. I blinked, trying to see.

With effort, I pulled myself up, still unable to hear much, still unable to make sense of the activity around me. Occasional bursts—screams—broke through the over-whelming pounding in my ears. Disoriented, I got to my feet, gripping the side of the seat.

Mouth hanging open, Pinky stared. But not at me.

I followed her gaze to the floor but couldn't hear my own scream. "Evelyn!"

She was slumped on the floor, with her back against a seat, her legs spread like a rag doll's. Her head lolled side-ways and her eyes widened and narrowed, as though she were trying to keep herself awake. One hand clutched at the neckline of her uniform, grasping at the fabric even as blood leaked between her fingers.

"What did you do?" Still unable to hear myself, I dropped to my knees next to Evelyn. I cradled her head, trying desperately to remember whether it would be better to lay her down or keep her upright. Down, I thought, as I wrapped an arm around the back of her neck. I tried to convince myself that it was a flesh wound. Maybe Pinky had hit Evelyn's shoulder.

"Easy," I said, not knowing if she could hear. I had the presence of mind to wrap my fingers around her wrist. Her pulse was weak, her breathing labored. "You're okay," I lied.

Muffled noises from above. I disregarded them.

A kick to my side I couldn't ignore. Still on my knees, with my back to the rest of the cabin, I twisted. Pinky had regained control. She brandished the gun above me while the rest of the passengers watched like an audience frozen in terror.

As my hearing began to return, I made out what Pinky was saying. "Back up, back up. Get away. Get back."

She kicked me again. "You, too."

"But what about—" As I turned to the injured woman, the words died on my lips. The hand grasping at her neckline fell to her side, limp and lifeless. The ragged movement of her chest ceased. Her eyes went still and blank. Half open, half closed, they made her look like a sneering mannequin. Desperately, I repositioned my fingers in a futile search for a pulse. Nothing. I tried again, this time pressing hard against her carotid artery. No beat, no life. "Evelyn!" I shouted, as though I could wake her.

Pinky raised her voice: "Get up. Look what you made me do."

Though shaken, I was unharmed. I grappled to my feet, facing her. "You killed her."

Her face betrayed her fear. She was as shocked by what she'd done as I was. Before I could get another word out, however, she'd shoved the still-smoking gun into my breastbone. I could feel the heat, smell the acrid residue. I didn't look down even as she pushed me backward, my heels bumping against Evelyn's still form as my shoulder blades hit the wall. "You did this," she said. "You stupid idiot."

She realized that her back was to the rest of the group one split second after they did. Adam, Bennett, and Matt had started for her. She waved the gun in a semicircle, forcing them to retreat.

"See? See?" Pinky rasped. "I told you not to mess with me. You all did this to her. It wasn't my fault. You tried to trick me, and now one of you is dead." She grabbed my hair with her free hand and forced me to my knees. "Any of you makes a move and this one is next."

My hearing had returned enough to know that the plane's cabin had gone silent at her pronouncement. All I could make out were soft sobs and hiccups of fear, but I couldn't tell who they came from.

"Now." Pinky took a deep breath in a studied attempt to settle herself. "Unless you get me off this plane safely and without any cops around, more of you are going to die. Is that understood?"

Chapter 15

THE ENTIRE SHOOTING COULDN'T HAVE TAKEN
more than thirty seconds. Forty-five at most. On my knees,
my back to the aisle, wedged between Pinky's legs and
Evelyn's lifeless form, I bit my lips hard, doing my utmost
to maintain control. My body rebelled. Shaking harder
than Bootsie did when we went to the vet, I probably would
have sunk to the floor had I not been held upright by my
hair.

A sharp noise from the front of the cabin—metallic and
fast—caused Pinky's grip to tighten, and the hot pain in my
scalp brought tears to my eyes.

A male voice behind me. "What's going on here?"

The instant Pinky let go of my hair, I dropped my hands
to the floor and crawled to the window, twisting to see the
co-pilot's stunned expression. He'd startled Pinky enough
that she'd lowered to a crouch and now held the gun in both
hands. "Don't move," she said.

His lips formed silent words in an attempt to speak. A

detached part of my brain recalled his name. Robert. He could manage only fragments at first: "We heard a . . . What did . . ." When his gaze lit upon Evelyn, his eyes grew large, his mouth dropped open.

With enough of a head start, and the gun back firmly in hand, Pinky had the advantage. "Shut up," she said. "It wasn't my fault." She angled herself so as to keep me and Robert in her sights. We were the only two close enough to make a move on her, something I wasn't steady enough to attempt.

Comprehension began to dawn on co-pilot Robert. His face changed. Brows dropped low over suddenly steely eyes. Resolve took over for confusion. "Give me that," he ordered, reaching for Pinky's gun.

She jumped back.

"Do not," came a voice from the rear of the plane. Rudy's. He stood. "The pilot will be calling to find out what is wrong. On the intercom." He pointed to the work area at the front of the plane. "You must not shoot the co-pilot, or we could have danger."

Pinky smiled at Rudy then, an arrogant, self-satisfied smile. It was the weirdest feeling watching her take all this in as though enjoying herself. "Well, then, we ought to tell him everything is all right back here."

Rudy hesitated.

"Take care of that, you hear? Tell the pilot that everything is fine and dandy back here."

He lurched forward, looking unsure.

"Go on," she said, waving the gun. "What are you waiting for?"

Co-pilot Robert was across the aisle, standing in front of my original seat. In order to make it to the head of the airplane, Rudy would need to pass between Pinky and Robert. Could I attempt to wrangle the gun from Pinky using Rudy as a distraction? I wasn't confident in my abilities on that score. We'd seen how well that turned out.

Would the co-pilot make a move? The look on his face made it clear he was trying to make sense of all this. "What do you want?" he asked in a soothing voice. "Maybe I can help."

Rudy advanced two steps.

"Fat chance of that," Pinky said. Her body language told me she was feeling stronger again. She'd drawn herself taller and dropped the second grip on the gun. "I'm in enough trouble for screwing this up already."

"From whom?" I asked.

Rudy passed in front of Robert. Pinky turned to answer me. "You'd be surprised—"

Robert lunged for the gun, pushing Pinky's arm—and aim—upward. Mercifully, the firearm didn't discharge. Surprised by the attack, she spun as she fought back, screeching and clawing as he gained control of the weapon. Using arms, legs, and fingernails, she dug at him as I leapt into the fray and tried to pull her down.

One step ahead of me, Rudy grabbed Pinky and slammed her against the fiberglass wall, causing the gun to pop out of her hand. If this had been a movie, she'd have been knocked unconscious. Instead, she rolled onto her hands and knees, crawling like a robot doll to the weapon, now inches from Robert's shoe.

Rudy wasn't finished. He reached down and grabbed Pinky by the head, spinning her upward to her feet.

I heard the crack when her neck broke. Quiet, yet profoundly loud even over the din, it was a sound I knew would haunt me forever.

She dropped to the floor. I didn't need to check for a pulse. Instinctively, I looked at Evelyn. Two women rendered suddenly lifeless, both now no more than rag dolls.

Noise burst around me in relentless explosions. I was vaguely aware of Bennett pushing his way through the frantic group, making his way to my side.

He placed a hand on my shoulder, but I didn't look up. "Gracie, are you all right?"

"We'll never know," I said, still staring at Pinky. "We'll never know who she was working for. Not anymore."

There were cheers, cries, applause. Co-pilot Robert and the rest of the passengers congratulated Rudy on rescuing us from Pinky's inexplicable wrath. I shut them all out.

Bennett put his arm around my shoulders. "Come sit down."

I pointed to Evelyn. "Why did she panic? We were so close." I finally met Bennett's sympathetic gaze. "We could have stopped Pinky. I felt it." I swallowed past the rising heat swelling my throat. It hurt. Everything hurt. "Without anyone getting killed."

"I know." He tugged gently. "Let's get you away from this."

I had to ask. "Did I cause this?"

"No." There was no hesitation. He stepped back, grabbing both of my shoulders, holding me in place with his penetrating gaze. "You did everything to stop this from escalating. Pinky, whoever she was, is responsible for this tragedy. No one else."

"But . . ." my voice was near whispering, "you said yourself that I always drum up trouble."

"Gracie." The stare grew ever more forceful. "This wasn't your fault."

"How did she get the gun?" This time my voice cracked. "I'm the one who checked her purse. Did I miss it?"

"Of course not. She must have had it on her person."

"I should have been more thorough."

"Come on." With no more fight left in me, I allowed myself to be pulled along through the celebrating horde. We were jostled and bumped as the SlickBlade people high-fived one another. I looked back. Two people who had been alive an hour ago were now dead.

My limbs practically collapsed beneath me as Bennett
sat me down. He took the seat closest to mine, leaning forward and clasping both my hands in his warm ones. "Close
your eyes," he ordered.

"I don't think I can." Adrenaline that had kept me going—
and kept me alive—was melting away now that danger had
passed. My strength dissolved as instantly as cotton candy
in a downpour, rendering me loose, unsteady.

"Close your eyes," he said again as he released me
and eased back. "I won't leave. I'll watch over you. Try to
relax."

I AWOKE WITH A JUMP, MY FEET HITTING THE
floor as my fingers gripped the armrests. Half standing,
disoriented, I scanned my surroundings. "Where am I?"
Blinking myself into alertness, my mind registered that I
was aboard a plane in flight. That my heart was heavy. That
something had gone terribly wrong.

In a flood of awareness it all rushed back to me. Pinky.
Evelyn.

I sat again, possibly even less composed than I'd been a
second earlier. "No," I heard myself say. The word bubbled
up from deep within, unbidden.

Bennett was at my side in an instant. "The altitude shift
must have woken you. We're landing."

Still gripping the sides of the chair, I tried to see what
was happening in the rest of the compartment. Everyone
from SlickBlade had returned to his or her seat and Rudy
was up front, talking on an in-flight phone. Bennett filled
me in. "The pilot has radioed ahead, and the authorities
will be questioning us all before we disembark."

I took a shuddering breath.

"I'm glad you were able to sleep a little," he said.

"Did you sleep?"

He smiled. It was the first light moment I'd experienced in many hours, and the sight of his weary grin took my breath away. "I dozed. You were up there in the middle of it all, Gracie. It was too close."

I leaned my head back. It *had* been too close. For both of us. "What if the police can't find out who Pinky was working for?" He opened his mouth, and I knew it was to chastise me about keeping my nose clean. I interrupted before he could utter one word. "The police will do their best but right now it's all tied up in a bow: a murder, a guilty party, and a hero who saved us all. To them, this is a closed case."

I knew that the moment we were back at Marshfield, I'd pull Frances and Tooney in and enlist their help. My heart swelled for a moment, in anticipation of being home among friends—if you could count Frances as such—where familiarity could help me regain my equilibrium. The lightheartedness was fleeting, however. Too much had happened too fast. And I'd been part of it all. Yet again.

"I can't help thinking that this is all my fault."

Bennett was silent a moment. "No, it's mine. If Pinky had been successful in drugging my food, Evelyn might still be alive."

Appalled, I said, "You can't think like that."

"Don't you see? That's how you got involved in the first place: protecting me. If you're going to blame yourself, then I must share culpability."

The two women accompanying SlickBlade began complaining the moment the aircraft's wheels touched down. "It's bad enough we had to ride with dead bodies," one of them groaned. "Now we're stuck sitting here until the police let us go."

Her companion nodded. "Ridiculous."

I didn't think it was ridiculous in the least. Just the opposite. I was disappointed to discover that my concerns had

been justified; the authorities seemed to accept that they'd
been presented with a fully encapsulated crime. I wouldn't
say they were derelict in their duties, but I would say that
they seemed pleased that this one would be wrapped up by
the time the shift ended.

Pinky killed Evelyn. Rudy killed Pinky, protecting us.
How much clearer could it get? Case closed. I held out hope
that Detective Williamson, a fiftyish, flat-nosed fellow, who
wore a weathered trench coat à la Columbo, might dig a
little deeper. Although we'd garnered the FBI's and CIA's
attention, Williamson—a homicide detective in Charlotte—
was the designated point man.

During my interrogation, conducted in a small room in
an administrative section of the airport I'd never encountered before, he asked me about the drugs I'd seen Pinky
add to Bennett's plate. Leaning back against a blue plastic
chair that squeaked, he studied me as he pressed for answers as to why I thought Bennett may have been targeted.
Across the small table from him, I kept my hands folded in
my lap and wished to heaven that I had answers. I did my
best to suggest—without appearing as though I was trying
to do his job—that Pinky's background might be worth a
look.

"Do you have any idea what her real name was?" I asked
him. "I mean, who was she?"

His head had been bent as he scratched notes in a bat-
tered book that had to be as old as his coat. With a weary
look and a crooked grimace, he sucked in a deep breath.
"Well, that's the million-dollar question, isn't it? We've got
the flight's manifest but other than the name Priscilla Edge-
water from Brooklyn, New York . . ." He held up a hand.
"Yeah, we've run a background check. So far we're coming
up empty."

"You mean she doesn't have a criminal record?"

"I mean we can't find her. Name's probably an alias."

My stomach dropped. "There has to be some way . . ."

His frown softened. "Don't give up hope yet. She'll be fingerprinted. If she's in the system, we'll have a better chance of discovering her identity."

"And if she's not in the system?"

He went back to scribbling notes. "Makes my job harder, is all."

"But you will continue to investigate?"

His sharp glance made me worry I'd overstepped my boundaries. "What do you think?" He leaned forward, both elbows on the Formica table between us, notebook in one hand, pen in the other. "I'll be frank with you, Ms. Wheaton. We may never find out why this Pinky person wanted your boss dead. We'll do our best to reconstruct where she came from and what she was doing on that flight, but when the killers get killed themselves, the truth often dies with them. I'm not going to give up today, tomorrow, or the next day. I'll track this down as far as I can take it, but I want you to keep in mind that we may hit a brick wall."

Wasn't that encouraging? "Thanks," I said.

We went over a few more details, and he released me.

I shook his hand. "If there's anything I can do to help . . ."

His mouth twisted upward at the corners. Not a smile—I got the impression this guy never cracked loose—but acknowledgment. "I'll be in touch, Ms. Wheaton."

Back in the private lounge area the charter company had designated for us, Williamson summoned Jeff for his turn. Drunk or sleeping for the bulk of the trip, he'd be a whole lot of help. I made my way over to Bennett. He'd gone through his interrogation right before me.

"Are you in a rush to leave?" I asked. I glanced up at the clock on the blue wall above the swishy doors and realized we'd landed more than two hours ago.

"What did you have in mind?"

"Couple things are still bothering me." I indicated the other passengers still in the waiting area: Adam of Slick-Blade and his bandmate Matthew, with Millie resting on her haunches next to him. Everyone else had taken off. Airport security had been kind enough to bring our bags here, saving us the added headache of having to locate them after the long ordeal. "I'd like to ask them a few questions."

"Go ahead," Bennett said with a squint. "As long as you tell me what you discover."

"Deal."

As I made my way toward Matthew, Adam sauntered over to intercept. "That was one heck of a trip, wasn't it?"

"It was."

"Roughest flight I've ever been on."

Wasn't that the understatement of the year?

"My heart goes out to that woman Evelyn," he went on. "She deserved better."

"Do you know if she has family?" I asked. "This is going to come as a real shock to them."

He wagged his head. "No idea."

Adam shuffled in place, clearly believing he needed to continue the conversation. On a whim, I decided to include him as I cornered his bandmate. "Do you mind if we ask him"—I pointed to Matthew—"about Pinky? I got the impression he didn't know her very well, and yet they seemed to be traveling together."

Delighted to be of assistance, Adam joined me as I crossed the small lounge. Waxy smells of floor polish and fast food combined in this fundamentally utilitarian room. Faux leather seats were littered about the area in attached groups of three. Matthew slouched in the center seat of one of these groups, head dropped back facing the ceiling, one leg crossed over the other. If it weren't for the hand holding Millie's red leash, the fingers of which were tapping out a rhythm only he could hear, I'd have believed he'd fallen asleep.

Adam and I sat on either side of him, our weight causing the connected seats to wobble. Matthew sat up quickly. "What happened?" he asked, looking alarmed. "Did they call me?"

"I wanted to ask you a few questions," I said, "before the police do."

"Is that allowed?"

"It doesn't seem to be a problem." Two officers had been stationed inside the lounge area, purportedly to make sure we didn't leave before being questioned. They didn't seem to have an issue with us talking amongst ourselves.

Although I'd been involved in this entire situation from the very beginning and knew that we had no plan to corroborate or conspire, I still thought it was shoddy police work. The authorities had been handed a solved crime in a shiny, jet-shaped package. All they cared about now was filling out the paperwork.

Adam followed my gaze and apparently my train of thought. He lifted his eyebrows and grunted.

I addressed Matthew. "Here's what I want to know: You brought Pinky into the group—"

"If I would have known she was packing, I would never have—"

"Slow down," I said, "I'm not placing blame, I'm trying to understand. According to Detective Williamson . . ." I waved in the direction of the interrogation room ". . . the name Pinky provided was an alias. We'll never find out who was behind her actions if we don't know her real name."

He folded his arms and stared out at nothing. "I don't know it."

Adam sat sideways in his chair, elbows propped on his

open knees, fingers clasped. He gave a patient sigh. "Come on, bro. Listen to the lady. All she wants is to ask you a couple questions. Quit acting like an idiot here. Nobody thinks you had anything to do with that poor stewardess getting killed. But if there's some way you can help . . ." He let the thought hang for a moment before he chucked Matthew on the shoulder. "Maybe you should chill a little here and listen to the questions before you jump down our throats."

Matthew leaned forward again. Not acquiescence. More like resignation. I knew he wasn't about to launch into the conversation and beg me to question him, so I started in without waiting. "Did she give you her real name?"

Hunched over now, he shrugged. "Just Pinky."

"Where did you meet her?"

"At the club. Last night. She was hanging around backstage and in between sets told me she had some problems and needed to get back home to the States."

"What kind of problems?"

Matthew grimaced. "Said her mother was sick." He blew raspberries. "The oldest con in the book, huh? And I fell for it. She said that her mother had been taken to the hospital and that she might not make it more than a day or two. She said she didn't have money for a flight and did I know anyone heading to the East Coast?"

I exchanged a glance with Adam, whose brow furrowed over concerned eyes. It appeared as though he wanted to say something, but kept quiet as Matthew continued.

"I felt sorry for her. It wasn't like she was into me or anything." He seemed to seek our acceptance on this point. I nodded. "I sure wasn't into her. She was nice enough, but as soon as we got to the plane, she didn't even bother faking it." To punctuate his words, he leaned down. Millie anticipated his move and flopped onto her back so he could rub her stomach. "When I told her we had a jet scheduled for the next day, she was all over me, begging me to let her come along. I said it was okay as long as Slick said it was."

He glanced over to Adam, who let out a low whistle. "Sounds like she targeted us specifically. No idea why. We get hangers-on from time to time," he explained. "Nobody as wacky as this chick, mind you. Anyway, I was busy with the sound mixing guy at the club—he wasn't getting me because of the language issue—and I agreed without really thinking about it too hard. I'm sorry."

Heaven help us if the rest of the world were this gullible. "I guess it's almost like picking up a hitchhiker," I said. "You take your life in your hands."

"We've picked up lots of hitchhikers on the bus. Plenty of times," Matthew said, as though that absolved them.

Adam apologized again. "We blew it. There's no disputing that. And we'll do whatever we can to help." He nudged Matthew. "Won't we?"

"Yeah, sure."

"If it's any consolation to you, Grace," Adam continued, "we're in it pretty deep, too. That plane isn't ours." He shot a glare at Matthew as though warning him not to interrupt. "It hasn't been announced yet, but we'll be the warm-up band for Curling Weasels at their next concert."

"Whoa," I said. "They're huge."

"Yeah, and they're none too happy about this." Adam held out a hand as though the waiting room symbolized all we'd been through. "We're keeping that info on the down-low. If you don't mind."

"Got it."

"If the press finds out, they'll spin it into a convoluted conspiracy." Adam met my gaze with his concerned one. "That won't help you get answers. Once the media gets wind of Curling Weasels' involvement, they won't care what really happened, and we can kiss the truth good-bye."

I pulled a couple of business cards out of my purse,

scribbled my cell phone number on the back, and then handed them to Adam and Matthew. "I'll keep the Weasels out of this as much as I can," I said, "as long as you promise to get in touch if you find out anything."

Matthew stuck the card in his back pocket. I wondered if he'd toss it at the first opportunity. In contrast, Adam held the card in both hands. "I promise," he said.

When the door opened and Detective Williamson called Matthew to come in next, Bennett and I said good-bye to Adam. Within minutes we were safely ensconced in the backseat of one of Bennett's cars and finally, blissfully, headed home.

"Don't worry, Gracie," Bennett said. "Once we're back at Marshfield, we'll be able to shake off all this unpleasantness."

I nodded, but only to be polite.

Chapter 16

IT WASN'T JET LAG OR MY INTERNAL CLOCK being messed up that had me at my desk before six the next morning. It was a need to grab hold of my bearings before the day got away from me. Although my capable assistant, Frances, had been left in charge in our absence, there was still much to do to catch up.

I had a slew of tasks I needed to cross off my list. First and foremost, I wanted to find out more about Pinky. I'd have to draw on every resource I could. In the past, Marshfield had used a service, Fairfax Investigations, to look into sensitive matters on its behalf. Their offices weren't open yet, so I left them a voicemail to call me. I debated leaving a voicemail for Ronny Tooney, but was afraid of waking him. He'd become an ally of sorts, but I decided to call him at a more respectable hour.

Until then, I started through the tidy piles of notifications Frances had so precisely placed on my desk. As I read reports from the various departments, my mind wandered back to my homecoming late last night, with Bootsie snuggling close as I lifted her to my chest. Having waited up for me, Scott had shouldered the luggage and tugged it in through the back door, while Bruce pulled me into a huge bear hug that threatened to squeeze Bootsie out of my arms.

My roommates had been as overjoyed to see me as I was to be home. Even though I struggled with fatigue, I insist they bring me up to date on all that was new at Amethyst Cellars, their wine shop, everything that had happened with Bootsie, and a few tidbits about the neighborhood. I took it all in, happily digesting the news but suspecting that they were avoiding one topic in particular.

"What about Hillary?" I'd asked. "Was her move-in day as big a production as we all expected?"

Bruce and Scott had exchanged a look before Bruce said, "We haven't seen her."

Scott had held out his hands. "There's been nothing going on over there since the day she arrived—which was pretty quiet, to be honest. No movement. Not a peep."

I thought about that conversation now as I sorted through the time cards, stopping for a moment to stare out my office window overlooking the verdant Marshfield gardens. It wasn't like Hillary to keep a low profile. The idea of her being our neighbor was almost too much to bear. Everything I knew about the woman screamed "Look at me." I couldn't imagine her having completed the move without taking out a full-page ad in Emberstowne's local newspaper and organizing a parade in her own honor.

As I'd snuggled Bootsie, I'd told my roommates what had happened on the flight across the Atlantic, and tried in vain to dismiss their concerns. The problem was, I was worried—a great deal more than I let on. As usual, however, Bruce and Scott saw right through my assertions that all was well now that the authorities were in charge.

"But who hired Pinky?" Bruce had asked.

That question haunted me now as I pulled the timecards closer and forced myself to focus. I hadn't had a reply for Bruce, and I knew I couldn't rest until I had answers that made sense.

The door to the next office opened and shut. A quick glance at the clock told me it was far too early for employees to be arriving. That left security or an intruder as the only options behind the noise.

I stood. "Hello? Who's there?"

Before I could make it to the door that connected my office with Frances's, she walked in, scowling. "Give me a fright, why don't you?" she demanded. "What are you doing here at this hour?"

I opened my mouth to automatically respond in kind to her snippy tone, but was surprised by the sudden rush of affection I felt for the purple polyester–clad woman glaring at me. I was glad to see my cranky assistant, and shocked by such an unexpected reaction. The two deaths on the flight home yesterday had clearly wrought havoc with my emotions.

I managed to instill enough sarcasm into my truthful reply to keep her from falling over in a faint. "I missed you, too, Frances."

"Humph," she said, turning her back to me as she trundled away.

I followed her to her desk. "How did it go while we were gone?"

She pulled her beige purse off her shoulder and dropped it onto the desktop with a heavy thud. "Is that why you're in early? To check on what I've been doing while you and the Mister have been gallivanting all over the globe? Let me tell you something—"

"I'm here early because I need your help," I said quietly. "Bennett's in danger."

Her mouth clamped shut, tadpole eyebrows bunched together over her alarmed, beady eyes. "Be more specific."

I took a seat in front of her desk and pointed. "Sit down. I need to bring you up to speed."

As I retold the story of Pinky's attempt on Bennett's life, her subsequent killing of Evelyn, and how Rudy had saved the day by taking Pinky down, Frances's eyes by turns went wide then tightened. Her mouth opened and shut as she struggled against the urge to interrupt. It dawned on me about halfway through the story that this was one of the rare times I was able to bring news to her. Frances always seemed to have an ear to the ground and a finger on the pulse of Emberstowne. She was always ten steps ahead of me. Not this time.

"Wait, wait. That can't be the end of it," she said as I wound to the conclusion of my tale. "Pinky must have been in cahoots with someone else." Frances's face reddened. The tadpoles squished together. Her disapproving eyes sparked with anger, and little bubbles of spit gathered in the corners of her mouth. "Why would anyone want to kill the Mister?"

"That's what we"—I wiggled a finger between us—"have to find out."

She sat back a little bit. She blinked. "You and I?"

"There's no way we can accomplish all this alone, though. We'll need help."

Reaching for the phone, she said, "I'll call Fairfax."

"Already done." I pointed to the clock on her desk. "I think it's a decent enough hour to call Ronny Tooney now, too. I'll do that in a minute."

She sniffed. "Like he could handle something this important."

"He's done pretty well for us in the past."

"Pheh," she replied. "He got lucky and he knows it."

I let that pass. "Bennett has his WizzyWig board

meeting this afternoon," I said, "But I'm seeing to it that he doesn't go alone."

She gave me one of her cheeky glares. "How do you plan to protect him? Tuck a gun into your skirt and play bodyguard?"

Dealing with Frances required grappling with her frequent grousing, including that fun quip. "I called Terrence yesterday," I said, exercising extreme patience, "on the ride back from the airport. He and a couple of his staff will accompany Bennett to the board meeting today." I arched my brows to prevent her from jumping in before I'd finished. "And before you snarl, yes, I've already gotten Bennett to buy into this arrangement."

"Snarl? *Humph,*" she said again, scowling.

"Bennett mentioned that Vandeen Deinhart is particularly upset about this new acquisition. Bennett is positive Deinhart wouldn't try anything drastic to keep the deal from going through, but you and I both know better than to trust anyone. Especially where money is concerned. Has anything unusual been going on here?" I asked.

Her little eyes relaxed ever so slightly, and when she asked, "Wouldn't I have alerted you if there was?" her words had a bit less bite.

"Of course you would have," I said smoothly. "I only ask because now that you know what happened on our flight, you may interpret things differently."

She considered that. "Best of my knowledge, nothing amiss."

"Good. I guess," I said. "I almost wish we had something to look into."

"Yes, well." Frances worked her jaw in a way that let me know she was about to unload a big piece of news. "There's more. Nothing to do with the Mister. Not precisely." She slammed her mouth shut and struggled for control. Her lips writhed, making me believe she was attempting to keep from spewing in an angry eruption.

I sat back a little, but knew my assistant well enough to hazard a guess. I kept my tone even. "Frances . . . did something happen between you and Hillary while we were gone?"

"Did something happen?" she repeated in a voice loud enough to startle staff on the first floor. "I'll say it did. I'm sorry you and the Mister had the kind of trouble you did on that airplane, but I had my hands full with that . . . that . . ."

Her face had gone bright red and I was afraid she might explode in front of me. "What happened?" I asked.

She took a breath, calming down enough to answer with steady, rather than crazed, fury. "That businessman of hers—that, that . . ."

"Are you talking about Frederick?" I supplied. The week before Bennett and I had taken off on our European jaunt, Hillary had dropped a couple of bombs on us: She was moving to Emberstowne, and she was launching a new interior design enterprise with a fellow named Frederick. From what we could tell, she wasn't interested in him romantically, but I would lay odds that she'd used whatever feminine wiles were at her disposal to manipulate his cooperation to ensure financial backing for her fledgling business venture. "What happened?"

"That headstrong girl will be the death of me." As her angry spittle threatened to provide my second shower of the day, it occurred to me how often Bennett had used the same description when referring to his stepdaughter. "I told her she wasn't allowed in the Mister's rooms while he was gone, but did she abide by the boundaries I set?"

I waited.

"Of course she didn't," Frances went on. "That girl has never had respect for authority. Somebody needed to teach her a lesson when she first came to live here. I'm telling you, if she were my daughter—"

"What did she do up there?" I asked to keep Frances focused.

"Took photographs. Lots of them."

I sat back, confused. "You mean 'took' as in stole or borrowed, or 'took' as in captured images with a camera?"

Frances's cheeks puffed. Her face flushed red. Clearly, I'd interrupted her diatribe with a stupid question. "She's using *pictures*"—Frances pantomimed operating a camera—"from the Mister's quarters to create a portfolio for herself."

"Whoa, wait," I said. Frances favored me with a look of congratulations for finally catching on. "She didn't design those rooms. Bennett hired professionals."

"I reminded her."

"Years ago," I continued. "Those rooms haven't been changed in decades. She can't waltz in here and claim them as her work."

Frances wiggled her head. "You think I didn't argue that point? Hillary says it doesn't matter. She believes she's fully capable of creating those kinds of designs, so why not pretend she did?" Frances waved her hands in the air dismissively. "Of course she claims that this is only temporary. Says she's borrowing the rooms just long enough to build up her own clientele."

"But that makes no sense."

As though reading my mind, Frances asked, "Hard to have a battle of wits against an unarmed opponent. She's a twit."

In spite of myself, I laughed then sobered as I rubbed my temple. "I can't fight this battle right now. There's too much at stake here. Bennett could be in danger." I stopped, then corrected myself. "Forget 'could be.' I'm sure he is. I can't let anything distract me from protecting him. Once we get to the bottom of that"—I hoped we could do so quickly—"then I'll tackle the Hillary problem."

Frances snorted, but didn't disagree with the plan. "Have you called those two Keystone Kops down at the police department yet?"

Although this matter was not in our local detectives' scope, the two of them, Rodriguez and Flynn, might be able to lend assistance. Or at least provide guidance. "Not yet," I said. "I was waiting to tell you first."

"I'll take care of that. Is your morning free?" she asked, picking up the phone. "Can you meet them in an hour?"

"I'll make it a priority to meet them whenever they can get here." I sent another quick glance at the clock. "It may be too early for them."

She sat up, poker straight. "Too early to protect the Mister? I think not."

I stood to return to my office. "I'll be here."

"Good," she said as she dialed. "Let me sort through some business. I have a few other pieces of news you may be interested in hearing, too."

From the shrewd look in her eye, I deduced she had news of Jack. My stomach did an anticipatory flip-flop, as it usually did when I thought of him, but I tamped down my curiosity, reminding myself that there were bigger issues to deal with at the moment. Truth was, I'd had a great deal of time to think while Bennett and I had been away, and I'd come to a decision of sorts.

I'd no sooner stepped into my office when Frances called to me. "They'll be here in less than a half hour."

The woman might annoy most of the staff with her nosiness and dogged determination, but she took care of Bennett. I couldn't ask for more. "Thanks, Frances."

Chapter 17

ON THE OTHER END OF THE PHONE, BENNETT didn't mince words. "I'll be leaving in twenty minutes. With or without Terrence."

"Can't you wait until he shows up? Your board meeting is scheduled for two in the afternoon. Why are you leaving so early?"

"You really have to ask?" he said. "After all that happened, I plan to confront Vandeen Deinhart personally."

I gasped so hard I nearly choked. "Is that wise?"

"Do you believe me incapable of taking care of myself?"

How to answer such a loaded question? "Of course not."

"Then why do you insist on assigning a babysitter?"

"Terrence won't be there to babysit. He'll be there to keep an eye on things. Someone is out to get you. We need to take precautions."

"We don't know that anyone has targeted me. That Pinky may have been telling the truth when she said she was trying to poison the dog."

"If you believed that, you wouldn't feel the need to confront Vandeen."

"My goal is simply to eliminate suspects. I don't believe for a moment that he's responsible, but until he's cleared, we will all waste valuable time investigating him. I will not have my head of security running around on a fool's mission."

Bennett was being obstinate and we both knew it. I tried again. "Pinky was up to no good. We can agree on that much, can't we?"

He muttered a barely audible, begrudging assent.

"I'm convinced she was on a mission." I heard him take in a breath as though to interrupt. I kept talking before he could argue. "Terrence is objective . . ." *And trained,* I wanted to add. "It can't hurt to have him accompany you, right?" Again, I plunged on before he could say anything. "Let him talk with Deinhart while you're there. Get his take on the guy."

"Too late. I've already scheduled an early meeting with Vandeen. He was reluctant to meet until I told him I was having second thoughts about the merger."

"Are you?"

"Anyone in his right mind would have second thoughts about working with Vandeen. That's good enough. I'm set to meet him an hour from now. You know how much I deplore tardiness."

I did. Rubbing my forehead with my free hand, I wracked my brain for any excuse to stall. Coming up empty, I lifted my head to see Frances in the doorway, holding up a finger. "Hang on," I said.

"There's no point in trying—"

"It's Frances," I said. "She needs something."

At the mention of my assistant's name, Bennett quieted. "Find out what it is. And be quick. I don't have much time."

I placed a hand over the mouthpiece and sent her a quizzical look. "What's up?"

She spoke in a stage whisper. "I got hold of Terrence. He's on his way."

I raised my eyes, thanking the heavens for my eavesdropping, busybody assistant. Before I could ask, she said, "He's five minutes from here."

I mouthed, "Got it. Thank you," and returned to my conversation with Bennett. "Terrence will probably be upset, you know."

"Certainly not."

"I think he will be. You know he's had a tough time trying to prove his worth to you."

"With all the incidents we've had here, it's no wonder."

I lapsed into a wistful tone. "He was looking forward to going with you today."

"Don't feed me lines like that."

I waited.

He gave a low growl. "I did agree to this yesterday," he finally said. "How soon can he be here?"

"Five minutes?" I watched a happy gloat brighten Frances's expression. She gave a self-satisfied nod and returned to her office. I spoke again into the phone. "Why don't you stop down here before you leave?"

He made an impatient noise, but I could tell I'd won him over. "Trying to make sure I don't sneak out on my own, are you?"

I laughed. "You know me too well."

AFTER CALLING OUR WANNABE PRIVATE INVEStigator, Ronny Tooney, and bringing him up to speed, I hung up and sent him a quick e-mail. I didn't know what he might come up with, but from past experience I knew he'd give it his all.

I hit "Send" and sat back, thinking about that. I trusted Tooney, more than I would have ever imagined possible,

given the way we'd first met. Who would have predicted
him becoming part of the Marshfield family? I shook my
head just as Bennett strode in.

"I'm here," he said, making his way to my desk.
"Where's that security fellow?"

Frances appeared in the doorway between our offices.
In a singsong voice, she said, "Came in one second after
you did, Mr. Marshfield." She stepped aside to allow Terrence to enter.

"Humph," Bennett said. Addressing Terrence: "What
exactly do you intend to do to keep me safe, young man?
Jump in front of a speeding bullet?"

"Don't say things like that," I said.

With his hands behind his back and a tranquil expression, Terrence gave off a confident, quietly militaristic air.
"I'm hoping that won't be necessary, sir," he said. "My goal
is to stop anyone who means to do you harm *before* they
have an opportunity to do so."

Bennett folded his arms. "And I suppose she"—he nodded at me—"told you all sorts of frightening tales of conspiracies and murder plots."

Terrence slid a glance in my direction, but answered
without any trace of humor. "I've found Ms. Wheaton's in-
stincts to be consistently on target." He waited a beat. "I
believe I've heard you express a similar sentiment from
time to time. Or have I misunderstood?"

Bennett growled again then tapped his watch. "What are
we waiting for? Let's go."

"Yes, sir."

"One more thing," I said. They both turned. "Please,
don't eat or drink anything. Not one thing."

Understanding crossed Bennett's features. He gave a
brief nod. "Yes, Mom."

Rodriguez and Flynn's arrival halted the procession out
the door. Frances clomped toward them, her face flushed

with anger. I could practically read her mind—*how dare they walk in unannounced?* "May I help you?" she asked in a voice clearly meant to frost their preserves.

Rodriguez looked like he'd gained a few pounds in the weeks I'd been away. He'd blown past middle-aged spread and looked like he would soon leave portly in the dust. Tucking his chin into a wide, wobbly neck that draped over his collar like soft-serve ice cream on top of a brownie, he stared at Frances. "You called us, remember? Some sort of emergency?"

Time for me to step in. "I'm glad you're here, Detectives," I said. "I'll bring you up to speed in a minute."

Flynn had been scowling at Frances and now faced me with fire in his eyes. "What kind of trouble have you gotten into this time?" The younger detective hadn't changed since I'd seen him last. Wiry, with army-short hair and a tendency to attack first and analyze later, he no longer scared me the way he had when we'd first met. I'd seen a softer side of him recently. While it didn't change my overall opinion of the man, it did help to summon the patience necessary to deal with his tirades.

"Why don't you have a seat?" I swept an arm toward the chairs opposite my desk.

As the two detectives made their way across my office, Frances led Bennett and Terrence into hers, where two of Terrence's staff waited. I braced myself.

"What's this?" Bennett spun to face me. "It's bad enough you want me to look like a feeble old man who needs a companion to help him get around. You want me to be seen in public with three of these . . . attendants?"

"They aren't attendants; they're bodyguards," I said.

"I can take care of myself."

"No one doubts that." The last thing I wanted was for Bennett to believe I thought less of him in any way. Especially after seeing how old age had affected Nico Pezzati.

"Look at Marshfield. Look at all you've done to turn this beautiful home into a first-class museum and showplace. Look at all you've done for the people of Emberstowne, for your staff, for the people you care about."

"That's not what I mean, and you know—"

"Then think about those people. All of us who work here. All of us who care about you, who are part of your life. Remember how we lost Abe." I waited for that to sink in.

Bennett's shoulders drooped. "They thought he was me," he said softly.

"No one doubts that you can take care of yourself," I said. "But these guards—people who work for you—are trained to spot problems before they explode. They're protecting you, yes, but they're also protecting everyone here at Marshfield."

It had taken more effort than I'd anticipated, but Bennett finally seemed convinced. His chin came up and he wagged a finger at his protective contingent. "Let that be a lesson to you boys. Never argue with someone who's smarter than you are."

Terrence winked at me as he escorted Bennett out the door. "Tell that to the two detectives in there."

I hoped Flynn and Rodriguez hadn't heard Terrence's remark. Frances had, because she snorted. "Speaking of those two, you want me to bring in coffee or something?"

"That sounds wonderful, Frances," I said. "And when you bring it in, pull up a chair. I'd like you in on this conversation."

Again, her tadpole brows shot up in surprise, but she didn't comment. With a nod of acknowledgment she was gone.

"So . . ." Rodriguez stretched back in the leather chair as I returned to my office and sat behind my desk. "What's the problem? From what we can tell, you haven't had a murder here today. Not yet, at least. That's a step in the right direction."

"Thanks for that vote of confidence, Detective," I said, "and you're right. No murder here today. Unfortunately, however, Bennett and I were involved in a murder on our flight home."

Rodriguez leaned forward. "Involved?"

Flynn leapt into the conversation. "You're suspects?"

"Sorry to disappoint. We were mere witnesses. The thing is, although an innocent woman was killed, I believe Bennett was the real target."

Rodriguez blinked slowly and sat back. "So that's why there were news cameras camped outside the estate's front door."

My voice went high and limp. "There were? I was hoping to keep this under the media's radar."

"They were shouting questions I didn't understand," he said. "What the heck is a Curling Weasel?"

"They're a band. Musicians." Oh, geez. Adam was in deep trouble now.

With a skeptical look, Rodriguez pulled out his notebook and pen and perched them atop his ample midsection. "Maybe you'd better start at the beginning."

When I finished, Rodriguez's gaze was more alert and Flynn's slightly more relaxed. Exactly the responses I'd expected. It was clear that they both believed me, with Rodriguez now eager to jump into action, and Flynn less willing to point the finger of blame.

Frances rejoined us, bearing treats. Aromatic wisps twisted into the air above the bright coffee mugs, tantalizing us with cheerful caffeine as she set them before us, one by one. Sad to say that the two officers had been in my office enough times that we didn't even need to ask them how they took their brew. Frances had included a plate of cookies and a mug for herself. She grabbed that last, cupped it in two hands, and lowered herself into a nearby chair. Flynn sent her a glare of disdain then looked over as though he expected me to toss her out.

"Thank you, Frances," I said. "We're all up to date now."

The younger detective fidgeted as he refocused on the matter at hand. "You're trying to tell me that the altercation on the airplane happened because Bennett Marshfield was targeted, but you don't know by whom and you don't know why."

"There are only two possibilities I can come up with." I knew how odd my guesses would sound to these men, and I hesitated.

"We're listening," Flynn said, his eyes bulging with impatience. He hadn't touched his coffee, yet as usual, he was the jitteriest of the bunch.

I talked about Bennett's concerns with regard to Vandeen Deinhart and I told them about the board meeting today. Rodriguez nodded. "If Deinhart was behind the original attempt, he won't try anything today. Not while the press is sniffing around Mr. Marshfield." He continued to scribble notes. "When will this sale between the businesses go through?"

"They're supposed to settle that question this afternoon."

Rodriguez frowned. "We'll work under the assumption that it's soon. What's this other possibility you mentioned?"

I bit my lip then plunged on. "There was this skull . . ."

Flynn practically shot out of his chair, sloshing his coffee. "A human skull?"

I mentally smacked myself in the head for giving him such an opening. "Let me start again. When we were in Italy, we visited a friend who showed us a piece of art. An extremely valuable piece—a skull sculpture."

Flynn's free hand loosened its grip on the chair's arm, and he regarded me skeptically. I went on to explain how Bennett had tagged the skull as a fake, but how his friend

Nico Pezzati apparently was unaware that his priceless treasure had been replaced by a phony.

"What did Pezzati do when Mr. Marshfield pointed out the counterfeit?" Rodriguez asked.

"He didn't," I said. "But we're afraid Bennett's reaction might have been noticed."

"Who was in the group when this happened?" Rodriguez asked, jotting notes again.

I listed everyone: Signor Pezzati; his daughter, Irena; Angelo, the personal assistant; and Cesare Sartori, the art dealer. I'd made a copy of the little man's business card and handed it to Flynn, who stared at it with contempt. For a flash of a moment, I saw what he might have looked like as a little boy. I wondered what had soured him so badly on life.

"What's this Angelo's last name?" Rodriguez asked.

I didn't know.

Frances sat just outside our little triangle, watching our interplay with impatient eyes. "I'm sure I could find out for you if you need it."

Rodriguez rolled his tongue around in his mouth, like he was rearranging a meatball—a pretty tasty one, from the looks of it. He finished by smacking his lips. "Let's hold off on that. You said yourself that Mr. Marshfield didn't make any accusations. And the thief who stole the original skull—if it really was stolen—might not have even been present when you were there."

"But—"

The older detective wagged his head. "It's too thin. This business problem on the other hand"—he went back to slogging his tongue around in his cheek—"that we can look into."

"I realize that a theft that occurred in Italy is out of your jurisdiction—"

Flynn barked a laugh. "I'll say."

"But what if—"

A slow smile broke over Rodriguez's soft features. "You can't help yourself, can you Ms. Wheaton? Planning to help investigate, are you?"

I didn't answer.

Frances sniffed. "Seems to me she's had more success finding murderers than you two have. I think you ought to listen to her."

"That's the problem, y'old busybody. Nobody asked you to think."

"Whoa." I stood, pointing a finger at Flynn. "That was uncalled for."

Rodriguez reached over—a futile attempt to calm Flynn down. But the younger man wasn't paying attention. With hot anger shooting out in almost visible sparks, he stood, too. "The two of you have been our biggest problem. If you'd stay out of our way and let us do our jobs—"

"Then what?" I asked. "If we left you unchecked, our murder rate would skyrocket."

Flynn's face went white, then red. Without looking at Rodriguez, he said, "We're done here. Good luck keeping your boss safe," and stormed out of the room.

Rodriguez heaved a deep sigh as he stood to leave. "I apologize for my young colleague."

I waved his attempt away, ashamed of myself for letting my anger show. "My fault. I shouldn't have allowed it to escalate."

Frances, who'd thrown the verbal jab that had started this skirmish, stood with her arms folded across her chest, looking smug. I knew better than to expect any apologies from her.

Chapter 18

AS SOON AS THEY WERE GONE, FRANCES
dropped the self-righteous performance and reminded me
that she had more news to share. "You're not the only one
who's had troubles these past few days."

"You told me about Hillary," I said. "What else?"

"Well . . ." She sat. I did, too. "We've gotten three landscape architects interested in working for us. Two of them
seem *particularly qualified* to pick up where Jack left off."
With the sly look that accompanied this pronouncement, I
took that to mean that the two in question were young,
handsome, and single.

"What about the third?"

"She's new to this part of the country." Frances made an
I-just-bit-into-a-lemon-face. "And she's single."

"What's wrong with that?"

She stared as though the answer were obvious. "Fox in
the henhouse. Reverse the genders. You *know* what I mean."

Taken aback, I said, "Excuse me?"

"She would be competition," she said with excruciating patience. "Right about now that's the last thing you need."

I rubbed my eyebrows in frustration. "Nice to know you're looking out for me, Frances."

"Anytime," she said, totally missing my sarcasm. "I have the two other landscapers scheduled for interviews this week."

"With me?"

"Who else?"

I shook my head. "Until I get to the bottom of who's after Bennett, I can't allow myself to be distracted."

Her mouth curled downward and her familiar raised-chin defensive posture returned. "When I set up these interviews, I had no idea you'd be bringing a murder back with you. How was I to know?"

"You couldn't have known," I said, absolving her. "Let's reschedule them. And add in that female landscaper, too."

"You can't be serious."

"Frances," I said, "we will not discriminate. No matter how convinced you are that this fabulous woman will swoop in and destroy my chances for personal happiness. It just wouldn't be right."

She took that in with characteristic scorn. "Suit yourself."

MY PHONE RANG A SHORT WHILE LATER. "Incoming," Terrence said when I answered.

"What happened?"

"We're heading back to Marshfield. Right now. Can you get a meeting room ready?"

Confused, I found myself sputtering. "I don't understand. Who wants to meet at Marshfield? Why are you on your way back so early? Did Deinhart try something?"

"Deinhart pitched a fit when he saw us. He accused Mr. Marshfield of making a spectacle by bringing bodyguards.

which of these people might be Vandeen Deinhart. Of the twelve newcomers, five were women. Of the seven males, four were of ethnicities that wouldn't likely match the surname. That left three potential suspects.

The group milled about, talking among themselves in the way people who have worked together do. Polite, stilted. Theo approached each member asking what he or she would prefer to drink. He was joined by another butler, who took orders on the other side of the room.

The group was dressed conservatively: dark suits and crisp white shirts; bright ties for the men. Bennett spotted me and made his way over just as I zoomed in on a gentleman in his sixties who stood at the far window, hands clasped behind his back, scowling. He wore his middle-aged paunch with confidence and style. Taller than my five-foot-eight, he had a full head of dyed red hair, sideburns tastefully left white. It had to be Deinhart.

I made my way toward Bennett, noting belatedly that he wasn't alone. With him was a thin-to-the-point-of-emaciated man with deep-set, haunted eyes and a bit of a limp. I judged him to be a few years older than me, and a few inches taller, too. His dark suit coat would have looked more filled out on a wire hanger. I hoped he was wearing suspenders because that drooping belt couldn't be working.

Bennett made introductions with a cheerful glint in his eye. "Grace, I'd like you to meet Vandeen Deinhart. Van, this is Grace Wheaton. She runs Marshfield Manor and is my most trusted advisor."

Though taken aback by the fact that Deinhart looked nothing like I'd imagined, I offered my hand, resisting the urge to wince as his cold, sweaty palm crushed against my warm one. Deinhart's voice matched his physique—high and raspy. "Pleased to meet you. Bennett speaks of you often." From the unmistakable aroma that rolled out as he spoke, he had to be a four-pack-a-day guy.

Before I could say a word, he stepped a little closer. His eyes were set so deeply I couldn't even make out their color. "I hope you know you aren't allowed in this meeting. Board members only."

"Wouldn't dream of it," I said as though he hadn't just been extraordinarily rude. "I'm here to ensure you have everything you need before the meeting begins." I indicated the far wall of the dining room, where appetizers were being set out atop one of the antique sideboards. "We've prepared a few offerings for all of you to enjoy." Turning to Bennett, I asked, "Will your guests be staying for a late lunch? Early dinner?"

"Unfortunately not," he said, eyes still glittering with amusement. "These important people have busy lives. We don't want to delay them unduly." I could practically read his mind. *Get them out of here as soon as possible.*

"Very good." To Deinhart, I said, "It was nice meeting you."

The other board members were beginning to choose seats. I hurried over to Theo and let him know that as soon as he and the rest of the staff had taken care of our guests' needs, they should take their leave. "But you'll want to stay nearby just in case."

"What about you?" he asked. "Will you return to your office?"

"I think I'll remain up here. I can get some work done in the study. I'll ask Frances to bring my laptop."

He nodded, finished rearranging the buffet's display, and gestured for the other servers to follow him out. I trailed behind.

Deinhart crossed the room at a quick enough clip to cut me off before I reached the door. "Ms. Wheaton," he said, with a clammy hand to my forearm. "A moment?"

I glanced around for Bennett, but he had his back to me, in deep conversation with the dyed red–haired man I'd originally believed was our quarry. I shifted my attention to the question at hand. "Is there something you need?"

"Your assistance." I felt surrounded by his personal cloud of smoke as he stepped closer, invading my personal space. "As Bennett's trusted advisor, you need to inform him that this business venture he's attempting is a terrible mistake."

"Why would I do that?"

"You wouldn't want anything bad to happen to Bennett, would you?"

"Is that a threat?"

"Don't be silly." His brows came together and he stepped even closer as though to encourage me to keep my voice down. I stepped back. "I'm merely trying to help."

"Of course you are."

My sarcasm was not lost on this man. "Mark my words, Grace," he said. I hated that he used my name with such easy familiarity. "I'm giving you good advice." He turned to leave, but threw one more comment over his shoulder, in a whisper. "Don't underestimate me."

I WAS DEEP INTO CRAFTING A STAFF MEMO about changes from our health-care provider when the phone rang. I'd set up a workstation of sorts in Bennett's study and had asked Frances to route any important calls to the phone there, so I shouldn't have been surprised. Still, I jumped.

"Grace Wheaton," I said.

Frances was on the other end. "The Mister's friend Signor Pezzati is on the line. Wants to talk with him."

"Bennett is still in the board meeting."

Her tone took on an impatient air. "I know that. But Signor Pezzati is beside himself. Extremely agitated. I asked if he'd be willing to talk with you, and after some convincing, he agreed."

"Agitated? About what?"

"How would I know?" she asked in a huff. I wanted to remind her that she supposedly knew everything, but maybe her powers didn't reach across the Atlantic. "I'll put him through."

A moment later I thrust the receiver away from my ear. Frances had put the call through, all right, but Pezzati had taken that very moment to shout orders—or complaints, it was hard to tell—in aggravated Italian. From what I could tell, the recipient of his anger was the bearlike Angelo. I waited for Pezzati to finish his high-octane harangue before bringing the phone closer.

"Signor Pezzati?" I began. "Are you there?"

"Ah, Grace! I am so sorry to bother you. My good friend is in a meeting, yes?"

"He is; I'm sorry I won't be able to disturb him. Is there anything I can help you with?"

He made a noise in his throat. "He trusts you. I suppose I must."

I tried again. "I'll do whatever I can."

He mumbled something unintelligible. "Perhaps I should not share a confidence, but my dear friend Bennett explained more about the nature of your relationship."

"What did he tell you?"

"He told me about his father. With your grandmother."

In a rush, I remembered how Pezzati's attitude toward me had changed after my return from the washroom that first day. Bennett certainly hadn't wasted any time. "A blood relationship has never been proved."

"Only because you haven't yet agreed to a test."

I took a breath. "It seems you and Bennett have no secrets from one another."

"This is precisely why I am willing to talk with you in his absence. I have a problem. I need his help."

Chapter 19

"WHAT HAPPENED?" I ASKED.

"I believe my son is stealing from me again."

I pinched the bridge of my nose. "How can that be?" I asked. "He lives here in the States and you're—"

"Who else could it be? I have recently discovered that he has been in contact with one of my employees. Secretly."

I thought about how Bennett believed he might have seen Pinky working at the villa but I kept that to myself for the moment. "What's missing?"

"Money, of course. My accountant noticed discrepancies in the household finances. Funds have been drained over a considerable length of time. Small enough amounts to escape scrutiny. I was lucky my accountant thought to look more deeply. It is obvious to me that my son didn't want me to suspect."

"How could he have—"

Pezzati's ire flashed. "By working with Antoinette, how else? She lived here as my trusted cook, which gives her full access to my home. Who knows how much she has stolen for Gerard? How much she kept for herself?"

Antoinette? I didn't know whether I was more relieved or distraught over the fact that Pezzati apparently had no clue about Pinky, or about his missing skull. Well, not yet at least.

"Bennett will want to talk with you about this the minute he gets out." I eyed the door, wondering how much to share with Signor Pezzati. "He had an inkling . . ."

"Of Antoinette's deceit?"

"No," I said quickly. "He . . ." Stalling, I said, "He . . . wasn't sure your possessions were secure. He wanted to ask you about that, but there were always others around."

Pezzati was silent for several long seconds. I could hear him breathing—a soft, yet labored sound. "What was it he wanted to know?"

The news about the skull being stolen—or, more accurately, the news of it *allegedly* being stolen—shouldn't come from me. After all, Bennett hadn't yet proven the switch. "Signor Pezzati," I began, "you and Bennett have been friends for a long time. You should wait for him to explain it to you."

I could practically see him shaking his head. "I do not accept that. What if Antoinette was not working alone?"

Even though Rodriguez and Flynn believed my theory was a long shot, I couldn't discount the nagging suspicion bouncing around in my brain. With Pezzati already aware of theft in his home, how much would it hurt if I told him about the skull?

"First, I need to ask you a few questions."

From the noise on the other end of the line, it was clear Pezzati wasn't happy with the delay.

I started with the question uppermost in my mind, "Who—that is, who specifically, arranged for our chartered plane home?"

"I do not understand. What does your flight have to do with my son?"

"Bear with me, Signor Pezzati." I wiggled forward in my chair, lowering my voice even though there was no one nearby. "When our original flight was canceled, someone in your home located that replacement flight. Do you know who made those arrangements?"

"I assume one of my servants."

"Which one?"

"How should I know? Was there a problem? If so, let me know and I will chastise whoever is responsible."

"There was a problem on the flight," I said in a hurry, doing my best to keep Pezzati calm. Failing. "I wanted to talk with whoever it was, to warn them that the police may be visiting as they investigate."

"Police? What sort of problem did you have?"

"Is Irena there?" Surely she would be easier to communicate with. Calmer, too. "May I speak with her?"

"What does she have to do with any of this?"

I would have loved to have asked if she'd noticed Angelo talking with SlickBlade while we were at Troppo or if she could recognize Pinky from a description. Trying to pry that information from Nico Pezzati would prove challenging to say the least.

"Nothing, really," I began.

"Then stop stalling and tell me what I need to know."

I drew in a deep breath at the rumbling anger in his voice. "Perhaps it would be better if you spoke with Bennett first."

"Young woman, you are trying my patience."

Just as I resolved myself to recounting Bennett's theory to Pezzati as gently as possible, I heard the unmistakable sound of the meeting breaking up. Layered chatter and boisterous blurts brought me to my feet. "I think Bennett may be available," I said. "If you wouldn't mind holding on for just a minute . . ." I didn't wait for him to reply. This room's phone was an old-fashioned corded model. I put the receiver down before hurrying out into the hallway.

Bennett and Deinhart stood apart from the rest of the group at the far end of the corridor. Engaged in deep conversation, neither was aware of my scrutiny. The rest of the board members were still emerging, talking among themselves as butlers herded them toward the staircase.

Reluctant to interrupt what appeared to be an important discussion, I dithered for a few indecisive seconds. The conversation between the two men intensified. Their voices rose. When Deinhart thrust a pointed finger into Bennett's chest, all bets were off.

"What do you think you're doing?" All thoughts of Pezzati forgotten in that snap of a second, I dashed across the room, vaguely aware of Bennett's startled expression. Hands on hips, I got into Deinhart's space, much the way he'd gotten into mine. "You are in Bennett's home. How dare you assault him?"

The momentary advantage I had in surprising the man caused him to take a wary step backward, but a heartbeat later, he'd collected himself. He leaned sideways to make eye contact with Bennett. "I see why you keep her around." He straightened. Referring to me as though I wasn't there, he continued, "She's certainly not bad on the eyes, but I find it hard to believe that she's not a curse. I mean, what with all the murders here lately . . ." His lips flatlined. "Makes a man think twice about doing business with you. No one wants to be carried out feet first."

Without another word, he spun on a shiny heel and started down the corridor at a quick clip. Theo, the butler, moved to intercept. Deinhart flung a hand in the air as though to dismiss any assistance. With a helpless shrug, Theo followed him anyway.

"Well," I said, furious now, both for myself and for Bennett. "He's a piece of work, isn't he?"

Bennett chuckled. "That's just his manner. His bark is far worse than his bite. Vandeen is out of sorts. The deal went through, exactly as we'd hoped, much to his disappointment."

"You're in the clear then? There would be no benefit to killing you to prevent closing this deal?"

Bennett placed a hand on my shoulder. "How did I get so lucky to have you watching my back? I hate to disappoint you, but this was just the second-to-the-last step." He wagged white eyebrows over crinkling eyes. "If I get hit by a truck, the deal's off. Today, however, we took an important step. Our legal teams will now finalize all the documents. Until the board and I sign and certify those documents, I'm still vulnerable."

He must have reacted to the look on my face because he was quick to change from teasing to comforting. "Don't worry so much, Gracie. Vandeen is no threat. At least not to my personal safety. When it comes to business, he's a worthy adversary, but he wouldn't stoop to such a despicable method of achieving his end."

"I'm not so sure about that," I said, then gasped when I remembered. "Signor Pezzati! He's on the phone." I explained the situation.

"My poor friend." As we strode toward the study, Bennett asked, "Did you tell him about my suspicions about the skull?"

"I was about to, but then the meeting broke up. I thought the bad news would be better coming from you." We crossed the threshold into the room, where the receiver still lay atop the table. "When I saw Deinhart poke you I couldn't stop from reacting. I'm sorry."

"No harm done, I'm sure." Bennett said. He lifted the

device. "Nico?" he said. He pulled the phone away from his head and looked at it the way people do when they're met with an unexpected noise. "Dial tone. He must have hung up."

"Oh no."

"It's just as well," Bennett assured me as he dropped the receiver into place. "I haven't yet had the chance to pull out my old photos of the skull. I've been holding out hope that I'm mistaken."

"Except you know you're not mistaken, don't you?"

He gave me a look, which was answer enough.

As distressed as I was to have caused Signor Pezzati the aggravation of waiting, I was silently relieved. In the man's worked-up state, he wasn't in any shape to discover that one of his most prized possessions was gone now, too. From the little I'd gathered about Pezzati, he was quick to make decisions, opting to listen later, but only when necessary. Bennett, a far more methodical person, would only feel comfortable talking to his friend once he had examined the photos and could present his proof with confidence.

"Where do you have these pictures?" I asked.

Bennett's eyes sparkled. "Come on, I'll show you."

Chapter 20

I FELT GUILTY LEAVING THE BUTLERS AND assistants to clean up after the meeting. Bennett was clearly unfazed. The gentle sounds of china and silverware being gathered faded as we headed down the corridor, and I thought about how living one's entire life in the company of servants sure made for a different outlook. Bennett was wonderful to his employees, generous and kind. His butlers, chauffeurs, and indeed most of the staff, would eagerly stand up for him because they knew he cared about them. For all his wealth and privilege, Bennett maintained an air of approachability. He was loved for that.

We took a sharp left into a part of this level I'd never visited before. Bennett caught my quick glance back at the busy staffers. "It makes you uncomfortable, doesn't it?"

I didn't understand what he meant. This part of his private rooms was illuminated less ostentatiously. The hall was narrower and all the doors on both sides were shut. "This area, you mean?"

He slowed to allow us to walk side by side. "Having servants do all the work. That bothers you."

I gave a one-shoulder shrug. "I'm not used to it."

His mouth twisted. "Even after the trip to Europe? You seemed to be able to relax and enjoy yourself when everything was taken care of for you there."

"Vacations are different."

"Are they now? Good to know."

The hallway opened into a wide expanse. I'd studied as many of the floor plans as I could get my hands on, though I knew from personal experience that not all the building's secrets were recorded on paper.

Years ago—during Marshfield's era of live-in servants—this area had been one of the spots staffers gathered at the end of their shifts, to share stories, complain about their days, or sit in rocking chairs and do mending. There were other, similar spots throughout the mansion. This one, new to me and a good distance from Bennett's regular living quarters, appeared to have been abandoned a long time ago. While there was no apparent dust, nor cobwebs—every room was kept clean—the creaky-floored expanse felt lonely and desolate.

Bennett seemed charmed by my fascination with the forgotten space. I wanted to take a moment and breathe in the memories that had been created here. When my grandmother had worked at Marshfield, had she been part of the crowd? Or was she off on one of her secret rendezvous with Bennett's father?

Not that I believed I'd be able to conjure up any spirits or know for certain what life here had been like, but even as my hand grazed the curved beauty of the wainscot rail, I felt the power of the past.

"We'll come back another time. For now, this way." He made a right into an even narrower hall, which came to an abrupt stop after about ten feet at a munchkin-sized door set into an *A*-shaped wall. Crouching, he grabbed the door-knob. "I have no idea why they made this entry so small," he said as he pushed his way in.

I ducked and followed him, finding myself in an attic that—despite the short door—had high enough ceilings to allow us to stand. Like so many other attics, it was full of hot dust and cobweb-filtered sunlight. Airborne motes, disturbed by our arrival, shot upward and slowly floated to silently land atop the furniture, steamer trunks, hundreds of boxes, and other echoes of the past that were stored here.

My breath felt thick as I said, "Wow."

"Indeed."

The exposed wooden eaves, the piles of . . . stuff . . . were like my attic at home. Like any attic, really. But this one went on and on. Bennett kept moving forward, pulling lightbulb chains to illuminate the area as we progressed. While the windows and occasional skylights helped, there were many hidden corners that were too dark to see into clearly.

I couldn't stop myself from pointing to all the boxes, "This is all your stuff, too?"

He turned to give me a penetrating look. "Are you suggesting I have too many possessions?"

"Far from it. I'm thinking about what a treasure trove this is. I could spend a month up here." Rotating in place, I took it all in then amended, "More like three months."

"I'm glad you approve," he said, then gestured. "Over here."

Bennett led me to a giant oak bookcase that was at least eight feet wide and six feet tall with glass doors every twelve inches or so. He moved to access one of the shelves, but I stopped him. "How in the world did something this huge get in here?" I asked. "There's no way it fit through the door we came through."

Bennett winked. "I'll tell you later. For now, let's have a look."

The oak-trimmed door opened with a goose-pimpling squeak. "It's been a while since you've been up here, I take it?"

Bennett didn't answer. He reached in to pull out a faded red leather album, the cover of which had been tooled in gold with the family crest. "I used to keep scrapbooks for each year," he said, giving a self-conscious shrug. With the side of one hand, he wiped off some of the dust.

"Why is it up here?" I asked as I peered around him. "Are there more of them?"

He half turned to give the bookcase an appraising glance. "Probably twenty, I'd say."

"But why—"

"Marlis didn't like anything around to remind her of Sally," he said. "Most of these scrapbooks are from the years before she died."

"Ah." That explained a lot. I'd heard about how jealous Marlis had been of Bennett's relationship with his first wife.

"I'm glad I didn't bend to her demands that I throw them away."

"What?" I asked, incredulous. "She wanted you to dump them?"

"Burn them, to be precise." He scratched the back of his head. "I should have realized," he said absentmindedly, "this was a compromise. One of many."

I bit my tongue. It wouldn't do well to speak ill of Marlis. She'd been gone for many years, although her personality apparently lived on in her daughter, Hillary.

Bennett dusted off the side of a steamer trunk and sat down. I joined him, taking another quick glance around before turning my attention to the album on his lap. What other priceless mementos from Bennett's life were stored up here, forgotten over the years?

He paged through the early part of the scrapbook, running his hand along every entry as though caressing it. He lifted and turned each thick page without comment, but as his gaze lit upon old black-and-white photos, postcards, and clippings from newspapers, he alternately smiled and looked wistful.

Dust settled around us, grit baked into my skin. Amid the occasional whispers of paper being flipped, Bennett heaved deep sighs. He still said nothing.

My nose itched. I wiggled it instead of scratching, hesitant to make a move that might spoil the moment.

Tiny corners had broken off the edges of several pages and as Bennett turned them, I could see how brittle the paper had become. These albums needed to be returned to the main floors where they could be preserved. They were, after all, Bennett's history.

"Here we are," he said in a voice barely above a whisper.

I leaned closer. A thick portrait of Bennett and Nico—they were instantly recognizable—sat centered on the brown page. The black-and-white photo's edges were worn and rounded, and below their grinning shot, with their arms across one another's shoulders, a caption was scrawled: *First week in Paris.*

"Looks like you two had fun."

"It was quite a year." Blinking, he turned to me. "I would love to explain the story behind every photo, but that's not what we're here for, is it?"

"I wouldn't mind."

With a wry smile, he kept turning pages. "The skull adventure happened right about . . ." He pointed. "Here."

The two young men posed for a shot in front of the gallery they'd spoken of, the skull held between them. "Who took the picture?"

Bennett laughed. "Nico approached a couple of girls who happened to be walking by. Wound up with one of their phone numbers, too, if I recall correctly." He flipped another heavy page. "Here is where we took a few ourselves."

There was one of Bennett posing with the skull in his "Alas, poor Yorick!" pose. Then a similar one of Nico doing the same.

"The girls had moved on by then," Bennett offered. "We took turns with the camera. I took this one"—he pointed to a shot of his friend studying the skull in deep concentration—"when Nico wasn't looking. That's when he found the mark."

"And you took a picture of it?"

Bennett pulled reading glasses out of his breast pocket and placed them on his nose. "Several." He pulled the album closer, scrutinizing every shot. "Here," he said, lowering the book onto my lap. "Those three. Take a look."

I brought the album closer because, although the photos were clear, they were relatively small. "I see it," I said, half in delight, half surprise. "The mark. It's as clear as anything." It was. There was a deep gouge in the skull's right side, roughly resembling the *P* shape Bennett had mentioned. My turn to point. "Right there."

"You sound shocked. Did you doubt me?"

"Not for a minute," I said sincerely. "But seeing the mark so vividly after handling the actual skull myself makes it more real." A new weight settled on my shoulders. "You are the only person who can prove that the skull has been stolen and replaced."

"How would anyone know that I even suspect it happened?"

I thought back to that moment in Pezzati's gallery, when Bennett had called me over to examine the sculpture. "Whoever stole the original had to have been in the room at that time."

Bennett grumbled, skeptical. "I can't believe I reacted in any way that might have drawn attention to my surprise."

"Think about it," I said. "What if the thief *was* in the room with us? That person would know that the skull was fake, and as you and Nico talked about finding it, they would realize there was a chance you might have noticed the replacement. They'd be hyper-aware." He nodded as I went on, "Could you imagine their terror when you picked it up and examined it?"

"I wish I would have paid closer attention to everyone's reaction."

"Me too," I said, trying to remember. "It was you, me, Nico, Irena, Angelo, and Cesare. I didn't think to notice them—I was so focused on you."

He patted my hand. "Who can we eliminate? Besides ourselves, of course."

I wrinkled my nose. "Nico. He's the only one."

Bennett was silent for a thoughtful moment. "Unless my old friend is disposing of his possessions in an effort to collect the insurance money, I'd have to agree."

The comment took me aback. "You don't think that's possible, do you?"

He hesitated. "Nico has always been less . . . scrupulous, shall we say . . . than most in regard to legal matters. Where others see lines that shouldn't be crossed, he sees technicalities and loopholes."

"Insurance fraud is a lot more than a technicality."

"It is," he said. "I highly doubt that Nico would stoop so low, even if he were having financial difficulty. I'll find out more when I talk with him. He'll be honest with me."

If I were running a scam, the last thing I'd want to do is admit to it over a transatlantic phone call where I couldn't be certain who was listening in on the other end.

Bennett continued, almost talking to himself now. "I shouldn't have spoken ill of my friend. He's been known to play fast and loose from time to time, but this . . ." He let the thought hang as he heaved a deep breath. "This is not his style. I'm sure he's the victim here. I'll call him later and let you know."

"I'd appreciate that," I said. Closing the album, I stood. "And I'd appreciate something else as well."

Bennett waited.

Holding the album in one arm, I gestured with the other. "How about we bring these treasures back down into your rooms where they belong?"

"Who am I to argue with the manager of Marshfield?" He made his way over to the bookshelf and began removing albums, one by one. There were thick ones and slimmer versions, and it became clear that we wouldn't be able to carry all of them in one trip.

I offered to come back later and carry the rest.

"On one condition," he said.

"What's that?"

"That you and I make a date." He eyed the piles in my arms and his, and the remaining books on the shelves. "Several dates," he amended. "To go through these. I'd love to be able to share some of our family history with you."

Shifting the weight in my overloaded arms, I said, "I couldn't think of anything I'd like more."

Chapter 21

"ARE YOU STILL WORRIED ABOUT BENNETT?" Scott asked me that evening.

The three of us sat together in the parlor—me in my favorite wing chair with Bootsie asleep on my lap, and Scott sprawled across the long sofa while Bruce sat squeezed into the end nearest me, eyeing his partner's comfort with bemused envy.

"Of course," I said. "I can't very well sit with him day and night, though. Not that he'd allow me to."

Bruce pointed at Scott's feet, crossed on the cushion next to him. "You care to share a little room with me?"

Scott sat up at the sofa's far end. "Better?"

Bruce didn't hesitate. He swung his legs onto the cushions Scott had just vacated and crossed his arms behind his head. "Much."

Scott whipped a pillow at him, catching him straight in the face.

"Boys," I said. "Remember, it's all fun and games until somebody rips the fabric."

My gentle reminder that the sofa was old—it had been my grandmother's—was not lost on the two of them. "Sorry, Grace," Bruce said, returning to a seated position. "It was just that kind of day at the store today. I think we're both punchy."

"No harm done."

Bruce picked up the conversation where we'd left off. "You can't mother him, as much as you may want to. Bennett's a man who's used to looking out for himself. He's used to succeeding, too. You start hovering, he's going to feel weak. You don't want that."

I'd come to the same conclusion. "That doesn't mean I shouldn't be vigilant where his safety is concerned."

"True enough," Scott said. "Speaking of safety . . ." He elongated the word and exchanged a look with Bruce. "You were too wiped out last night for us to ask but . . ."

I knew what was coming and braced for it. Bootsie must have sensed the tension because she woke up, stretched her little white paws across my knees, then bounded over to the couch to sit between the two men.

"We couldn't help but wonder if you'd come to any conclusions. I mean, we were curious if you'd thought about what you said you were going to think about—"

Bruce interrupted Scott mid-sentence. "You beat around the bush better than anyone." To me, he said, "What have you decided to do about Jack?"

The two of them faced me, looking like a pair of matching bookends, leaning forward with their elbows perched on their knees, waiting for my answer with eager attention. Bootsie watched me, too, as though she completely understood what was going on. Maybe she did.

"I have given it thought. A lot of thought." Mimicking their position, I placed my feet flat on the floor and leaned forward. I'd made a decision, all right, but saying it aloud made it real.

Even though it was only the three of us here, I felt my pulse race. "Here's the deal: I can't deny that I'm attracted to Jack. I have been from the start."

They both nodded, eyes wide as if to say, "Duh!"

"Bear with me." I started again. "The more I thought about it, the more I realized that I value Jack as a friend. I definitely don't want to lose that. He's a decent guy. Kind, fair-minded—"

"Good looking," Bruce suggested.

"Yes," I laughed. "That, too. What I didn't realize was the baggage he was carrying and how heavy that burden was. How much it affected his entire life."

I stopped to choose my words. "The thing is, once I got it, it was too late. He'd pulled away."

"Hurting you in the process," Scott added.

"And that's why I hurt him when he finally came around." I shook my head, remembering. "Little did I know. They say that relationships are all about timing. That's an understatement."

"So . . ." Bruce had inched forward. "You're not answering the question."

I was about to. "I realized a truth on this trip. I came to the conclusion that the cons to pursuing a relationship with Jack far outweighed the pros. He and I already had our chance. It was time to move on. No matter how much I believed that he and I would make a good couple, I convinced myself I needed to cut ties and move on."

"Why do I sense a 'but' in there?" Scott asked.

"But." I heaved a deep breath. "I came to another conclusion too: I'm not a Vulcan who lives by logic. I'm human. I can't ignore my emotions."

"And?"

The truth was hard to admit. "I *have* to try again.

Unfinished business. Besides, I want to. Even knowing the risks. Jack may not be right for me, but how can I know for sure unless I give this relationship one more try?"

I waited for their reaction. Nothing.

"Well?"

They exchanged a glance I couldn't parse.

"Come on," I said. "This took a lot to divulge. Say something."

Scott opened his hand toward Bruce, who took the floor. "While you were gone, we decided that the best thing we could do for you was stay neutral. So we are."

"You're joking."

Bootsie began grooming herself. She'd evidently become bored with the conversation.

"It's not like we're disinterested. We're *very* interested in what happens next." Scott looked to Bruce for support before continuing. "It's just that we've given you some bad advice: 'Go for Jack' when the timing wasn't right. 'Go for Mark,' and we all know how that turned out. . . ." His mouth twisted. "We're sorry, Grace. We only want what's best for you."

"Problem is," Bruce chimed in, "we don't know what that is. So we vowed not to say a word, no matter what you decided."

I tried again. "You're kidding, right?"

They didn't answer. Bootsie stopped grooming long enough to look at me. I think she and I were in agreement.

"Any bad decisions I made, I made on my own. None of that was your fault."

"Maybe not," Bruce said. "Consider us a jinx then. We believe it's better if we keep future opinions to ourselves."

"Huh." I sat back. "You're obviously not kidding. I guess I need to understand this new neutrality. Does this mean that I shouldn't tell you what happens when I go to visit Jack tomorrow?"

Scott's face broke out into a huge smile. "You plan to talk to him *tomorrow*?"

I laughed as Bruce rolled his eyes. "Real impartial there," he said, then turned to me. "We definitely want to hear everything. And we'll try"—he shot an exaggerated glare at Scott, who was working hard to adopt a dispassionate expression—"to keep our opinions to ourselves. For your sake, Grace."

I laughed, feeling good knowing that, despite their professions of objectivity, my roommates were behind me on this one. "Sounds fair."

BY THE END OF THE NEXT WORKDAY, I WAS feeling like a champ, quite proud of myself for having gotten so much accomplished. I'd made copies of Bennett's skull photographs yesterday. Today, I returned the originals to their albums. I decided to keep them in my office until Bennett and I made time to browse.

With Frances's assistance, all my outstanding *to-dos* were now crossed off as *dones*, and I'd even worked ahead on a couple of tax and reporting issues. I'd been hired as curator, but my job often felt more like that of a conglomerate's CEO.

I felt particularly great about the investigative work I'd managed on Vandeen Deinhart. Though I had to admit that his background didn't scream "attempted murderer," I didn't like the man. He wasn't my top suspect, and my gut told me he was innocent of the in-flight attempt on Bennett's life.

Problem was, I didn't have a top suspect, and until I did, Deinhart couldn't be crossed off the list. I called Fairfax Investigations and Ronny Tooney to ask them both for updates. Fairfax had little more than background to share on the names I'd provided—information that more or less duplicated what I'd been able find out for myself through a few Internet searches.

Tooney, on the other hand, promised to get back to me soon because there was a lead he'd uncovered and intended to follow. When I tried pressing for details, he said it was too early to share, but not to be concerned. Even if his theory bore results, he promised that it didn't pose immediate danger for Bennett.

I hung up, knowing Bennett was safe as long as he remained within Marshfield's guarded walls. Additionally, Terrence's team was under strict orders to accompany him if he went out anywhere. I knew Bennett chafed at the round-the-clock attention, and I didn't know how much longer I could get him to agree to bodyguards shadowing him wherever he went.

While I was thrilled that no one had tried to kill Bennett since we'd returned, I couldn't help but believe that whoever had been behind Pinky's attack was simply waiting for a new opportunity to strike. I hoped to heaven we'd figure out who it was before they made any fresh attempts.

"Good night, Frances," I said on my way out.

She glanced at her watch. "You're leaving close to on time today."

As always with Frances, it was hard to determine whether that was an innocuous comment or an attempt to dig for dirt. Experience warned me to assume it was the latter. Either way, I knew better than to share my plan to reconnect with Jack. With Frances's gossipy superpowers, Jack would be liable to hear all about it before I even made it to my car.

I acknowledged her comment as noncommittally as I could. "Might as well get an early start on the weekend."

She sniffed. "That two-week vacation must have worn you out."

I ignored the sarcasm by turning the tables. "Any special plans for the next couple of days?"

My question flipped a switch, the way I knew it would. She blinked away her glare and turned her attention to a pile of papers on her desk. "Did you get a chance to approve the time sheets?"

She knew I had. This was her way of deflecting attention away from what she did every weekend. The woman had a right to her secrets, even if she didn't respect others' rights to the same. Still, I had a sneaking feeling that someday I'd know why she was always unavailable from Friday night until Monday morning.

"I sent them out to our payroll company an hour ago," I said. "I could have sworn I told you."

She didn't look up. Frances despised being wrong. For her to pretend that she hadn't remembered spoke volumes. Whatever she was hiding, it was important enough to color her cheeks and keep her gaze averted. She mumbled something unintelligible.

I started to say, "If there's nothing else—" when her desk phone rang. She gave me the universal sign for "don't leave in case it's for you," and answered.

She listened for a moment then said, "She's walking out the door, why?" A moment later she gave me a quizzical look as she continued to talk to the person on the other end. "Did he say what he wanted?"

Another moment. I stepped closer to the desk, straining to hear, but all I could make out was a tinny mumble, muted by Frances's head against the receiver.

Her expression darkened. "I don't think that's a good idea."

I took another step forward. "What's not a good idea?"

She held up a finger. "After all she and the Mister have been through?" She made a noise that sounded like *pheh*.

"I don't think so." She shot me a look that asked, *Can you believe this?*

I had no idea. I wanted to snatch the phone out of her hands and demand to know what was going on. "Who is it?" I asked.

Another "wait" finger. "You can tell him I'll tell her, but he'd better not hold his breath."

With that she hung up, grousing.

"Who was that? Who's 'he'?"

Frances folded her arms across her ample bosom. "Can you believe the nerve of some people?"

"No, I can't. Now tell me what you know."

"One of those men from the band, Slickwhatever, is here. Wants to talk with you."

"Which one?"

"Said his name was Adam."

"Oh my gosh," I said, "maybe he's remembered something about Pinky. This is great."

"I don't think he's here to share clues with you," she said. "Not according to what Doris said."

The tone of her voice made me wary. I stopped myself before bolting out the door. "Why? What did Doris say?"

"He's carrying a bouquet of flowers."

Chapter 22

MY FREE HAND FLEW TO MY FOREHEAD.
"What?"

"You're blushing," Frances said unnecessarily.

Was I? I hadn't given Adam any signal that I was interested in him. Not in the least. "Maybe he brought flowers just to be nice?" It sounded lame, even to me.

"Uh-huh," she said, unconvinced. Making a little shooing motion with her hands she said, "If I'd *known*, I'd have told Doris to send him up. Go on now, hurry before he leaves."

"There's nothing to 'know,' " I said. "I'm sure he's here to give me an update." I frowned. "At least I hope that's why he's here."

I flew down the stairs, eager to find out what he had to share, though puzzled by the idea he'd brought flowers. The attraction I'd felt for Adam, both on the plane and afterward, when we conversed in the waiting room, had been purely platonic. At least on my end. This visit of his, coming out of the blue, was throwing me for a loop. Flowers? There had to be a mistake.

Or . . .

I stopped dead in my tracks.

I'd made it into the part of Marshfield that was open to visitors on the tour and was about to take the main staircase when I remembered another man who had taken recent interest in me. I shuddered, recalling how *that* had turned out.

Resuming my course, I took the center steps down as quickly as I could manage while disjointed thoughts raced through my brain. I'd been intent on visiting Jack today. Intent on talking with him about rekindling whatever we thought we'd had. Adam's arrival threw an unhappy detour into my plan.

When I reached the main floor with the front desk in view, the first thing I saw was Adam's backside. He was leaning over the desk, his right arm perched atop it, his left hand holding a bouquet of colorful blooms down by his side. As I approached, I heard him ask who Frances was. "So this woman says I should leave, but then says I should stay? Why can't I just talk with Grace directly? Let her decide if she wants to see me or not."

I tapped him on the shoulder. "Hey, Adam."

He straightened at once, surprise and pleasure leaping to his features as the handful of flowers sprang up between us, bringing with it a gust of sweet air.

"Grace," he said. "I didn't know . . . I mean, I wasn't sure if I should call first, but I thought maybe if I did . . ."

He stopped himself mid-sentence and handed me the bouquet. "These are for you."

I accepted the rainbow collection of pink and red roses, purple irises, orange and yellow daisies, and lush greenery. I took an appreciative sniff.

Unencumbered now, he ran his hands through his hair. I was glad he hadn't shown up wearing the black wig. "I wasn't sure if this was such a good idea. I mean, I probably should have called first but decided to take a chance because I thought if I called you might politely tell me to bug off."

I think he must have read confusion on my face because he hurried to explain: "I thought you were awesome on that plane. You stayed cool and pulled together. You didn't freak or melt down. I never told you how impressive that was—how remarkable I thought you were. I figured I should, and in person is always better."

"Thank you," I said, "for the flowers and the compliment." Touched by his disconcerted rambling, I had to struggle to maintain my guard.

He pointed to the profusion of color in my arms. "After all you did, I couldn't come empty-handed. That wouldn't be right."

Doris was a lot older than Frances, but she operated in the same grapevine. I ignored her growing smirk. Rather than keep up this conversation for the benefit of our front desk clerk's entertainment, I motioned for Adam to follow me. "Come on, I'll show you around a little."

Alarmed, he pointed to the desk. "I didn't pay my entrance fee yet." Digging for his wallet, he said, "Hang on."

I gave his arm a gentle tug. "It's on the house. Besides, it's almost closing time. Too late in the day to get your money's worth." Marshfield wouldn't shut down for another hour to allow the stragglers to finish their self-guided tour of the manor, but we had stopped accepting new guests for the day. "We'll hit one of my favorite spots instead."

Doris had been watching this little banter with wide eyes. She anticipated where I was headed and cupped a hand to her mouth to call out, "They stopped serving tea at four."

Like I didn't know that. "Thank you, Doris," I called back.

"So this is where you work, huh?" Adam's gaze swept up and down each wall, taking in as much as he could. "It's magnificent."

I chose not to rush him, instead providing light commentary as we meandered through the many rooms. He seemed to appreciate the bits of trivia I shared, and even asked a couple of questions that made me believe he wasn't a stranger to the world of antiquities. I led him deep into the house to one of my very favorite spots to wow first-time visitors—the Birdcage Room.

As we stepped into the sunny, two-story area, Adam drew in a sharp breath. "Wow. This is incredible. I thought you meant this room was full of birdcages. This is like being *in* a giant birdcage." His voice echoed in the emptiness as he took a long look around. This late in the day, tables and chairs were vacant. The harp was covered, its musician gone until morning. We made our way across the room to the giant, curved wall of windows that overlooked the patio and south gardens.

We stood next to each other facing outward for a solid count of twenty. When I turned to him, I discovered that he was studying me, as though waiting for me to resume the conversation. I shrugged. "I have to admit to being surprised to see you," I said. "I take it your band is performing in the area?"

"No."

"You . . . you came out here just to see me?" I asked, trying hard to keep the incredulity in my voice to a minimum.

"You were phenomenal on that plane."

Although his flattery seemed sincere, I wished he'd stop. "I assume you have news, or you've discovered something about Pinky." I didn't want to get my hopes up, but I couldn't help myself. "Is that why you wanted to see me?"

He continued to face the wall of windows, clearly frustrated by my oblivious nonchalance. If my guard had been up slightly before, it was running at full red-alert now. Moon-eyed men didn't show up on one's doorstep without good reason, I reminded myself. I'd been pulled in before by a smiling face and a hidden agenda. I wasn't about to make the same mistake again.

Ever polite, however, I gestured. "Let's sit and talk awhile."

Once we were settled near the windows, with the flowers forming a colorful barrier on the table between us, I leaned forward. "Your visit here comes as a bit of a surprise. I'm hardly prepared for it. Do you mind if I hit you with a few questions?"

He broke into a relaxed smile. "Fair enough," he said, "shoot."

"Have you remembered anything more about Pinky? Has anyone in the band been able to come up with a lead we might be able to follow?"

His brows came together briefly. He'd probably expected me to lead with something more personal. Shifting in his seat, he leaned forward and spoke quietly. "That Detective Williamson came to visit us yesterday. Wanted to clear up a few issues with Matthew. He showed up right before our concert," he said, adding, "We played to a sold-out crowd. It was a smaller venue than what the Curling Weasels are used to, but we weren't the warm-up band—we were on our own."

He had interesting eyes. Expressive and clear, watching me with an alertness that took me aback. The diamond stud earring was gone, but his face was as craggy and acne-scarred as I'd first observed. Like Tommy Lee Jones, Adam had rugged, appealing charm. Didn't matter. There was no way I'd allow myself to be pulled in by a compelling stranger who just happened to be around when I needed him and who just happened to find me wildly attractive. Not again.

The pride in Adam's voice was evident. I smiled encouragement. "That's wonderful." Waiting a beat, I asked, "Did Williamson have any news?"

Adam's expression dimmed. "He told us he was able to track her movements back a few days, but asked us not to share that." He gave a wry grimace. "I guess I just did, didn't I? I never mentioned I was coming here, but I wouldn't expect he meant to keep it from you."

"He knows her real identity then?" I pressed for more. "What is it? Did he tell you where she'd been before the charter flight? Who she worked for?"

"I can't remember her real name. Williamson asked if it sounded familiar, but it didn't. To me or to Matthew."

I bit my bottom lip, wishing he would remember. "Was it close to 'Pinky' or completely different?"

He concentrated, staring out the window again. "I can't remember. All I know is that I never heard it before. Sorry."

"Was it an American name? Italian?"

He brightened, happy to be of help. "Definitely not Italian. I can tell you that. It was a pretty ordinary name, as I recall. The big news, though, is that this woman—whoever she was—has a criminal record here in the States."

"For what?"

"He wouldn't tell us."

"Those two women who were with your band on the plane," I began, "did they have any information to share that they didn't mention?"

It was his turn to look confused. "I haven't talked with them."

"I assumed they were band wives. Or girlfriends."

He threw back his head, eyes crinkling into small slits as he belly-laughed. "No, no way. Not a chance."

"They seemed to be part of your crowd and . . ."

"They're hired groupies."

I shot him an "Are you kidding me?" look. "Come again?"

He scratched the top of his head. "I've been in the music business for a long time, and this band we've got now is the best I've ever worked with. Our agents think that the more we behave like a top act, the more we'll be viewed as one."

"Oh, come on," I said, "even little garage bands have groupies. You're head and shoulders above that level. Don't tell me you don't have fans."

He made a so-so motion. "We do have fans. Quite a lot, actually. Contrary to popular belief, however, most of them don't jump on a plane to follow us to Europe. Beyond that, a lot of our fans don't fit the stereotype. Groupies are supposed to be eager, fast, and easy." His cheeks went red. "We haven't gotten there yet."

"But you hope to."

"The other guys do. Me, I'm not into the party scene. I love writing music, love playing it. I want the world to sing the songs I write." He got a pained look in his eyes, as though remembering a past hurt. "All the rest of that stuff? You can keep it."

Klaxon warning bells sounded in my brain. Oh sure, I thought. Come here unannounced, act all sweet and unpretentious. A wannabe rock star who didn't crave fame and fortune? Spare me.

Maybe Adam *had* played a role in this conspiracy. Maybe he was trying to get close to me, hoping I'd let down my guard. *Play along.* At least until I knew what his angle was.

He was still talking. "Big names like the Curling Weasels have real groupies. We're nowhere in the same league as the Weasels, you know that."

"Count your blessings."

"You don't like hard rock?"

"I don't like their sound, sorry," I admitted. "When the Weasels come on the radio, I switch stations." I leaned across the table and whispered, "Don't tell them that, of course. I haven't heard a lot of your original stuff, but what I heard in Florence was great."

"Thanks," he said, grinning now. "I'd love for you to come to one of our concerts. As my guest."

There it was. The invitation oozing out as innocently as anything. "Thank you," I said pasting on as sincere a smile as I could muster. How could I keep him close enough to determine his true motivation without putting myself in harm's way? "I don't get to concerts very often. In fact, encountering you at that bar in Florence was the first time I'd been at a live music event in a long time. How did you get that gig?"

He talked about his agent, their manager, and all the other clubs they'd played in Europe during their two-week trip. I piped in with questions asking for specifics regarding individuals, locations, and details. I thought for sure that he'd drop a familiar name—one that I could tie to Pinky, or Angelo, or Cesare. Maybe even one tied to the Pezzati family.

Adam was an engaging storyteller, gregarious now that he had my attention. He gestured with wide arms and expressive brows. Most of his stories were tales of mishaps on the road. He told them in such a light, self-deprecating way that I couldn't help laughing, despite my unwavering resolve to stay objective. I eventually turned the conversation back to the flight, and tried again, unsuccessfully, to pin him down—to uncover a clue that he might unwittingly divulge.

We talked a little more about our harrowing experience on the plane and Pinky's possible motives. I made a mental note to contact Detective Williamson at my earliest opportunity, but when I asked about him again, Adam shifted positions and shrugged. It was clear there was little more I'd be able to glean from this line of conversation. And if Adam couldn't help me, I saw no need to keep talking.

I stood. "Wow, Adam, I can't tell you how much I appreciate you coming all the way out here to give me this update."

He got to his feet, looking shocked at the abrupt end to the conversation. His gaze fell to the flowers on the table, as though asking them for advice.

Here it comes. Staving off what I knew was coming, I plastered on a cheerful smile and pointed toward the door. "We'll be shutting down soon. You wouldn't want to be trapped." I winked. "Lots of history in this house. You never know when you might encounter a ghost."

"I'll bet you could get out," he said with a sly smile. "I'm sure you've got all the codes and keys. Am I right?"

Zing. I felt the hot warning shoot up my back. "Nope," I lied. "Security handles all that. I have to go through them for everything."

I picked up my flowers and led the way out. As we walked back to the front of the home, uniformed guards walked by in sets of two, giving credence to my fib. They were doing a final sweep of the grounds before locking the tourist sections up for the night. Doris had closed up the front desk. "Leaving so soon?" she asked Adam with a not-so-subtle eyeball of the flowers. "I thought you might be here for the weekend."

"Nope," I said, heading off any chance of that conversation gaining traction. To Adam, I said, "It was so nice of you to stop by. You'll let me know if you hear anything else about Pinky or if you hear more from Williamson, won't you?"

"Sure."

I waited for him to leave. He didn't.

Doris had stopped what she was doing and was watching with undisguised interest.

"Uh," Adam said. "I forgot to ask. Do you know of any good places to eat? I don't plan to leave until tomorrow morning."

"Doris," I said, "do you have any of those Emberstowne pamphlets we used to keep back there?"

She grumbled about having already locked up, but pulled out her keys and obliged us. "Here you go," she said as she opened the fold-out map and pointed. "Your best bet's here," she said, "on Main Street. But you better get moving. All the good places crowd up quick on the weekends."

"Thank you."

Doris locked up again in a hurry this time, as though she was afraid I might ask for another small favor. She came around the desk and started toward the back of the house, where there was a passage to the employees' underground garage. She raised a hand over her head. "See you Monday, Ms. Wheaton."

"Good night," I said to her back.

The giant house fell suddenly silent when she disappeared around the far corner. All the security guards were off to their posts. "Thanks again for coming," I said.

Adam looked around. "Sure gets quiet here fast."

"It's a big house."

He took that in. "Lots of secrets in these walls. I can feel them."

He may not have meant his comment to sound menacing, but it did. "The front gates are locked up," I said. "There's one last shuttle waiting outside for an all-clear from security. You'll want to grab that one, or you'll be stuck here all night."

He got an amused look on his face, but didn't share whatever had put it there. Slapping the booklet against his palm, he said, "I guess I'll go then." He seemed to be waiting for me to stop him. I stepped to the side and opened the front door. As promised, the white shuttle bus idled outside.

He started out, but stopped and turned in the doorway. "I came all this way to ask you something I should've asked you back in that waiting room when we landed."

Here it comes.

He worked up a shy smile. "Are you . . . single?" He was either sincere or one heck of a great actor. I wondered, briefly, if I wore a flashing neon sign that read "GULL-IBLE" in all caps over my head.

"I'm . . ." How to answer? Without a quick quip at my disposal, I opted for the truth. "I'm not in a relationship at the moment. But that . . . may change."

He tilted his head. "Oh?"

I wasn't about to explain my situation with Jack. I shrugged. "Time will tell."

"I guess asking you to dinner tonight would be out of the question then."

"I . . ."

"One dinner couldn't hurt? Could it?"

"I'm sorry. I have plans."

He smiled and nodded. "Thanks for talking." He held up the Emberstowne pamphlet. "See you around."

Chapter 23

JACK'S OFFICE WAS DARK BY THE TIME I GOT there. The tiny, candy-apple red storefront trimmed in bright white had lush greenery spilling from wide flower boxes beneath its picture window. I'd been afraid of this. Adam's unexpected appearance had done more than rattle me; it had thrown me off schedule. I'd intended to talk with Jack here, alone, quietly.

I'd counted on it being a Friday night and there not being a lot of last-minute business. I could say what I had to say then take my leave. Topmost on my list was letting him know that I missed his friendship. I didn't harbor hope of Jack jumping at the chance to rekindle whatever we thought we might have had at one point, but I wanted to plant the seed. Seeing as how Jack had been Marshfield's landscape architect until very recently, the analogy felt apt.

It had taken every ounce of courage and belief in myself to bring me to this moment. Now that I'd made the decision to talk with Jack, I chafed at the delay.

A shadow crossed the back of the office. I cupped my hands to peer in through his front window. Maybe he was still there.

The shadow stopped moving, then waved and made its way forward.

Jack's younger brother, Davey, opened the office front door, causing the bells overhead to jingle a hello.

"He's gone for the day, Grace. Anything I can do for you?"

Davey was kind enough not to make a big deal out of my unexpected appearance at Jack's front door. Davey had been witness to much of the trouble Jack and I had gone through, and I believed he, too, was hoping we'd find common ground.

After a harrowing escape from a dire situation not all that long ago, Davey had gone to work for Bennett as a personal assistant. From all accounts, that was working out wonderfully for both of them. "What are you doing here tonight?" I asked. "I thought you gave up garden work."

"Jack couldn't open a few documents on his computer. Turns out he needed a software upgrade. Simple fix. Now he can get back to studying."

"How is he managing to keep the business going and study for his law degree at the same time? That's got to be tough."

Davey gave a sad smile. "He's been through tougher."

We both knew what he meant. Taking my leave, I said, "I guess I'll see you around."

"Jack's at Hugo's," Davey said. "At the bar. I told him I'd meet him when I was done, and I'd planned to head over there now. If you don't mind, maybe you could stop by and let him know his computer's all set."

"Davey . . ." He was setting me up and we both knew it.

"You'd be doing me a huge favor. Honest."

"I don't believe that for a minute."

"Come on." Davey grinned. He looked so much like his brother, it took my breath away. "Hugo's is only a couple of blocks away. What can it hurt?"

I STEPPED OUT OF THE WANING SUN INTO THE relative cool and low-lit Hugo's. The young hostess greeted me with an expectant look and a bright smile. I pointed and said, "Going to the bar."

"No problem, have a nice time."

I scooted around her and made my way past the few tables up front, taking pains to avoid making eye contact with anyone. This wasn't my ideal scenario for a talk with Jack, and the fewer witnesses, the better. I hoped to sneak in unobtrusively and sneak out again without anyone the wiser. Although I didn't know everyone in Emberstowne, Frances had plenty of eyes and ears among the residents, all of whom seemed to know that I was the manager of Marshfield.

The place was filling up quickly, as Doris had predicted. This was our town's busy season and by seven there would be lines out the door. I ducked around the next corner into the bar area and spotted Jack right away.

He sat at the far end, near the wall, with about six empty stools between him and the rest of the bar's patrons. I decided there was enough piped-in music and ambient noise to cover our conversation. The best I could hope for.

I took a deep breath, tugged at the hem of my blouse, and made my way over.

He had a beer in front of him, his arms stretched across the bar on either side of his glass, his eyes forward. Lost in thought.

I slid onto the stool next to him. "Hey, Jack."

He turned to me, startled. "Grace."

"Davey said you'd be here. He asked me to tell you that your computer's all set."

"That's great," he said, blinking. "Where did you see Davey? Is he here?"

I was spared answering when the bartender meandered over. "What would you like?" he asked.

Right about then I could have gone for a martini, or two, but decided this was better done clearheaded. "Just water," I said with an apologetic shrug. "I'm driving."

"Driving?" Jack asked as the bartender filled a glass and placed it on the bar next to me. I thanked him. "You're not that far from home."

"I'm here straight from work."

He gave me a quizzical glance, but didn't ask.

"I stopped by your office," I began. "That's where I ran into Davey."

"You came to see me?"

Water was cool relief down my suddenly clogged throat. What had I been thinking coming here?

"Trouble at Marshfield with the gardens?" he asked. "I checked in with Old Earl while you were in Europe; he assured me there were no issues."

I placed the glass back on the bar, keeping a grip on it. I studied my hand as though it belonged to someone else. "No trouble. You left the place in pristine condition. You trained the staff well. They're keeping up."

He took a deep drink of his beer. "Then this is a personal visit?"

"I guess it is." There was no turning back now.

His eyes were clouded, sad. I didn't know how to read that, although I clearly wasn't getting the positive vibe I'd hoped for. Expected, even. He ran a finger along the *J*-shaped scar on his cheek and I remembered him telling me how it got there. How his life had spiraled out of control so many years ago. I thought about how my involvement in his history had caused so much recent pain among his family. No matter what Bennett said to the contrary, I felt responsible. I *was* responsible.

Maybe this had been a bad idea, after all.

Thank goodness for the dim lighting. My face had gone hot.

All the perfect phrasing I'd come up with earlier as I'd envisioned this moment was lost when my words came out in a blurt. "I miss talking with you."

The pain in his face dissolved. "I've missed talking with you, too."

We suffered an awkward moment where we each took sips of our drinks and then both started talking at the same moment.

"How was Europe?"

"What's going on with you?"

We did that "laugh, No-you-go-first" thing. I insisted, and Jack asked me again about Europe. I frowned.

"You didn't enjoy yourself?" he asked.

"We had an incident on the way back," I said. "Probably better if I tell you about it another time."

Concern jumped into his eyes. "Incident? Was anyone hurt?"

I nodded, realizing how good it would feel to be able to tell him about all that had happened. "I think Bennett may be in danger."

He stared. "You can't say something like that and leave me hanging."

My heart raced. I struggled to come up with the right way to ask if he'd like to come back to the house to talk, or at least go somewhere quieter, when he interrupted. "Maybe you could stop by the office again one of these evenings. Or I could visit you at Marshfield."

That wasn't the sort of date I'd been hoping for. His eyes had taken on a dark melancholy. I didn't know why.

"Sure," I said, knowing my disappointment showed.

"Grace," he said, and the end of all my hope was in his voice. "I would love to talk more about this . . ."

He was about to say "but," when a slim, tanned arm snaked around the back of his neck. The owner of the arm pulled him close. "Jack," she said. "Who's your friend?"

There was pain in his expression. Embarrassment for me, probably. Not like I needed any help in that department. Mortification rose up as "Back off, he's taken" vibes rolled off her like steam out of an iron. She'd read my intentions, and she was clearly staking her claim.

Curvy, with her extra weight in all the right places, she loosened her pull on Jack, but stayed close enough so their shoulders touched. Her hair was short and spiky, her dark eyes hot with curiosity. She wore tight jeans, cowboy boots, and a gauzy white blouse over a bright pink tank.

"Becke, this is Grace. Grace, Becke."

"Oh," she said, stringing out the word into two syllables. "I should have guessed. I've heard so much about you."

So much for all my high hopes. "I've heard a lot about you, too," I said, getting to my feet. Thank heavens I hadn't ordered anything. No need to fumble through my wallet to settle up. "Here. You can have my seat. I was getting ready to leave anyway."

She tilted her head. "That's not how it looked to me."

"Becke," Jack said quietly.

There wasn't a lot of room between us, so when she took a step forward, we were almost nose-to-nose. She was about my height, but outweighed me by at least thirty pounds. "Jack's moving me into his house this weekend. Did he tell you?"

My face practically pulsed with heated humiliation. All I wanted to do was get out. Now.

Barely aware that Jack had jumped off his stool and was speaking to Becke, chastising her, it seemed, I drew on every reserve to force a smile. I might feel absolutely stupid right now but there was no way I was going to let her think she'd had anything to do with it. Nope. I'd managed to pull that off myself.

"I hadn't heard. How wonderful. Congratulations to you both."

Jack's angry glare at Becke made me realize that he, at least, had hoped to spare me this public degradation. Too late. Ignoring Becke, I faced him. "When you have time, let me know. I'd still like to get your input on that other matter. But don't bother"—I sent a pointed look toward his companion—"unless you'll be able to keep it confidential."

With that, I turned away and walked with purpose to the front door. Let Becke chew on that for a while.

Stepping out into the evening air was like jumping into a dark pool on a hot night. As Hugo's door swung shut behind me, I held a hand against a light post and stared up at the sky, filling my lungs with the fresh, humid air. "Why do I do these things to myself?" I asked rhetorically.

Letting go of the post, I started for my car. The streets were busy with tourists wandering in and out of the Main Street shops. As was my habit, I rehashed the conversation, realizing that I was a little bit proud of myself for not backing down under Becke's withering gaze. "Let her have him," I said aloud.

"Do you mean that?"

I spun to find Adam right behind me. As was obvious from his breathless question, he'd run to catch up. "What are you—?"

"I'm sorry," he said, taking a step back. "It's just—" He jerked a thumb toward Hugo's behind us.

"You weren't in . . ." I felt my face go red yet again. "You didn't . . ."

He met my gaze, straight on. "I was having dinner. You obviously didn't see me."

"No," I said. "I didn't."

"I'm sorry, Grace. I didn't hear anything. Honest. The body language, though." He had the decency to look ashamed. "I take it that's the guy you were hoping to connect with?"

Although it was none of his business, I had no oomph left to tell him so. "That obvious, huh?"

Adam threw a scathing glance back at the restaurant. "He's a fool."

My pride was hurt, my guard was down, and I knew that continuing this line of conversation with Adam was a bad idea. "Or very, very smart."

Adam looked confused.

"I have terrible taste in men," I said. "Consider yourself officially forewarned."

He grinned. "I'll take that as a compliment. I mean, seeing as how you don't seem particularly smitten with me."

I laughed. A genuine laugh. "Touché." I started for my car again. "Thanks for that."

He fell into step next to me. "Happy to oblige."

"I'm going home now," I said, hoping he'd take the hint.

"I'll walk you there."

"I've got my car."

He made a noise that sounded like "Mmm," but kept up with me.

Logic told me I should be wary of his attention. After all I'd been through, how could I not be? Yet, the streets were teeming with happy, Friday-night tourists, and I had to admit, I didn't feel especially vulnerable or unsafe. Chatting politely, I pointed out Amethyst Cellars and bragged a bit about my roommates' success there.

Despite the fact that my gut told me that Adam was harmless, the logical part of my brain reminded me that I'd been wrong before. I kept alert as we continued to the next block, paying less attention to my surroundings than I did to him, worried he might try for a whole-body grab and stuff me into a nearby vehicle within full sight of all the people around us.

"This is a pretty town," Adam said. "I can see why you love it here."

"I never said that I did."

He gave me a shy grin. "Not in so many words."

If I was stuck with him for another block, I figured I might as well push for more information. "I plan to get in touch with Detective Williamson as soon as I can. I'm hoping he can shed some light on everything that happened. Can I ask you a favor?"

"Please do. I'd be happy to help if I can."

"Would you mind sending me Matthew's contact information? I have to believe he knows more about Pinky . . ." I'd been about to say "than he admits," but realized that might sound accusatory. Instead, I hedged, ". . . than he actually realizes."

"I can do that," he said. "I've got your cell phone number. I'll call you with the information."

"Let me give you my personal e-mail address, too. Sometimes that's faster." I stopped walking to dig out pen and paper from my purse. Thinking it would be easier to write on the hood than balancing the items in my hand, I gestured, "Maybe we should do this at my car."

That's when I saw the man standing next to my little Civic. Familiar, though out of context. Less than a second later, I remembered. Startled, I instinctively grabbed for Adam's arm. "That's Rudy." Paper crumpled in my fist, I pointed with the pen. "That's him. Isn't it?"

As the words tumbled out of my mouth, it hit me that both men appearing here on the same day was too strange to be coincidental. I jerked my hand back. Realization made me jump away, closer toward the street. Away from Adam.

"Why is he here?" I asked with dripping accusation.

Looking as shell-shocked as I felt, he didn't seem to notice my tone. Instead, he started forward after Rudy, moving fast. "Hey," he called.

But in the three heartbeats it had taken for us to react, Rudy had turned away, immediately swallowed up by the crowd in the dark. Streetlights, designed more for ambience than for bright illumination, didn't help as Adam gave chase, with me not far behind.

At the next intersection, however, I stopped short. What if that had been the plan? Get me to follow. Separate me from the crowd?

Out of breath, more from alarm than from exertion, I gave up pursuit, feeling a peculiar sense of déjà vu.

I hurried back to my car, eager to get away. I'd just unlocked the driver's side when Adam appeared next to me. Sweat beaded above his lip and along his hairline. He rested an arm along my car door's frame, effectively blocking me from getting in.

"What are you doing?" I asked.

Oblivious to my question, Adam said, "I called Rudy's name, but he didn't turn. Do you think we were mistaken?"

"I think you should get your sweaty arm off my car."

He stepped back, looking confused. "Why are you angry?"

"Why do you think?" Simmering resentment—at myself for being so gullible—shot my words out unchecked. Empowered by the crowds, knowing he couldn't harm me if I created a scene, I advanced on him. "Do I have a neon sign over my head? Is that it? How does Rudy figure into this equation? Huh?"

His bottom lip went slack.

I took another step forward. "Huh?"

"I don't know what you think." Adam's voice was low. "I'm just as surprised to see him here as you are." He closed his mouth and scratched the side of his head. "I can't speak for Rudy, but I can tell you that I came here to see you. That's it." He gave a self-conscious shrug. "I like you. Whatever I did to make you angry, I'm sorry."

He offered a half-hearted smile, and for the second time that day said, "See you around."

Chapter 24

ADAM DISAPPEARED INTO THE NIGHT AS EASILY as Rudy had. I shook my head, staring down the block, my breath coming in short gasps, my heart beating a rhythm that was at once panicked and furious.

When I finally managed to get myself under control, I drew in a deep breath of the muggy night air, and congratulated myself on handling that as well as could be expected. With a precautionary glance in all directions, I finally opened my car door and slid behind the wheel.

A folded piece of paper sat under my wiper blade, one corner lifting up in the faint breeze as though waving hello. Wanting to be noticed.

I clambered back out, grabbed the white sheet and opened it. On it was written: *Rudy (flight attendant)* and a local phone number.

I remembered having offered a blanket invitation to come visit if he was ever in the area. I hadn't expected him to simply show up without calling, of course.

Misery and embarrassment settled on my shoulders like an itchy blanket that I wanted to throw off but couldn't find the strength to lift. I'd all but accused Adam of conspiring with Rudy. I rubbed my clammy forehead, ashamed to realize that I'd behaved a lot like Flynn. Accuse first, ask questions later.

Still standing outside my car I stared down the street, hoping to catch a glimpse of Adam. Did he deserve an apology? I wasn't sure.

Why did I feel like such a jerk?

I WAITED UNTIL THE NEXT MORNING TO contact Rudy, leaving a voicemail for him at what turned out to be his hotel. In my message, I expressed surprise at his visit and I encouraged him to return the call.

Bootsie watched me putter around the kitchen, winding between my legs as I soaped up the morning mugs and dunked them under the warm running water. She wasn't used to me being home—both because I'd been out of the country with Bennett for so long and because I'd spent most of the week at Marshfield catching up. "It's Saturday," I said to her.

She sat on the dark rug we used to protect the kitchen's wood floor from wild sudsy splashes. What difference we thought it made to the scarred oak was anyone's guess, but it made us feel proactive. That was my new mantra these days. No longer would I accept situations or people at face value. In order to protect myself, I needed to maintain a shield. My blemishes might not be as visible as my floor's, but the scars ran much deeper.

I finished tidying the kitchen, showered, and, once I'd decided it was respectably late enough on this weekend morning to bug Detective Williamson, I pulled out his card and dialed.

His clipped "Williamson" interrupted the first ring.

"This is Grace Wheaton," I began.

"You got my message then?" he asked. "I was afraid I'd called too late last night."

He must have left a message at Marshfield. "As a matter of fact, I'm calling because Adam from SlickBlade told me you'd discovered information about Pinky. Is that true?" I half expected Williamson to react in surprise, to discount Adam's assertion. That would prove once and for all that the lead singer of SlickBlade had made it up.

"He came to tell you about that in person?" Williamson said. The disbelief in his voice, coupled with the implied substantiation of Adam's story, made me frown, despite the fact that information on Pinky was exactly what I wanted right now.

"You mean you found her?"

"That Priscilla alias slowed us down for a while but we found her. Diane Waters. But the info about her living in Brooklyn didn't change." He rattled off her birth date. A little quick math. Pinky had five years on me. I would have guessed ten.

"Who was she working for?"

Williamson snorted. "That's the thousand-dollar question. Born and raised in the city, she lost her share of jobs before picking up and relocating to Europe about ten years ago."

"She was living in Florence, then?"

"This Diane was a nomad. We're still backtracking. I can't say where she was living. Not yet."

This wasn't sounding promising. "What did she do to support herself?"

"Odd jobs. Maid. Office work when she could get it. We're still investigating. No solid career path, if that's what you're asking."

I asked Williamson if Pinky might have had any

connection to Vandeen Deinhart here in the States, or Cesare, the art expert, in Florence. He hedged.

"I left that message for you out of courtesy, Ms. Wheaton." His voice strained for patience. "There's no proof that
she was working for anyone. She may have simply cracked.
This Diane was clearly a disturbed individual. Let's not
imagine conspiracies."

I wasn't imagining, but I bit my tongue rather than risk
his wrath. At this point keeping the lines of communication
open was paramount.

Changing the subject, I injected perkiness to my voice.
"By the way, remember Rudy? The flight attendant who
ultimately killed Pinky?"

Williamson grunted the affirmative.

"He's here." I waited a beat to let that sink in. "In
Emberstowne."

Williamson started to reply. I cut him off. Maybe if I fed
him a few details he'd come up with conspiracy theories of
his own. With any luck, they'd match mine. I kept my tone
light. "He showed up the same day Adam did. Isn't that a
weird coincidence?"

"You saw them? Together?"

"Adam came to see me at Marshfield. Rudy left me a
note."

Through the phone line I heard the paper shuffling. I
waited until he spoke again. "Did they say what they
wanted?"

My cheeks grew hot and I was grateful Williamson
couldn't see my blush through the phone. "Adam asked me
out on a date," I said quickly. "I have no idea about Rudy. I
left him a message. Haven't heard back yet."

"You think he's there for romantic purposes as well?"

"I'm not the sort of woman who inspires men to traverse
the globe to ask me out."

He made a noise. I couldn't discern its meaning. "Thank

you, Ms. Wheaton. If you talk with either of these men again, please ask them to call me."

I started to say, "Will you let me know—" but he'd already hung up.

MY DOORBELL RANG LESS THAN AN HOUR later. Bootsie scampered ahead of me, curious as always. We had a small living room adjacent to the front door, set off from the foyer by oak pillars set atop rectangular dividers. She leapt up onto the top of the base nearest the door and lifted her white-splashed nose in the air, waiting for me to allow our visitor in.

"Hillary?" I said. Unable to prevent my shock from showing, I struggled to find a polite way of asking what she was doing on my front porch. "What a surprise," was the best I could manage.

Even though it was still early, the day was swelteringly hot. You'd never guess it to look at Hillary, whose blonde hair was pulled back in a sleek low ponytail. She wore a navy-and-white-striped sleeveless tank over white cropped pants. She belonged on a yacht, not my dilapidated front porch. I pushed open the screen door to allow her in, making sure Bootsie didn't make a break for escape. I know I wanted to.

Hillary smiled as widely as I'd ever seen, making me even more wary. She carried a dish, covered in aluminum foil. "Thank you," she said, making her way in. "Now that we're neighbors, I thought I'd stop by and say hello properly." She handed the dish to me. "Here. I made them myself."

I peeled the foil back to reveal a mountain of gorgeous, gooey raspberry bars individually displayed in crisp paper serving cups. "Hillary, you shouldn't have," I said. "You're the new neighbor. I'm supposed to be bringing goodies to your house as a welcome."

She waved me off. "Why stand on ceremony?" she said. Very un-Hillary-like. What was she up to?

I closed the front door and noticed that she'd bent over to cup Bootsie's face in her hands. The little mongrel was eating up the attention with half-closed eyes and an audible purr. "Look at this sweetheart. I didn't know you had a cat. Boy or girl?"

"Girl. Bootsie."

Hillary eyed her up and down. "Still a kitten, isn't she?"

"You know cats?"

"Always. Baxter's my only prince at the moment, but he's getting up there in age. Almost twelve."

I invited her to sit in the parlor while I put the raspberry bars away in the kitchen. To my surprise, she followed me in and pulled out a chair at the table. Okay. Casual it is. I changed my trajectory and placed the dish of sweets between us.

"Can I get you something to drink? Coffee?"

She demurred, folding her hands atop the table and tilting her head in such a way that she was studying me from beneath artfully mascaraed lashes. The coquettish move, if meant to disarm, was utterly lost on me. I dragged out the chair and sat, bringing our gazes level.

"You're probably wondering why I'm here," she said.

That was an understatement.

"You said you wanted to be neighborly." I pointed to the dish of raspberry bars.

"That's the main reason, of course." She gave a quick smile, acknowledging that we both knew she'd come up with an excuse to cover her real agenda.

Hard as I tried to come up with a possible explanation for her presence at my kitchen table, I couldn't. I waited, selecting a raspberry bar from the tempting pile. *I should pull out plates*, I thought, then gave a mental shrug. Each bar had its own pastel cupcake paper. Good enough.

"I do have one other reason." Another flash of teeth. "I'd like to ask a teensy favor."

My cell phone rang. Was that relief on Hillary's face? The interruption gave us both breathing space. I didn't recognize the number, though the area code told me it was a local call. I stood up to answer, making my way toward the front of the house for privacy even though this could turn out to be nothing more than a pesky telemarketer. "Hello?"

"Is this . . . Miss Grace Wheaton?" The heavy accent and halting English was a giveaway, but to be polite, I let him go on. "This is Rudy." He hurried to clarify, "The flight attendant from the plane," as though I wouldn't be able to put that together. "I am very happy you have seen the message I left for you."

"Yes, I did," I said, speaking slowly. "Although I have to admit I was surprised to hear from you."

"I am apologetic if I am intruding."

"Not at all," I said, crossing the dining room and parlor to put some distance between me and Hillary. There was nothing particularly secretive about this phone call, I realized, but I still preferred to keep Hillary's nose out of my business. I made it to the living room by the front door. "What brings you to Emberstowne?"

"The authorities required me to remain for several days in the United States and I have not yet secured a return flight assignment."

"An impromptu vacation for you, isn't it?"

He laughed, but I wasn't sure he'd understood.

Which reminded me. "How did you know which car was mine?" I asked. "To leave the note, that is."

This time when he laughed I could tell he meant it. "You are well known here. I asked several shopkeepers about you and everyone knew you and recognized your car. I could only think of that."

"I'm glad you did."

"You and the elderly gentleman were so kind after our . . . incident on the airplane. You both invited me to visit your beautiful mansion. I intend to do so."

"It's Bennett's home, not mine, but it's wonderful that you're taking time to visit. I know you'll enjoy it. I'd love for you to tour as my guest." Thinking fast, I considered ways to arrange to meet him. "If you're free later today or tomorrow, I'd be happy to escort you."

"My apologies. I have already made a plan for today and the next. Will you be available on Monday?"

"I will. When you get to Marshfield, give them my name. Don't pay an admission fee. I'll come down to get you."

"You are a most gracious host," he said, and thanked me for my time.

"See you Monday," I said, and hung up.

I returned to find Hillary bending off the side of her chair, dangling a tiny catnip-filled mouse on a string in front of Bootsie, laughing as the kitten batted at it with her pillowy pink paws.

"You said something about a favor?" I asked when I returned.

Enraptured by the cat, she didn't seem motivated to reveal what it was, so I prompted, "What do you need?"

She sat up, allowing Bootsie to grab the play mouse with her teeth. A moment later, the kitten was batting it around the wood floor, chasing and pouncing as she bounded around the room. Hillary fingered one of her glittery silver earrings. The triple hoops' gentle jangling made the room's silence more profound. She kept playing with the metal, weighing her words, it seemed.

Buying her time and giving in to temptation, I took a bite of the dessert and exclaimed over its deliciousness. I wasn't lying.

She nodded her thanks, eventually finding her voice. "Papa Bennett hired me."

This was news. I ran my tongue over my front teeth, where sticky fruit and streusel had decided to take up residence. "To do what?"

The wounded look on Hillary's face was not put on. I had no idea what I'd done to offend her. Her tone was almost pitiful when she asked, "Did you forget that I'm an interior designer?"

"Of course not," I said, scrambling to repair whatever damage I'd inadvertently caused. I might not like the woman, but I didn't want to hurt her. "It's just that we recently renovated several of the mansion's rooms. There aren't any due for rehab soon. None that I know of," I amended quickly. Bennett was generous and believed in second chances. Thirds, fourths, and fifths, even. In Hillary's case, they were probably in the double digits by now. "What rooms will you be focusing on?"

She fingered the earring so forcefully I was afraid she might rip it off. "That's just it. He didn't hire me to work at Marshfield."

My gut understood before my brain did. The raspberry bar did a perfect little backflip in my stomach. The words came out before I could stop them. "Then where?"

She had the good sense to look embarrassed. "Here." With her elbows on the table, she lifted her hands to the air and wiggled her fingers. "Your house."

Bootsie leapt into my lap at that moment, allowing me a precious second to compose myself. I stroked her face, thinking about how Bennett and I had discussed renovations here. Heaven knew the place needed it. If my neighbors were privy to this conversation right now, they'd burst into spontaneous applause.

I struggled for composure. "I don't know about that," I said.

Now that the truth was out, her words came fast, furious, and filled with the Hillary-level confidence I was used to.

"Listen, I can't start right away. I have another client to work with first."

I shook my head. "You misunderstand. I don't know that I'm ready for any renovations. Not yet."

She was not to be dissuaded. "I told Papa Bennett that you would be my first priority, but then this other project popped up." Leaning forward, she spoke in a confidential whisper even though the only one in earshot was Bootsie, "Honestly, I think Papa Bennett believed I would never land a client of my own. But I did. And there's no way I'm going to let this man down. He's very special. My first real client—wealthy *and* handsome," she said with a squeak in her voice. "That's why your project will have to wait."

"I don't think—"

"I understand this comes as a surprise. I also know that you haven't had a chance to see my work in person. I can change things around here." She gave the house a cursory glance and I got the feeling she was working hard at trying not to wrinkle her nose. "You'll love my ideas. I guarantee it."

"Hillary." The gravity in my tone must have caught her attention because she blinked. "I know the place needs work. The outside alone has years of updating ahead of it. The inside, however"—I paused to look around—"is comfortable. We may not have the best, the newest, or the shiniest of décor, but it's home."

She started to speak, but I talked right over her. "Believe me, I appreciate what you and Bennett are trying to do." That was a bit of a stretch. "After this first one, I'll bet you'll gain so many new clients that you won't even have time for this project." I said a quick prayer that that would prove true. "This isn't a good idea, Hillary."

She'd leaned back as I talked, not looking angry or disappointed in the least. I got the impression she was letting me have my say. In my passionate argument, I'd stopped petting Bootsie, and the kitten nosed my hand, hungry for more attention. I scratched behind her ears.

"Papa Bennett told me that my first job here was to focus on the outside." The corners of her pert little mouth curled up. "Interiors to come later. And"—she rolled her eyes—"he made me promise to listen to whatever you had to say."

"You're an *interior* designer," was the only thing I could think of.

"That doesn't mean I don't have what it takes to change your haunted mansion into a Painted Lady."

"This is hardly a haunted mansion."

Hillary made a face. "Whatever. The thing is, I can make a difference and I intend to. Unless, of course, you forbid me from helping you. Papa Bennett warned me that might be the case."

I heaved a deep sigh.

Hillary folded her arms across the table and leaned forward. "Bennett cares about you. A lot. It's obvious you care about him, too. Maybe he hired me because he wants to give my business a good start." She made a so-so motion with her head. "Forget the maybe. That is why he's doing it. Doesn't matter. I need the business and I have every intention of making doubters eat their words. Here's the thing," she went on, "he's doing this to help me, yes, but he's doing this for himself, too. Everyone in Emberstowne knows where you work. Don't you think it's embarrassing that the woman who manages Marshfield lives in a house that's in such a state of disrepair?"

I felt a paradigm shift. Months ago, I'd consented to Bennett's offer of help when the roof needed work, and I'd accepted assistance graciously on a few other matters of upkeep, but when it came to changes that were less necessary for living and more desirable for appearances, I'd rebuffed his offers.

Of course my eyesore house was an embarrassment to

Bennett. Why hadn't I realized that myself? I held my head
in my hands, resisting the urge to rub my eyes, which would
only exacerbate my cat allergies.

Bootsie, forgotten again, bounded off my lap and disappeared around the corner.

Numb, I reached for the only lifeline I had left. "You say
you have another client you need to work with first?"

Hillary bounced in her seat, surprised and clearly pleased.
"You won't be sorry. I promise."

I already was.

Chapter 25

FRANCES MARCHED INTO MY OFFICE MONDAY morning. "You're in early," she said.

Why did every sentence out of her mouth always come out sounding like an accusation? I looked up. "Nothing gets by you, Frances."

"The Mister wants to see you," she said with a glint in her eye.

I put down my pen to ask her about that when the phone rang. I answered.

"Good morning, Gracie," Bennett said. "I need to talk with you as soon as possible. Do you have a few minutes now?"

"Absolutely," I said. "I have a matter to discuss with you, too."

"I'll be right down."

Frances had been listening in, the corners of her down-turned mouth curling ever so slightly into a self-satisfied smile.

I stared up at her. "I was here before you this morning. The phone in your office hasn't made a peep. How in the world did you know?"

The twisty lip curls deepened. "I have my ways."

BENNETT SETTLED HIMSELF AT MY DESK while I shut the door between my office and Frances's. "This will be a private discussion, I take it?" he asked.

"Hillary came to visit." I perched my backside on the edge of my desk and folded my arms. "You hired her to work on my home?"

Bennett didn't flinch. "We've talked about this. You agreed to let me help."

"But . . . Hillary?"

"Two birds with one stone, eh?" When I didn't smile, he leaned forward and fixed me with a bright blue stare. "We won't let her run roughshod over you. You get the final say on all matters regarding your home."

I didn't budge.

"Time to come clean." He drew in a quick breath through his nose. "Here's what you don't know: I've cut her off." Reacting to my startled look, he went on, "I'd been providing her a generous allowance over the years. Hillary's never had to work a day in her life." The way his jaw set and the crinkles around his eyes deepened, I knew this was hard for him to admit. "I should have been a stronger parent when she was young. I was afraid of her, truth be told. She wasn't my blood and I believed I had no rights in raising her." He sat back and flung his fingers to the air. "Yet, here I am, watching her blow fortune after fortune with nothing to show for it." He shook his head. "They say it's never too late to learn. It took me too long, but I finally did. That's why I cut her off."

"Completely?"

He hedged. "I agreed to buy her a home as long as it was here in Emberstowne. The rest is up to her."

"So that's why she moved back."

"Maybe it isn't too late for her to learn, too."

I digested all this. "I had no idea."

"Hillary made me promise to keep it quiet until she settled in. Her pride is hurt."

That explained a lot. Always the gentleman, Bennett sought to help us both at once. Little did he know how much his stepdaughter's very presence grated on my every nerve. I thanked heaven that Hillary had snagged a client on her own. That bought me a little time, at least. "We'll put off this discussion for now," I said. Personal matters safely off the table, I opened the door between my office and Frances's to make it easier for my assistant to eavesdrop. "What did you want to talk with me about?"

"Two things."

I sat at my desk and waited for him to continue.

"First, and I believe this will come as no surprise to you, the pilot who flew us out to Europe, the one you so aptly nicknamed 'Milquetoast' has been cleared of all assault charges."

"What happened?"

"A case of mistaken identity. The charter company called me personally to let me know the details. Shortly after we departed on our fateful flight home, the pilot was released. All charges dropped."

"Isn't that convenient?"

Bennett met my gaze. "I thought so as well. The charter company is bending over backward to assure me that they screen all their pilots and staff extraordinarily well and that this situation was not their fault." Hands on his lap, he lifted his fingers as though to say, "What can you do?"

"What was the second thing?" I asked.

"Nico." Bennett got right down to business. "I wasn't

able to get in touch with him until yesterday," he said. "He's fighting chest congestion and is hoping it doesn't give way to pneumonia." Bennett's face clouded. "It's tough getting old. We're not as resilient as we'd like to believe. For Nico to be fighting health problems while he's chasing down thieves . . ."

"You told him about the skull, I take it."

"I had to. Nico is understandably distraught to think the skull may have been stolen. He's beside himself."

"I can only imagine," I said. "What does he plan to do about it?"

"That's the thing." Bennett crossed one long leg over the other, leaning back. Intertwining his fingers atop his silver-white hair, he pursed his lips and squinted up toward the ceiling. While his posture remained ramrod straight, his thoughtful, relaxed position was new. He looked different, younger. For one brief moment, he no longer seemed a sep-tuagenarian billionaire; he looked like a thirty-something businessman, problem-solving a particularly confounding challenge.

I waited.

Drawing a deep breath through flared nostrils, Bennett lowered his gaze to meet mine. "He wants to come here. To see the photos for himself."

"He doesn't remember the mark?"

"He most definitely does."

"Then why come here?"

"Nico doesn't have any pictures of the mark on the skull. He neglected to have that done when he set up his gallery."

"Cesare fell down on the job," I said. "The question is, was that an oversight or was it intentional?"

"So you don't trust the greasy little man either, do you?"

I laughed, despite myself. "Apt description. Truth is, I don't know who to trust." I thought about Bennett's admission that Pezzati sometimes played fast and loose. "If anyone."

Bennett adopted a faraway look again. "There's more. First of all, I'm uncomfortable with my old friend making this extensive trip while he's fighting illness. He promised he would wait until he was up to it, but Nico can be stubborn."

"Tell him not to come," I said. "I'll scan copies and e-mail them." A stutter-second later, I asked, "He does have e-mail, right?"

Amused, Bennett said, "I suggested that option. People of my generation aren't as out of touch as you youngsters believe."

"I never said *you* were out of touch."

He made a conciliatory motion with his hand. "You're too polite to say so, but I was behind the times until Davey started helping me out. But we're getting off point here. Nico is determined to come out here for another reason. He believes that if he brings the skull and we compare it with the photos, he'll have his proof."

"Here or there, the proof will be the same. I don't understand his need to travel across the ocean to see the pictures in person."

Bennett's mouth twisted. "He has more on his agenda." Raising his voice, he spoke over his shoulder, "You getting all this, Frances?"

From the doorway: "Loud and clear. Keep going."

Bennett's eyes sparkled when he turned to face me again. "That woman. I don't know why she doesn't simply stomp in and make herself comfortable."

She poked her head around the jamb. "Then who would stand guard out here to make sure no one else eavesdrops? Did you think of that?" Ducking back out of sight, she shouted, "And for the record, I do not stomp."

Bennett's wiry brows arched in amusement. "Noted," he replied. Then to me: "About Nico. He has it in his mind to scoop up my pictures and take them and the skull to New York to confront Gerard."

"What proof does he have that Gerard is behind the embezzlement?" I held my hands up, not understanding. "How much money are we talking about, anyway?"

"In American dollars, Nico has lost several hundred thousand over the past few months. They're digging now to see how far back the problem goes."

Incredulous, I asked, "How did no one notice that kind of money being routed through the kitchen?"

Bennett held up both hands in a helpless gesture. "When you trust your staff—"

"There's no oversight?"

Again, the helpless expression. "I realize how lucky I am to have you watching out for my interests."

"I still don't understand how he knows Gerard is behind all this."

"The accountant dug deeper. He found evidence of communication between Gerard and the cook. I'm sketchy on the details, because Nico had difficulty communicating through fits of coughing, but that's the impression I get. The cook is under arrest, but swears she's innocent. Of course."

"Do you realize that it's been less than a week since we visited there? How did all this come to pass so quickly?"

"I get the impression the accountant had begun looking into the books before we got there. Apparently that big guy, Angelo, was instrumental in arranging for this audit."

"Huh," I said. "There goes my theory of Angelo being the bad guy."

"There's another factor I was unaware of until now."

"What's that?"

"Nico intends to bequeath Villa Pezzati to his town, structuring the transfer much the way I have structured my gift to Emberstowne upon my death."

"Why would he do that when he has children?"

"You know his opinion of Gerard." Bennett waited for

my nod before continuing. "Nico is afraid that Gerard will come after Irena. I got the impression he believes his son might weasel his sister's share out from under her." Bennett shook his head, looking very sad. "Nico is providing comfortably for Irena, of course. He simply wants to keep the estate out of his son's hands."

I sat back, digesting all this. "That's huge."

"Indeed."

"Why did Angelo call for an audit, then? How does he figure into all this?"

"I was reluctant to push Nico for details."

I crossed my arms on my desk and leaned forward. "Could Angelo have framed the cook? I understand we only met the woman for a minute or so, but she hardly struck me as the thieving type."

Frances shouted from the other room, "It's always the ones you least suspect."

Bennett and I exchanged a look. "I'll keep that in mind," I said.

MID-AFTERNOON, IT OCCURRED TO ME THAT Rudy had never shown up to tour Marshfield. Either that, or he'd neglected to ask for me. I was about to call down there to ask Doris if she remembered seeing anyone who fit Rudy's description, when my cell phone rang.

I glanced at caller ID. Ronny Tooney. "Good to hear from you," I said when I answered. "Did anything ever come from that lead you mentioned?"

Traffic, shouts, whistles, and rumblings in the background made me strain to hear. "Maybe," he said. "What was the name of the guy you visited in Italy? Mr. Marshfield's good friend?"

"Nico Pezzati."

Squeals, like those from a braking bus, filled the beat of

silence between us. A moment later he said, "You mentioned him in passing, that's why it's familiar, but you didn't give me that name to investigate."

I sat up a little straighter, a curious *zing* running up my spine. "He isn't a suspect."

Crowd sounds filled the phone space. Much too busy for Emberstowne. Even in the middle of tourist season. "What aren't you telling me, Tooney? And where are you?"

"That list of names you gave me. I ran them all down as far as I could take them. I couldn't find your Pinky character, though. If I had a last name—"

"Detective Williamson identified her." I provided the basic details about Diane Waters of Brooklyn and waited for Tooney to write everything down. "Why did you ask me about Nico Pezzati?"

"I'm in New York City."

The background noise finally made sense. "Why?"

"You said you'd cover expenses. I flew out through Southwest. They were about ten dollars more than taking a train, but I thought it was worth it to save time. I didn't schedule a return flight. I can take the train back if you want."

"I'm not quibbling about costs, Tooney. I want to know why you went out there."

"Every name you gave me came up empty. Nothing. It was either they didn't exist, or if they did, there was nothing pertinent to report."

I rolled my wrist in a silent "Hurry it up" movement, even though he couldn't see.

"You know I always want to do a thorough job for you. You've trusted me so far, and I don't want to blow it."

Exasperated, I couldn't keep my impatience from showing. "Cut to the chase."

He smacked his lips. "I went back and tried again.

Digging deeper this time with every name. Still came up mostly empty."

"Mostly."

"Until I looked more closely at the leader of SlickBlade."

I sucked in a breath. "Adam?"

"The very one."

My hand gripped the receiver so tightly I was afraid I might crack it in half. "He was here. Friday. He came to see me."

"Ah . . ." Tooney said as though that explained something. "He's back in the Big Apple today. I spent the last couple hours following him. The guy lives in an upscale apartment overlooking Central Park."

"Why? Why follow him? What happened?" As usual, Tooney wasn't talking fast enough for me.

He explained, "The guy is rich, no question about it. Has a personal driver but seems to prefer walking."

"Pinky lived in Brooklyn," I reminded him. "Maybe there's a connection."

"I'll look into it."

"Tell me more about why you followed Adam."

"You told me that SlickBlade didn't own the chartered plane—that it belonged to the Curling Weasels."

"That's right."

"When SlickBlade and everyone else on the list came up empty, I decided to check out the Weasels. See if anything popped."

Where was Frances when I wanted her to listen in? Too late, I remembered she'd left the office to run an errand. "What did you find?"

"Do you know who manages the Curling Weasels?"

I shook my head, despite the fact Tooney couldn't see. "Who?"

"A guy here in New York. He works out of a fancy office

a couple of blocks away from Times Square. Adam from SlickBlade is up in that office right this minute, meeting with that manager. Want to know what his name is?"

I held my breath.

Tooney raised his voice to be heard over a sudden traffic crescendo. "He goes by Jerry Pezz," he shouted, "but his real name is Gerard Pezzati."

Chapter 26

THE MINUTE I HUNG UP WITH TOONEY, I dialed Williamson, eager to convey the information about Adam's connection to Gerard Pezzati. Irena told me that her brother was ashamed of his living conditions and begged her not to visit. She sent him money to help keep him going. How despicable to scam one's sister like that. Bennett had said that Nico was afraid of Gerard weaseling the estate from Irena. How apt that he managed the super successful Curling Weasels.

"The connection between the two has got to be important," I told Williamson. "It's too much of a coincidence, otherwise."

The detective had me repeat what Tooney had reported, twice. "You understand this is all hearsay," he said.

"Ronny Tooney is a private investigator." The words tumbled out of my mouth with surprising ease. Even as recently as a half year ago, I would never have predicted my voicing such fervent support of the man. "He uncovered this as part of his investigation."

Williamson grunted. "I'm not saying I'm convinced, but you've got that flight attendant . . ."

"Rudy. He said he might come visit today, but I haven't seen him."

"The fact that he's wandering around town is curious. You had the lead singer from SlickBlade trying to get close to you, too. There are allegations he may have connections to your friends in Italy, and those Italian friends are on their way to visit."

"We have to wait until Signor Pezzati is healthy enough to travel."

"Whatever. There's too much going on in your little hamlet to ignore. I'm coming out there."

"That would be great," I said sincerely.

"Don't wait up for me," he said. "I'm taking a detour to New York to verify some of what your personal P.I. came up with. When I get to Emberstowne, I'll want to coordinate with your local P.D. Any idea who runs homicide out there?"

I gave him both Rodriguez's and Flynn's names. "I've worked with them before."

"Somehow that doesn't surprise me."

I didn't bother hanging up. I merely clicked to get the tone and dialed Rodriguez. As I did so, I heard the door to Frances's office close. A moment later, her chair squeaked. Good. She was back.

"Ms. Wheaton," Rodriguez said in surprise when I identified myself. "I was just about to call you."

"Isn't that a coincidence," I said. "What's up?"

"We're closing the books on Vandeen Deinhart. The guy's clean. Clean enough that my spinster aunt could run a white glove across his forehead and hear it squeak."

"That's almost poetic, Detective."

"Don't get used to it. I'm only telling you that because Flynn and I plan to start looking elsewhere for suspects."

About time. "Elsewhere?" I prompted.

"We think it's time to take a second look at your Picasso skull theory."

Took you long enough. "Great," I said, then shared with him what Tooney had called to tell me. I also mentioned Detective Williamson's involvement. "Whatever you and Detective Flynn need, let me know."

"We'll be in touch."

I hung up and made my way in to see Frances.

"What did the dynamic duo have to say?" she asked.

"It's what Tooney had to say that's the most interesting," I said. Frances's eyes went wide, her brows jumping in silent surprise as I told her about the connection between my would-be suitor, Adam, and Signor Pezzati's son, Gerard.

"That's a little too cozy for comfort," she said.

I shared what Bennett had told me about Pezzati bequeathing his estate to the town. "Gerard is out of the will completely. I guess this is his way of negotiating his own inheritance."

"If he's a hotshot New York manager for that band you mentioned . . ."

"Curling Weasels."

". . . Then it sounds as though he's well off. Why jeopardize all he's worked for by stealing from his father?"

"A sense of entitlement, perhaps?" I suggested. "I've heard of instances where kids believe their parents owe them." I thought about my own inheritance, and that of my sister. How differently we'd handled what our mother had left us. How differently we handled life. I shook off the memories. Too painful. "We know nothing about Gerard as a person. We don't know how he managed his apparent success. He may have built his empire by stealing funds from others."

Frances clucked disapproval. "When Signor Pezzati arrives, will he stay with the Mister or at the Marshfield Hotel?"

"Bennett wants him to stay here. We were guests in his home, and Bennett believes it's only fitting to extend the same hospitality." I snapped my fingers. "That reminds me, I wanted to call before he leaves. I certainly hope someone besides Angelo makes the trip with him."

MARCO ANSWERED THE PHONE AND, WHEN I identified myself, was quick to remind me of his desire to visit the United States. "I believe Signor Pezzati is coming to visit soon," I said. Although these might not be the best circumstances under which to experience Marshfield, I was certain he'd find enjoyment in the trip. "Will you accompany him?"

"Unfortunately," he said, with great care to get the word out properly, "I am not to be included. Signor Pezzati requires me to remain here."

"I'm sorry to hear that. Do you know who is coming with the signor?"

"There is discussion," he said. "I believe Angelo."

I'd been hoping to hear that Irena would be coming, too. I asked to speak with her. Marco thanked me for my kindness and promised to call her to the phone. "She and her father are at dinner. Just a moment."

That's right; dinners there were later than we were used to here. It was well after eight in the evening at Villa Pezzati.

Irena came on the line, breathless. "Grace," she said with smiling exclamation in her voice. "So wonderful to hear from you."

"I'm sorry to interrupt your meal," I began.

"No, no. I'm delighted by your call. Father is beside himself with worry and believes you and Bennett can help him. This business about the skull is horrible. How could anyone do such a thing to my father?"

"He told Bennett that he believes your brother is behind it."

She heaved a sigh. "Such an accusation makes me very sad."

"Your father plans to confront Gerard."

"I know," she said. Her misery was evident. "I'm afraid this news is too much for his heart. Knowing how angry my brother makes him, I can't imagine how he will survive such an altercation. My father is constantly trying to protect me. This time, I need to protect him."

"So you're coming with him?"

"Unless Angelo has his way." She made a growling noise. "He tried to charter a jet yesterday—and leave without telling me. My father was in no shape to travel. He's only slightly better today."

"Whatever you do," I said, "don't take on additional passengers. Strangers, I mean." Thinking about Signor Pezzati and Irena alone with the burly bodyguard on the long flight over, I added, "Is there any way to leave Angelo behind?"

"I will try."

"Be very careful, okay?"

"Is it that bad?"

For about a second, I considered telling her about Gerard's connection to SlickBlade and the Curling Weasels. Although it wasn't proof that Gerard had engineered Pinky's spot on our tragic flight, the evidence was incriminating. Irena had enough to deal with. This could wait. "We'll talk when you get here," I said.

THAT NIGHT I FOUND MYSELF PACING THE house waiting for Bruce and Scott to get home. I'd told them about Hillary's new project, but now that I'd heard

Bennett's side of the story, I'd begun to rethink my initial knee-jerk refusal. My roommates knew how much I cared for Bennett. They knew about the potential blood relationship, too. I needed their advice.

For the fourth time in as many minutes, I checked the kitchen clock. It would be at least another hour before they were home. I decided to strap Bootsie into her harness and sit on the rickety front porch, hoping the evening air would help clear my mind.

The sun was doing its nightly disappearing act, purpling the clouds and shooting beams of shimmering orange out in its bursting farewell. I made my way down the graying, crooked steps to sit on the very bottom one. That would allow Bootsie the full six feet of her leash to explore whatever sidewalk, soft grass, and jumping bugs she could reach on the nearby ground. So engrossed was I in watching her belly-crawling antics that I didn't notice Jack until he was almost halfway up my front walk.

My breath caught in my throat. "Hi," I said in a strangled voice. He wore dress slacks and a collared shirt. Loafers that made no sound against the concrete. Too surprised by his appearance sauntering up my walk, I didn't have time to summon a dismissive "Oh, it's you" tone. Nope, in that one high-pitched "Hi," I communicated embarrassment from the meet-up with Becke the other night and my instinctive appreciation of him, looking all cleaned up and handsome.

"You busy?" he asked.

I shrugged. "Does it look like it?"

He closed the distance between us, crouching to pet Bootsie. "She remembers me," he said when she nuzzled against his hand.

I started to say, "She does that with everyone," but bit my lip.

He sat next to me, asking, "May I?" even as his back end met the uneven step.

My natural inclination was to apologize, and I started to form the words to express regret for interrupting his date with Becke on Friday. This time, however, I held my tongue. He'd come to see me. There must be a reason.

Crickets chirped, welcoming the rolling dusk.

He picked up a thick twig and began peeling at its bark with a fingernail. One long pale green line in a bumpy brown stub. "Becke's not moving in with me," he said.

"Change of plan?"

His face tightened. "She's moving into my dad's house. That's all it is. She and her kids are going through a bad time and my dad's house is, well, you know . . ."

I did know. While the paternal head of the Embers family served time in prison, the house remained empty.

"Having them live in it is good for everyone," Jack said, still scratching at the twig. More lines of pale green joined the first. "She catches a break, and I don't have to worry about vandals."

"We have that much vandalism in Emberstowne?"

Even in the rapidly waning light, I could see his cheeks color. He turned his attention away from the twig and met my wavering gaze. I wasn't feeling particularly strong right now, but I wasn't about to play the compliant female, either.

His mouth was so tight I could barely see his teeth when he spoke. "I'm doing a favor for someone I was once close to. Is that so wrong?"

"Very gentlemanly."

My sarcasm sat between us like a lump.

I kept my gaze averted for as long as I could. Tiring of treading the awkward silence, I reached for Bootsie, who wiggled away. "I should get in." I reached for her again.

"Wait," he said. "Please."

That surprised me into silence.

"Who was the guy you met outside Hugo's Friday night?" he asked.

I sat back. "You followed me?"

"I wanted to explain and to apologize for Becke's behavior. All I'm doing is giving her a place to stay, a home for her kids."

"She wants more, doesn't she?"

"I don't." He waited for me to make eye contact. "You know that, don't you?"

I lifted my gaze to the inky purple sky. Stars were out there, almost. I could feel their presence even if I couldn't yet see them. "Lately it feels as though I don't know anything."

"They say timing is everything in relationships."

Hadn't I just told myself that? "They do."

"Can we try again?" he asked. "Start over?"

I hesitated.

He handed me the twig. I could barely make it out, but he'd scratched a word in the little branch. It read, "Maybe?"

My stomach flip-flopped at the touching gesture. I swallowed as hope and memories of disappointment collided in my heart, making it swell even as it raced with fear and anticipation.

"Becke," I finally said. "She's going to be a force to contend with."

"I can handle her."

I squinted, barely able to see the shrubbery nearest the street now, but with sudden clarity when it came to mistakes of the heart I'd made in the past. I couldn't make those mistakes again. I turned to him. "I won't fight another woman for a man's affection or attention—"

"I don't expect you to."

Temptation was terrific. Gathering all the strength I could muster, I said the words that were right for me, right now. "Get Becke settled. Do whatever you need to do for her. It really is a great kindness you're offering."

"I swear there's nothing—"

Emboldened by the power of my decision, I reached forward and placed my finger against his lips. They were soft, warm pillows in the rapidly cooling night air, but I wouldn't allow myself to think about them right now. Not in that way. "I won't be 'the other woman' in Becke's world. She'll never be genuinely settled until she understands that you're not part of her new life. Until then, I won't be involved in the drama. I can't."

"I'm sure she'll understand soon. Very soon."

I wasn't so sure but smiled to be kind.

"Will you wait for me?" he asked.

I knew better than to say that I would. "One step at a time."

He nodded then tilted his head. "You never answered my question. Who was the guy who followed you the other night?"

I stared up at the sky again. "Trouble."

Chapter 27

FRANCES WAS IN THE OFFICE FIRST THE NEXT morning. "So." She threw off her reading glasses, allowing them to hang from the jeweled chain around her neck. "How's Jack? Is he selling you the line that his relationship with Becke is merely platonic?"

I stopped in my tracks. "I give up, Frances. How do you do it?"

Her chin poked upward. "What happened?"

I'd been barely able to find the words to tell my roommates about Jack's visit. I wasn't about to carry on with my telephone-tele-Frances assistant. Half the town would be chittering about it before noon. I raised my gaze to the ceiling. *Assuming they aren't already.* "Tell your grapevine that you have it on good authority that I'm still single and intend to remain so."

As her chin dropped, her lower lip jutted, and those eyebrows shot for the sky. I'd surprised her. "But I thought—"

"End of story."

To punctuate my statement, I headed straight into my office and shut the door. My desk phone rang a moment later. I picked it up without checking caller ID, thinking it was Frances calling to make amends.

"Yes?" I answered, realizing almost instantly that I'd made a foolish assumption. Frances apologize? Not likely.

"What gives, Grace?"

A male voice. Irate for some reason. I'd heard this voice before. Recently, too. I tried to place it. Not Williamson.

"Who is this?" I asked.

He wasn't letting up. "Where do you get off investigating me? If you wanted to know something, why not just ask?"

Boom. "Adam?"

"You're lucky we didn't press charges."

I matched his tone. "I don't know what you're talking about." Belatedly, I remembered. "Oh wait."

"'Oh wait' is right. Glad to see you have your memory back. Who is this Tooney stooge, anyway?"

I stood up, as though doing so would give me power. Tooney told me he'd been following Adam. And if Adam was in cahoots with Gerard, our would-be private detective could be in big trouble. "Don't hurt him. Please."

"Hurt him?" Adam's ire evaporated. "Why would I hurt him?"

"Because . . ." I stopped myself before giving anything away. "I want to talk with him." I imbued my voice with as much gravitas as possible. "I want to hear for myself that he's all right."

"What is wrong with you?" Adam asked. "You hired him to follow me, now you act as though I'm holding him hostage."

"Aren't you?"

"Oh boy." The soft scratching noise that traveled through the phone line led me to believe Adam was rubbing his face. "Your minion is down at the police station answering questions right now."

At the police station? I took a moment to process why guilty killers would involve the police. Came up empty. What I said was: "He's hardly my minion."

"You hired him to follow me. Why?"

Frances popped in. No surprise there. She sat at my desk, engrossed in my conversation. Receiver gripped to my ear, I knew how Bootsie must have felt last night, pacing behind my desk only as far as the corded handset would allow. At least it wasn't Frances holding the leash. I was too worked up right now to chase her out.

"What does it matter if you have nothing to hide?"

Adam's voice was low, more curious than agitated now. "What's going on over there?" he asked. "You must have had a good reason for having me tailed." He sounded almost hopeful. "What is it? Help me understand."

I wasn't about to share my theories with him.

He took my hesitation as reluctance. "Your investigator shouted Jerry's name when he was talking on the phone with you. Why would you be interested in him? I thought you said you didn't even like the Curling Weasels."

"I don't."

"Then tell me what's going on, Grace."

Anger got the best of me. I knew better than to throw caution to the wind, but all the fear for Bennett that I'd kept bottled up, all the panic I'd felt on that flight, all the disappointment brewing around whatever it was I had with Jack, erupted in a volcano of spite. "Why don't *you* tell *me* what's going on? How convenient that you're working with Gerard Pezzati. Did you ever think to mention that?"

He started to speak, but there was no stopping me now—steamrolling over anything or anyone in my way. "You came here to Marshfield. I trusted you. What were you trying to do? A little reconnaissance? You didn't get the job done right the first time, so you're back to try again? How much is Gerard paying you?"

Heat suffused my face in a way that made it feel as though all the blood in my body was likely to geyser out the top of my head. "Consider yourself forewarned." My words chomped out like angry bites. "Come anywhere near Marshfield Manor. . . . come anywhere near Bennett, and I will see to it that you're hauled off for good."

He was silent. "I . . . don't know what to say. Nothing you're saying makes any sense."

"Where is Ronny Tooney?" I demanded. "Send him home. Safely. Now."

"Grace." Adam's voice was soft and low.

"Don't make me come after you."

He cleared his throat. "I'll see what I can do."

I slammed the phone back into its cradle and resumed pacing. Frances sat silently, watching me. "That went well."

I thrust my hands skyward. "What would you have me do?" I said. "I can't find out who targeted Bennett, I can only surmise. If it's Vandeen Deinhart, we're at least almost out of the woods. Once Bennett signs the closing documents, Deinhart won't benefit from doing Bennett any harm."

"Rodriguez and Flynn don't think he's responsible," she reminded me.

"Thank you for that news flash. With their track record of hunting down killers, I thoroughly value their opinions."

She sat expressionless, unfazed.

"This Pinky. Priscilla. Diane. The dead woman." I paced, turning to face Frances with each statement. "She was working for someone else. I know it. We can't connect her to Gerard Pezzati, but we can connect her to Slick-Blade." I looked at Frances again. "Adam's band boarded the plane with Pinky in tow. Adam works with Gerard Pezzati."

Frances remained silent.

"What do I do? Wait for that Detective Williamson to show up? He's even harder to convince than Rodriguez and Flynn are. I need to uncover whatever connects Pinky to Gerard. It's got to be out there. All I need to do is find it."

"Maybe you should meet with Gerard Pezzati yourself."

I stopped walking. "Oh sure, I'll waltz over to his office, accuse him of stealing a piece of art worth millions of dollars, tell him I know he's been communicating with Antoinette, Pezzati's cook, in order to embezzle more, and that he's doing all this because he's been cut out of his daddy's will. To top it all off, I'll accuse him of attempted murder. Mind you, I don't have a shred of solid proof. How do you think that will go over? Do think I would even make it back alive?"

Frances stood, brushing her hands down the front of her lavender shirt. "I'm not suggesting you go in with guns blazing." She eyed me with an odd glint I hadn't seen before. "Even if your heart's in the right place, your aim is off. Way off."

My rapid breaths were slowing, the tension in my shoulders easing. "What are you suggesting?"

"You need to find out what connects Gerard with Pinky, right? Talk to the man. Pretend you hope to arrange a reconciliation between him and his father. Tell him that's why you hired Tooney. To get a read on the situation."

"After I just went off on Adam? They would never buy it."

"You won't know unless you try. New York isn't all that far. But for heaven's sakes, don't go alone. Take Terrence. Take a couple of the guys with you."

I didn't know what to say to that.

"I'll go with you, if you like."

I sat behind my desk. Like I had been last night, I was sorely tempted. I wanted answers to all my questions. Most of all, I wanted Bennett to be safe. But I didn't want to be stupid about it.

My cell phone rang. I glanced at the caller ID. "It's Tooney," I said to Frances. When I clicked in I didn't even say hello. "What happened?"

The wannabe private eye's voice was resigned, even sheepish. "I got busted."

"Talk to me, Tooney. Hang on. Let me put you on speakerphone."

When I did, he started talking. "I told you that Adam was a rich guy. Never dawned on me that he had body-guards watching out for people like me. They tagged me and took me down right after I hung up with you."

"Are you okay?"

"Couple of bumps and bruises from when they dragged me into their limo. The guys were professional. They took me to a quiet place and asked questions. Lots of questions."

"You sure you're okay?"

"I never told them who I was working for. They figured that out when they saw where I was from. I'm sorry, Grace. I would never knowingly give up that information."

I sighed. "It's okay. What did they want?"

Frances sat up.

"Weird," Tooney said. "Strangest thing."

"Explain," I said.

"They didn't seem to know what they wanted. They hammered me, asking why I'd been following that Adam."

"Physically hammered you?"

"Nah," he said. "That's an expression. When they came up empty they took me to the P.D. and threatened to press charges for stalking a celebrity."

"Why didn't you call me? I'd have bailed you out."

"Then the police would know who I was working for, and I didn't want to reveal your name. The bodyguards didn't tell the cops any of that, and I told you I wouldn't

ever give up that information as long as it was in my power
to keep it secret."

"I appreciate that, Tooney, but that's a little above and
beyond. How did you get out?"

"Charges dropped. They let me out and handed me my
stuff, and I called you right away."

"Huh," I said, exchanging a glance with Frances. "How
soon can you be back?"

He hesitated. "Should I catch a flight or take a train?"

"Fly back, Tooney."

"You know it's probably more expensive?"

I sighed. "Yeah, Tooney. I know."

Chapter 28

WHEN I HUNG UP WITH TOONEY, I FACED
Frances. "I like your idea of visiting Gerard Pezzati," I said.
"I especially like the idea of taking Terrence along."

"And me?"

"Why do you want to go?"

"Why should you have all the fun?"

I was spent. "You do realize we're talking about investigating murders and attempted murders. How on earth do
you count that as fun?"

She shrugged.

The desk phone jangled. "Who is it now?" I asked rhetorically. I grabbed for the receiver and saw the name on
the display, and my shoulders slumped.

"Who is it?" Frances asked.

I bit my bottom lip and decided to let it go to voicemail.
"Hillary." I knew Frances would eventually find out about
Bennett's stepdaughter renovating my house, but I intended
to put off that moment of disclosure for as long as possible.

Frances stood, preparing to return to her office, giving me a quizzical look. "How's that new business of hers coming along?" she asked.

"No idea."

"When do you want to leave? For New York, I mean."

I thought about it. "Signor Pezzati is due here in the next couple of days. Let's wait until we talk with him. I'd rather meet Gerard with all my facts straight." I stopped, realizing from the indicator light on my phone that Hillary had left a message. *Great.* "How does that sound?"

Frances twisted her mouth in disapproval. "You're the boss," she said, rolling her eyes. "I'm merely an assistant."

This would have been the perfect setup for me to tell Frances that she was so much more than just an assistant, but her peeve bugged me. I was still charged from my unsettling conversation with Adam and wasn't in the mood to placate my never-happy employee. I waited until she'd made it to her own office to call up Hillary's message, very glad that I had the capability of listening through the receiver rather than blaring it aloud in the room.

"Good afternoon, Grace. This is Hillary," she began, oh-so-professionally. "I understand that you've been in contact with Bennett Marshfield about our arrangement. I'd like to set up our first appointment whenever is convenient for you. We'll need to decide the scope of the project and share our ideas with one another. I'm booked this week with that other client I mentioned. As of next Monday, however, I'm wide open. Give me a call." She rattled off her new business number.

I hung up and rested my head against the back of my chair. I knew putting Hillary off until next week was no answer, but it sure felt good right now.

BENNETT STROLLED IN A LITTLE WHILE later. "Good afternoon, Frances. How was your day?"

She mumbled a reply.

"What was that?" he asked.

Glad to hear a friendly voice, I got up and made my way into Frances's office in time for Bennett to ask her another question. He turned to me. "What's this about New York?"

I glared at my assistant before explaining our plan to visit Gerard Pezzati.

"You think that's wise?" Bennett asked.

I wasn't in the mood to argue for fear that my agitation would get the best of me. "Plans aren't set in stone yet," I said. Then changing the subject, I asked, "What brings you down here?"

Bennett brightened. "I received a call from Irena earlier. They should be here tomorrow morning."

"Signor Pezzati is well enough to travel?" Frances asked. "Pneumonia is nothing to sneeze at."

Bennett held on to the back of a chair, the long fingers of both hands stretching down the tight leather. "I agree. They're expected to land shortly after five. That puts them here before seven A.M. I'll have their rooms set up and food brought in. I expect they'll want to sleep. Even traveling by charter can be exhausting."

"I wouldn't be surprised if they want to see the skull photos right away," I said.

Bennett's brows came together. "I suppose they might. I'm reluctant to allow Nico to push himself. He's under a great deal of strain, whether he cares to admit it or not."

"Would you like me to pull out the photos now?" I asked. "That way you have them at your fingertips when you need them."

"Certainly not. You're as big a part of this story as any of us. We'll arrange to view them all together. Perhaps if I tell them you're indisposed for a while, they'll take advantage and get some rest before we get into the real reason for their visit."

So thoughtful, yet so old-school, Bennett had been raised in a world where one waited for the proper time for such revelations. Nico Pezzati was making a trip across the world to see Bennett's proof. If it were my treasures we were talking about, I wouldn't be able to wait, and doubted Irena would, either.

"I'll look forward to seeing them both."

"There's one more thing. Irena says that she had some difficulty with Angelo about coming out here. He didn't want them to make the trip. I suppose we'll find out more about that tomorrow."

"Doesn't bode well," I said.

AS I PREPARED TO LEAVE FOR THE EVENING, my cell phone chimed the arrival of a text. It was Bruce. "Guy here asking for you. Good looking."

"Who?" I texted back.

"Won't give a name. Wants to surprise you."

Adrenaline flashed up, hot and fast. I didn't like this. Bruce and Scott had met Eric well before he'd run off with my sister, so I knew I was safe on that front. Who could it be? Rudy?

"Italian accent?" I wrote back.

"No. Tall, dark, handsome."

"Local?"

"Not sure."

I kept a finger poised, ready to Swype another reply, if only I knew what to say. Bruce and Scott's wine shop, Amethyst Cellars, would be hopping even though it wasn't the weekend. There would be lots of people around. Safe enough.

"What's your gut tell you?" I finally asked.

When I read his reply, I smiled. He'd typed: "Go for it!"

* * *

TWENTY MINUTES LATER, I WALKED INTO Amethyst Cellars, breathing in the familiar wine commingled with woodwork. The shop, with its busy, happy patrons holding sparkling glasses and socializing amid tasteful displays, always had an energetic, upscale vibe. I felt welcome here, despite the fact that tonight I had no idea who waited for me. I was neither jittery nor eager, but I was curious. Who was this mystery man?

A couple dozen wine-tasters at the counter had their backs turned to the front door and I couldn't recognize anyone. The chattering crowd appeared to be broken out into groups of twos and fours. I scanned the shop for any lone males, but came up empty.

Scott called me over. "When Bruce told the guy you were on your way, he said he'd be right back, and took off." He gestured vaguely. "You don't have any idea who he is?"

"Not a clue. You know everyone I know." A thought occurred to me. I placed both hands on the countertop and gave Scott a mischievous glare. "It isn't Jack, is it?"

"Not a chance. We wouldn't do that to you. Heck, if we knew who this guy was, we would have told you, no matter how much he insisted on surprise."

A customer waved for Scott's attention. He started to excuse himself, then stopped, focusing over my shoulder. "Speak about the devil. He's back," he said, then, "Whoa."

I turned, curiosity crashing like cymbals on concrete. The surrounding din of lively, casual conversation faded as my hearing and vision tunneled. "What are you doing here?"

Adam closed the distance between us, not smiling. "I'm sorry, Grace," he said. "I've done something to hurt you. I don't know what it is, but I'm sorry."

In his hands he held a bouquet of flowers. Twice, maybe triple the size of the bunch he'd brought me last time. He pushed the blooms into the space between us. Reflexively, I reached for them, then pushed back.

"I asked what you're doing here." I did a quick assessment. Plenty of people, potential witnesses. I didn't sense that Adam would risk anything in such a public environment, and the comfort of the crowd made me bold. "I told you to stay away." I was furious by his response—which was no response at all, so I went on, "Why did you have Ronny Tooney arrested?"

"You asked me to let him go. We dropped the charges."

"Why did you pick him up in the first place?" I asked. "Why didn't you tell me you worked with Gerard Pezzati?"

He held the massive flowers I'd refused to accept. "You asked me that on the phone. What is Jerry to you? Why do you care if I work with him?" Gesturing as he spoke, he wound up banging the bouquet against the back of a gentleman sipping white wine. The guy turned to give Adam a furious glance, noted that we were in the midst of an argument, and took a cautious step away.

We were creating a spectacle. Not exactly conducive to business, and the last thing I wanted to do was hurt Scott and Bruce. "Can we take this outside?" I asked. Warning bells sounded, but it was early enough in the evening. Light enough outside. Lots of people. How much trouble could I get into on the tourist-crammed streets of Emberstowne?

Chapter 29

BRUCE HEADED US OFF AT THE DOOR. "IS everything okay, Grace?"

"We'll be right outside," I said. "I don't want to disturb your guests." Shooting a malevolent look at Adam, I added, "Keep an eye on me though, okay?"

Adam exploded when we got outside. "What was that all about?" He threw his arms out in frustration, the blooms in his left hand bouncing brightly, as though shaken by his anger.

Two large men sauntered up behind him. They looked like the kind of guys who play bouncers in movies. Built like Mack trucks, they wore dark T-shirts stretched to bursting against ham-sized pecs over black jeans that were too tight to be comfortable. I pointed, less confident than I'd been a moment ago. "Bodyguards?" I asked. "Plan to rough me up the way you did Tooney?"

Adam rubbed his forehead with his free hand, muttering. "I don't know why I don't throw these stupid flowers

on the street and walk away from this nutty place." He
turned to the two men flanking him. "Go find something to
do," he said.

They exchanged a look but didn't argue.

"You try to tell me that SlickBlade is no big deal, yet
you show up here with bodyguards," I said, pointing toward
the departing figures. "We share a flight together with a
killer that *your* band brought on board, and you tell me you
have no idea who she was. Now I find out that you're in
cahoots with Gerard Pezzati." I fisted my hip. "What else
are you hiding?"

" 'In cahoots'?" As he mocked my words, his lip curled.
I got the impression he was tamping down a smile. The
jerk. "Did you really say that?"

"Don't change the subject."

"What I want to know is why you care so much about
my business dealings with Jerry Pezz. That's what I call
him, by the way. It wasn't until your friend—what's his
name?—Tooney—showed up that I remembered Pezz is a
shortened version of Pezzati. I've been working with the
guy for years. To me, he's Pezz."

"Convenient."

He raised the flowers, as though to make a point, belatedly realizing what he was doing. "This is stupid," he said.
He turned and scanned the immediate area. A fortyish
woman, walking alone, was about to pass us. She carried a
reusable grocery bag down by her side and seemed lost in
thought. He intercepted her, smiled, and handed the aston-
ished woman the bouquet. "A beautiful woman deserves
beautiful flowers."

I watched confusion, pleasure, and suspicion cloud the
woman's face, but before she could even thank him, he
stormed back over to me. "Where was I?" he asked.

The woman must have read the situation. She gave a

resigned shrug and continued on her way, a smile playing about her lips. I hoped she wasn't on Frances's team.

"You were about to profess your innocence, no doubt," I said with sharp sarcasm.

He ran both hands up and through his hair. "What does Jerry have to do with you?" he asked in exasperation. "Why would I even think to tell you that I know him? Did you expect me to provide you a list of every person I've ever met in my entire life? You didn't seem all that interested in me; why would I care about my association with Pezz?"

"Why *wouldn't* you tell me about your association with Gerard Pezzati? After all, I told you that—" I stopped as gears began to turn, making clunky connections in my head. I straightened, in delayed realization. "No, I didn't tell you," I said softly. Almost to myself. "Did I?"

Adam didn't answer. He pulled in his bottom lip and chewed on it. He crossed his arms and regarded me with narrowed eyes. "What am I missing?" he finally asked.

I held up a hand, asking him to wait, then covered my eyes as I tried to replay our interactions on board the plane, in the waiting room afterward, even when Adam had come to visit. I'd never mentioned the Pezzati family. To Detective Williamson, yes, but that was in my debriefing. Private. When Bennett and I had talked about the Pezzatis, it had been quietly, away from the others.

I raised my head, meeting Adam's watchful eyes. He was waiting for me to explain. I brought my hand to my mouth. "You didn't know about our visit to Nico Pezzati's villa in Florence, did you?"

He shook his head slowly, hands spread. "Who is Nico?"

I took a deep breath. Gerard Pezzati must have taken advantage of Adam and SlickBlade without their knowledge. I still couldn't figure out how the younger Pezzati had engineered Pinky's place on board the plane, but it was becoming evident that Adam had had nothing to do with it. "I owe you an apology."

"That's the best thing I've heard since I got here."

We needed to talk. Not standing here in the middle of a busy sidewalk, either. My guard still wasn't dropped enough for me to invite him back to my house. "Let's hit Hugo's," I said. "Your friend Jerry Pezz may have used you."

He gave me a patently unconvinced look, but didn't argue.

There were no open tables at Hugo's, so we settled ourselves at the bar with a draft beer for him and a glass of malbec for me. "Gerard Pezzati," I said in a low voice, "is the estranged son of Nico Pezzati, formerly of the United States, but now living in Italy."

Adam took a long drink of his beer, wiping a bit of the foam mustache before answering. "Jerry mentioned some family issues. He doesn't talk about it much. I get the feeling he's been hurt pretty badly."

"The way I hear it, it's the other way around. Did you ever ask how he got started? Why he refuses to talk to his father?"

"Doesn't sound like the Jerry I know, but it's none of my business."

"Could he be scamming you?"

Adam threw back his head to laugh. "You don't know Jerry at all, do you?"

I didn't answer.

He covered his mouth with his hand, and consulted the clock on his cell phone. "I know he had some family thing to go to tonight. Kid's dance recital or something. I don't want to bug him."

"Family?" I asked. "Kids?"

"Yeah," Adam said with a glint in his eye. "I think maybe you've got the wrong guy. You think maybe there are two Gerard Pezzatis out there? Stranger things have happened."

My brain whirled, making me dizzy. And it wasn't from the three sips of wine I'd had. "It can't be. Gerard Pezzati turned his back on his father years ago. He hasn't even tried to contact the man for fourteen years."

"Tell you what," Adam said, "Let's clear this up once and for all. Let's meet tomorrow—you and I—and I'll put you on the phone with Jerry. He can tell you if he's the guy you're looking for. If he is, you can ask him whatever's on your mind. If he's not—well, I guess that means you and I have a chance to be friends then, don't we?"

I studied his face for signs of duplicity. Couldn't find any. I'd been fooled by an attractive face before, however, and I wasn't about to walk into a trap, no matter how unlikely such a prospect seemed. "Meet you tomorrow?" I repeated slowly, wary again now. "Where?"

He'd lifted his glass, but stopped it halfway to his lips. "My suggestion makes you nervous. Am I still so frightening to you?"

I wasn't about to explain the reason for my caution. Too much had gone on in recent months to naively accept whatever strangers swore was true.

"I have a meeting tomorrow," I said, making it up on the spot. "Can I call you in the morning to arrange a time and place? Would that work?"

"Done." He took a swig of his beer.

With our agreement sealed, he relaxed, visibly. His smile was genuine, his body language open. "Interestingly enough," I said, "I'm meeting with Gerard's father and sister tomorrow. They're visiting Marshfield."

His brows came together. "What are the chances of that?" he asked rhetorically. A moment later, he thrust his chin up, eyes taking on a calculating air. "That's a pretty big coincidence, is it?"

I sipped my wine and didn't answer.

* * *

"WHAT HAPPENED?"

"Who was that guy?"

"Why were you arguing with him?"

Bruce's and Scott's questions made it through the back
door and into our kitchen before they did.

Bootsie dove off my lap and bounded to greet them as I
stood. "Busy night at the shop, huh? Sorry for causing a
scene."

Scott waved off my apology. "You provided entertainment. Those flowers he came in with were stunning." He
looked around the room. "Where are they?"

"Gave them away."

I explained over our evening snack. Today it was cheese,
strawberries, and chocolate. A perfectly sweet ending to a
day laced with sour notes.

"What do you hope to accomplish by talking with this
Gerard?" Bruce asked.

"At a minimum, I hope to ensure we've got the right
Pezzati."

Bruce shuddered. "Wouldn't that be a mess if you
didn't?"

"I don't want to think about it," I said. "Assuming we do
have the right man, I think I'll learn a lot by talking with
him. He's far enough away that he can't hurt me, so a little
poking and prodding won't get me into trouble this time. I
have no idea what kind of link I expect to find between him
and Pinky, but I know it's there."

"Be careful, Grace." Bruce said.

"I always am."

Scott wagged a finger. "And we've all seen where that
gets you."

Chapter 30

THE NEXT MORNING, I SAT AT MY DESK, thinking about how disappointed Frances would be when she found out I intended to talk with the elusive Gerard Pezzati on the phone. Our short-lived plans to visit New York City had evaporated with Adam's suggestion.

I'd gotten in early this morning to get a jump on what promised to be a hectic day, but I took a moment to stare out my windows at the gardens below. Jack had been instrumental in bringing the grounds to the exquisite level they now were. Too bad he hadn't devoted that level of attention to his personal relationships.

He seemed to be making a genuine effort to change the way he interacted with others. After all he'd gone through in his life, however, it would be a difficult process. I thought about the family's now-rocky relationship with their father. I thought about Gerard and how that father-son relationship seemed to have been tainted from the start. Such a shame. So much loss. On both sides of the Atlantic.

My desk phone jangled. Bennett.

"How are our weary travelers?" I asked when I picked up. "I take it they're sleeping?"

Bennett sighed, deeply. "Irena is here by herself. Nico couldn't make the trip after all. At the last minute, he ran a fever and his doctors wouldn't allow him to travel, fearing pneumonia. Irena said that she would have preferred to stay home with him while he recuperated, but he's adamant about getting this matter settled."

"I'm sorry to hear that," I said. "Although . . ."

"What's on your mind?"

I scratched my cheek, thinking. "Does she still plan on confronting Gerard? Signor Pezzati wanted a face-off with his son. Is Irena planning to follow through with that?"

"She hasn't indicated otherwise. Why?"

"Irena told me that she and Gerard stay in contact, despite the fact that the son wants nothing to do with his father. I may be in contact with Gerard later today. I'm wondering if there might be a chance to bring them together."

Bennett was silent for a thoughtful moment. "Taking the bull by the horns, eh, Gracie? I see where you're going with this. You want answers about Pinky and you think that by being a fly on the wall during what's certain to be an emotional conflict, you may find all you need."

"It crossed my mind."

"Irena is in one of the guest rooms now. As you predicted, she wanted to see the skull photos immediately. I told her you had them in a safe place. That's the reason for my call. How soon can you bring them up here?"

"I'd really hoped to talk with this Gerard before meeting with Irena . . ." I let the thought hang. "I suppose it can't be helped. I'll be up there—" My cell phone rang and I glanced at the display. To Bennett I said, "Detective Williamson is calling. Let me see what he wants, and I'll be up there as soon as I can."

I hung up one phone and clicked into the other.

"Ms. Wheaton," the detective said. "I have a few questions for you."

"Go ahead."

"That fellow you talked about in New York with the connection to the Curling Weasels?" It wasn't a question, though he phrased it like one. "Gerard Pezzati, doing business as Jerry Pezz."

"What about him?"

"You know we're talking preliminary fact-finding here, don'tcha? It's not like I can ransack the guy's office for information."

"I understand, Detective. Go on."

Before he could answer, I heard the outer office door open and close. Frances was in.

"I'm coming up empty," he said.

"Like he doesn't exist?"

"He exists, all right. That's not in dispute. Thing is, I can't tie him to our friend Diane, aka Priscilla, the one you know as Pinky. Except for the rock band members, I can't tie him to any of the other names you gave me, either. You need to keep in mind that when we've got an aka like this guy is, it takes a little longer to track all connections. I haven't given up, but it's not looking promising."

"You couldn't tie Pinky to any of the members of Slick-Blade either, could you?" I asked, even though I already knew the answer. "I mean, beyond them picking her up the night before the flight."

"Affirmative. I'm coming up empty. Either they're telling the truth or someone has gone to a lot of trouble to cover up tracks. You ask me my opinion, the band's claims ring true. Don't know what to tell you."

I didn't know whether to be elated or disappointed that Adam's story hadn't been shot full of holes.

"Thanks, Detective," I said.

"One more thing. Whatever happened to that flight attendant guy who contacted you? The one you saw hanging around town?"

"Rudy? I asked him to come visit here at Marshfield. Never heard a word. Why? Were you able to track anything down on him?"

"Nothing worth mentioning," he said. "His being a foreigner complicates my investigation, y'understand."

I sighed.

"You have a nice day, ma'am. I'll be in touch."

THE MOMENT THEO SHOWED ME INTO BENnett's study, Irena jumped to her feet, crossing the room in the time it took me to shift the file folder from my hands to snugging it under one arm. She grasped me by my shoulders and kissed me on both cheeks. "So wonderful to see you again, my friend," she said with a warm smile. She glanced back toward Bennett, who, gentleman that he was, had also risen to greet me.

"How was your flight?" I asked.

Bennett returned to his seat in a wing chair while Irena and I sat together on the adjacent divan. Theo hovered. "May I offer you coffee, Ms. Wheaton? Some other beverage?"

Neither Bennett nor Irena had any cups or glasses nearby. "No, thank you, Theo."

The butler turned to Bennett. "Anything else at this time?"

"Thank you, no." Bennett gave a vague wave. "Who comes in for dinner?"

"That would be Thomas, sir. With you having a guest in residence, I can stay longer today, if you like."

"I believe we can muddle through until Thomas gets here."

Theo nodded. "Very good, sir."

The moment he was gone, I turned to Irena. "How's your father? I understand he had a relapse."

She gave me a sad smile. "It is very difficult to watch such a vibrant man lose his strength so quickly." Pointing to a cell phone she'd placed on the low table between us, she asked, "You will not think me rude if I keep this nearby? A nurse is stationed there and will let me know if there are any changes in his condition. Angelo promised updates as well." She rolled her eyes. "For all his ignorance, he is devoted to my father. I cannot abide the man, yet he is there and I am not. I have no choice but to trust him."

Bennett reached forward, giving Irena's knee an avuncular pat. "Your father is strong. I believe he'll come through this."

Irena's eyes teared up. "I don't know what I would do without him. If he were to die, I would have nothing."

Hoping to lessen her melancholy by working together on proving that the skull was replaced, I set the file folder on the table. "Then let's get started."

Irena nodded and scooched forward to get a good look at the photos I'd brought upstairs. "I am hoping there has been some mistake and that the skull—one of my father's prized possessions—has not been stolen."

I opened the folder. "You can keep these," I said as she leaned over the black-and-white prints.

Bennett tapped a finger on one of them. "If we had the skull here, we'd be able to compare—"

"But the skull *is* here," she said, sitting up. "I brought it along. Father insisted. Let me get it." She hurried out of the room, talking over her shoulder. "He said that it's worthless anyway, so what harm was there in my bringing it."

When she returned with the skull in hand, she was still talking. I wondered if she'd stopped while she was out of earshot. "Father wanted you to see it for yourself, Mr. Marshfield," she said, placing it in his lap. "He's depending on you to sign an affidavit for the insurance company."

Bennett hefted the sculpture, examining it head-on before turning it over to check again for the tell-tale mark, explaining what it should look like and where it should be as he did so.

"Such wonderful adventures you and my father shared."

"I'm relieved to know this was insured," he said. A look of longing came across his features. "But the loss of the real skull is beyond tragic. So rare is it that an item is price-less in both monetary and sentimental value." He blinked away his sadness and returned to the business at hand. "Of course I'll be happy to do whatever I can to see that your father is reimbursed. I know how much paperwork is ahead of him."

Irena grimaced. "Tell me about it. An extremely valu-able piece of jewelry went missing several years ago. Father noticed it immediately. He contacted the authorities as well as our insurer. It was horrible. They all swarmed in and treated us like criminals—as though we'd stolen it our-selves." She shuddered.

"Was the piece ever recovered?" I asked.

She shook her head sadly. "We learned our lesson. Ever since then, Father has insisted on a full inventory once a year."

"Who's in charge of the inventory?" I asked.

"Angelo." She made a face. "He must be behind this forgery. I can't imagine how else it could have been accomplished."

Bennett placed the skull on the table between us, then leaned back, steepling his fingers in front of his lips. "An-gelo didn't strike me as a world-class collector. If he is re-sponsible for this theft, he must have connections in the industry."

"Cesare?" I asked, thinking of the Poirot-looking man we'd met at the Pezzati home. "Could he and Angelo be working together?"

She gave a very Italian shrug. "I am here only to enlist your help." She bounced a glance between us. "To ask opinions from both of you."

"Whatever we can do," Bennett said.

She leaned forward, separating the pictures with the tips of her fingers. "These are the originals, yes?" she asked.

"No, I have those in my office. Although they're still in decent shape, we thought it would be best to keep them safe. I made these copies for you. You're welcome to take them."

She nodded, gathering them up and tapping them on the low table, making their edges even. "I assume the insurer will need the originals."

Bennett agreed. "We will be happy to turn them over when the time comes."

"Thank you both, so very much," she said. "I'm sure our insurer will be in touch soon. That is all right with you?"

We assured her that it was.

"Wonderful. I am heartbroken that this happened to my father, but he is truly fortunate to have such good friends."

Her cell phone chirped. She scooped up the device and examined the text message. "My father is resting comfortably," she said, "but I wish to return home as soon as possible to help care for him. I will leave this evening, as soon as I confirm my plane is ready for the return trip."

"Whatever is best for you," Bennett told her. "But it would be a delight to me if you were able to stay for dinner."

She got up and kissed him on one wrinkled cheek. "Of course."

Her phone went off again, this time with a ringtone that signaled an incoming call. She took a look at the display and frowned. Tapping the screen, she silenced the device then glanced up at both of us with ill-concealed anger.

"Something wrong?" Bennett asked.

"My brother calling. I told him of our father's illness, yet he still refuses to see him." She shook her head, fuming. "I will return the call later. Let him wait."

"Your father believes Gerard is behind the thefts," Bennett said.

She wrinkled her nose. "I don't know what to think. I prefer to let the authorities sort everything out. And that is what they will do once they have all the evidence."

"You don't intend to confront Gerard the way your father planned to?" I asked.

"What purpose would that serve? He will deny any responsibility. If he is guilty, he will then know we suspect him. I don't see any good coming of such a meeting. No. I will go home and take great pains to ensure that my father's treasures do not disappear out from under my nose again."

Chapter 31

I'D SILENCED MY PHONE BEFORE HEADING
upstairs. Now, on my way back to my office, I checked it for
messages, discovering a missed call. The number was one
I didn't recognize; it had a New York area code. Whoever
it was had tried to call twice in the past five minutes.

Calls from out of state weren't unusual, but I was surprised that whoever had attempted to reach me hadn't left
a voicemail. The fact that they'd tried again me told me it
wasn't a wrong number.

I shrugged it off. As I took the turn and started down the
final flight of steps, my phone rang. I wasn't surprised to
see the same unfamiliar number. Time to find out what was
so important. I clicked to connect. "Grace Wheaton."

"Thank goodness. This is Jerry Pezz. You know me as
Gerard Pezzati."

I stopped my downward descent. "I thought—"

"Yes, Adam was supposed to meet with you this morning. I know. But this can't wait. I need to speak with you."

The staircase wound up above me to the skylight in the roof. It spiraled down to the sub-basement below. I got an eerie sense of being closed in. Of changes made without my knowledge. Or my consent.

"He gave you my phone number?"

"Could you meet with me? Wherever you want."

"Not a chance," I said with flash fury. Then, remembering the call Irena had refused, I added, "Irena should be calling you back soon. You have a lot to discuss with your sister."

"They've arrived? They're at Marshfield?" I couldn't decide whether the surprise in his voice was anxious or smug. "Will you allow me to come visit? I must see them. Please," he said. "I need to see my father."

"He isn't—"

"I know he doesn't want to see me. But I can't be this close and not make an attempt. I'll try calling Irena again. I'll beg to meet with them. If she agrees, will you allow me to come to your office? From what Adam tells me, you view me as some kind of ogre. I promise you, I'm simply a man who hopes to reconnect with his father before it's too late."

I bit my lower lip. Let Irena break the news to him that his father wasn't here. "Fine," I said, thinking that I'd be sure to have security nearby if Irena allowed the meeting. "But only if your sister says it's all right."

The moment we hung up, I thought to tell Irena about this latest wrinkle, but anger had me dialing Adam's number instead. No answer. Smart man. He must have known I'd ream him out. I'd agreed to talk with Gerard Pezzati, not welcome him as a guest of Marshfield. Too many unanswered questions. Too much at stake.

I pulled up my walkie-talkie and connected to security. Terrence was out of the building, answering a situation at the inn, so I left a message with the dispatcher. "I'm starting to feel the walls caving in," I told her. "I'd like him to keep a close eye on things."

"I'm sorry, Ms. Wheaton. There's a problem with one of the walls?"

I sighed. So much for sharing gut-level concerns. "There's nothing wrong," I said. "Not yet. I'm simply trying to keep ahead of trouble. Can you ask him to stay extra alert?"

"Yes, ma'am."

Frances stood up when I walked into her office. "Your friend Adam called here. He apologized profusely but swears he had no choice." The look on Frances's face told me exactly what she thought of that story. "Apparently he shared your contact information with Gerard Pezzati."

I held up my cell phone. "Just heard from him. Pushy guy."

She harrumphed. "So much for our trip to New York." Pointing toward my office, she said, "You missed a call a moment ago. I was on my phone and couldn't pick up."

"Did you check caller ID to see who it was?"

She pursed her lips. "What do you think?"

"And?"

"No name. A number I didn't recognize."

I returned to my desk and prepared to get started on reports that had piled up of late. Less than ten minutes later, I heard noise from the outer office. Frances had a visitor. There was a low murmur of conversation. Frances sounded ever so huffy as she came around the doorway and marched up to my desk.

I pointed to her office, mouthing a silent question, "Who?"

She gave an indignant head waggle. "You could have told me, you know."

I'd already gotten up and was making my way to the door when she grabbed my arm. "This wing ought to have better security. Any bozo can come in and ask for one of us and get escorted right up. We should put a stop to that. Doris brought this one."

She was right about the security issue; I made a mental note. "Who's here?" I asked again, this time aloud.

Frances made a smacking motion with her mouth as though she couldn't be bothered to answer the question. "See for yourself."

I didn't recognize the man standing next to Frances's desk. Mid-forties, tall and lean, he had a full head of dark hair worn long enough for it to curl a bit below his ears. Perfect teeth practically gleamed as he worked up a smile and moved forward to shake my hand. His eyes were familiar. Dark and tight with worry.

"Grace Wheaton?" He didn't wait for acknowledgment. "Jerry Pezz. But you'll know me as Gerard Pezzati. I know you're not happy to see me, but please hear me out."

In that instant I juggled all sorts of reactions: shock at the man's unannounced appearance, frustration at my ill-preparedness because Frances hadn't given me the courtesy of a heads-up, and panic. Could I be facing the very person who had engineered the attack on Bennett?

I relied on good manners to carry me through my discomposure. "I'm pleased to meet you," I said, ignoring Frances's *hmmph* of annoyance. She made her way to her chair and sat down hard. "After our brief discussion on the phone, I must confess I'm surprised—"

He cut me off. "I apologize for showing up here without forewarning. I tried calling Irena, but she has refused to meet with me."

"Then there really isn't much I can do," I said. "This is a family issue."

"Ms. Wheaton—may I call you Grace?"

I didn't answer.

He didn't really care. "You don't understand how

difficult it has been for me. With my father so close, I need to try. This may be the only chance I'll ever get to see him."

I opened my mouth to answer, but he cut me off again.

"I understand the difficult position I'm putting you in, but Adam tells me . . ." He flicked a glance toward Frances. "Is there a place we can talk?"

Not solely because it would buy goodwill with my assistant, though the thought factored into my decision, I adopted an authoritative tone. "Frances is fully apprised of the situation. We can talk here." I gestured toward one of the open seats across from her, but with a pained expression, he ran a hand up along his temple. He began to pace. Five strides took him to the far wall.

He turned and asked, "Do you have any idea how long it's been since I've spoken with my father?"

I didn't hesitate. "Fourteen years?"

His bottom lip went slack. "How do you know?"

"Your father told us when we visited him in Italy."

Gerard Pezzati blinked. "Why would he tell you that?"

"Isn't it obvious?" I asked. "He's hurt that you haven't been willing to connect with him."

Pezzati clapped arched fingers to his chest. "*I* haven't been willing to connect? *I?*" His hands returned to the sides of his head. With his elbows out and eyes clenched, he resembled a medium attempting to contact the spirit world. "This isn't right," he said. "Why would he say such a thing?"

His eyes flew open when I asked, "Are you trying to tell me that you've attempted to contact your father over the years?"

"Of course." His voice was high and thin. "Many times: when I married; when my children were born. My father has never met my wife or my kids. They are his grandchildren."

Fingers to my temples, I said, "Wait . . . that can't be right."

Gerard Pezzati strode toward me. "I need to see my father," he said. "I know he's here. Adam promises me that
you're an empathetic person. He calls you a kindred spirit.
Perhaps my father will listen to you. Please." Gerard's entire face tightened. Tears welled in his eyes. "I . . . I
miss him."

"I'm sorry, Gerard. Your father isn't here. Your sister
came alone. Your father is too ill to travel."

His clapped his hands over his mouth. "No," he said between tight fingers. "I've been afraid of this." He resumed
pacing, gesticulating in the air and raising his voice. "I
couldn't bear it if my father died before we have the chance
to reconcile. What can I do?" He turned to me. "Perhaps
you, or Mr. Marshfield, could intervene on my behalf?" He
clenched his fingers together in front of his chest, pleading.
"Please. My children need to know their grandfather."

It was a persuasive performance. But if he was telling
the truth about trying to get in contact with his father, then
Irena and Signor Pezzati had lied to us. Why would Bennett's elderly friend make up such a story? I had no answer.
All I knew was that I needed additional information. And
time to sort it out. I wasn't about to get either from Gerard.

"Leave your contact information with Frances," I said,
starting for my office. "I'll be in touch soon."

"Will you talk to my father? Will you ask him to allow
me—to allow my family—to visit?"

"What caused the split?" I asked. "Your father was
vague when we talked with him. Why are you and he
estranged?"

Gerard stiffened. His chin came up and his expression
changed. Like a curtain drawn across an open window, he
closed off with a suddenness that took me aback. "He chose
to believe a servant's word over mine. My father believed
that I sold one of his paintings and kept the money for myself. I would never do such a despicable thing."

"Was the servant Angelo?" I asked. Whoever he was, I got the feeling if he walked in right now, Gerard would tear him apart piece by little piece.

"I don't know Angelo," he said, shaking his head. "No, the man who engineered this windfall is most likely gone now. I pray that he is. How he was able to frame me—to convince my father that it was I who stole one of his irreplaceable treasures and fenced it on the black market—that I will never understand. The servant set me up well—to the point of adding unexplained funds to my accounts without my knowledge."

Perhaps reacting to the expression on my face—such a move seemed unlikely for a thief whose goal was to accumulate wealth—Gerard hurried to explain.

"The cash he added was a fraction of the painting's worth," he said. "But it sealed my guilt. I suppose the thief considered it a small price to pay for getting away with the theft. All fingers pointed to me. My father's was the one that counted." Gerard gave a sad laugh. "I couldn't tell what was more disappointing to him: that he believed I'd cheated my own family, or that I'd gotten so little for his prize."

"Didn't the insurance company investigate?"

Gerard shook his head. "My father was mortified by my supposed thievery. Refused to file a claim. Instead, he disowned me."

"If it wasn't Angelo, who was it?"

"His name was Rudolfo. Close to my age, but cunning and ruthless."

"Rudolfo. Rudy?" I exchanged a glance with Frances, who sat behind her desk, wide-eyed with surprise.

Gerard picked up on that. "You know him?"

I raised both hands, placating him while my mind raced. "I don't know. Perhaps."

Frances grabbed the phone. "I'll call Detective Williamson," she said.

Gerard was beside himself. "What aren't you telling me?"

I made eye contact, trying my best to steady the upset man with the calm demeanor I was working hard to maintain. "I will be in touch with you. Very soon." When he inched forward, I placed both hands on his forearms. "I promise. Leave your contact information with Frances and I swear that as soon as I discover anything for sure, I will let you know."

"This Rudolfo," he said, "he's still working for my father?"

"I don't think so." He relaxed slightly, so I went on, "I don't even know if the man I've encountered is the same one you're speaking of. Give me a little time."

Gerard glanced over to Frances, who was talking quietly on the phone. She picked her head up. "The detective would like to meet and talk about all this. He's not in town yet. Should I have him come by tomorrow?"

"Tomorrow?" Gerard's impatience teetered on explosive.

"You've waited this long. Let me talk with Irena. Let her know what's going on." To Frances, I said, "I never told Irena about Rudy. The guy on the plane, I mean."

Gerard's gaze bounced between us, utterly confused. "Plane?"

"Irena must know that it wasn't you who stole from your father," I said, trying in vain to come up with a reasonable excuse as to why Gerard's sister and father would claim that it was Gerard who refused to make contact after all these years.

"She has been the one person on my side through this ordeal. She's my staunchest supporter," he said. "If only she could make my father understand."

Alarm bells rang yet again. While the original family drama had nothing at all to do with the theft of the Picasso skull, I wanted to understand what was really going on.

"Let me take care of a few things," I said again. "I promise to be in touch."

The moment he was gone, Frances stood. "Do you believe him?"

"I don't know who to believe at this point." I headed into my office and picked up the phone, not at all surprised when Frances followed me in.

"Who are you calling?"

"Bennett," I said. "I'd like to visit with Irena again. We know Gerard's side of the story. Now I'd like to hear hers."

Chapter 32

BENNETT SOUNDED CONFUSED ON THE PHONE. "You're telling me Nico's son is in your office?"

"Was," I corrected. "He left a few minutes ago."

"I don't understand. How did he know to show up at Marshfield? What's his game?"

I regretted not keeping Bennett better informed about the SlickBlade/Pezzati association. "It's a long story. I'll explain when I come upstairs. Is Irena willing to talk? I have a few issues I need cleared up."

"She's arranging for her flight home, but I'll see if she has a few minutes . . ." Bennett put the phone down and I waited. A moment later he was back. "Come right up," he said. "We'll be here."

I'd made it into Frances's office when my desk phone rang. "I'll get it," she said. I stood in front of her desk as she held up a finger, indicating for me to wait. "Yes, yes," she said. "I'll tell her."

When she hung up, she said, "That was the Mister. He

says that he's been thinking about it and it may be safer to give Irena the original photos of the skull to take with her now rather than send them later. He says he's afraid they'll get lost in transit."

"He said that?"

"Word for word."

I twisted my lips. "They're his pictures, he can choose to do what he thinks best, but . . ." I let the thought hang. "I can't help but think Irena might have had a hand in this decision."

"My thoughts exactly."

I hurried to my office, grabbed the album, and placed it on Frances's desk. "Either Gerard or Irena lied to me about their family history. I can't imagine why." I opened the album and turned to the pages featuring the Picasso skull. Working gently, I plucked out the photos I'd given Irena copies of. "Here," I said to Frances. "Hold on to them for me. I'd like to keep them out of harm's way for a while."

"And you think Irena might cause harm?"

"She doesn't seem the type, but I'm not about to take chances."

I KNOCKED ON THE DOOR TO BENNETT'S rooms a few minutes later, abridged album in hand. "Gracie," he boomed as he stepped aside to allow me in. "You know you don't have to knock. Come right in."

"It's weird not to have Theo or another one of the butlers answer the door," I said. "But it does feel more homey when you do it."

"I prefer it this way, myself."

I followed him back into the study. "Where's Irena?" I asked.

He pointed toward the wing with the guest rooms. "Her flight has been delayed. Mechanical issue. She's on the phone with them now to pin down a scheduled departure. No sense in leaving here until she gets the all-clear. I know Nico will be relieved to have her back." He reached for the album and lifted it out of my hands. "And he'll be especially glad to have these."

"About that," I began, but was interrupted by Irena's return.

"Oh Grace, I am so happy to see you here. What a turn of events! My flight is back on schedule," she said, barely taking a breath. Spying the album in Bennett's hands, she walked over to him, still talking to me. "I can't believe my brother came to see you. He was here, in this house?"

"He left a short while ago."

"And this is the album with photos of my father as a young man," she said. "I am excited at the prospect of seeing all these wonderful pictures. I know these will give my father a thrill. I can't wait to show this to him."

She started to open the book, but I stopped her. "Your brother told me that he's tried in vain to reconnect with your father over the years. Yet you and your father claim that he hasn't even made an attempt in the past fourteen."

She gave me a patient smile. "I'm not surprised."

"What happened fourteen years ago?" I asked.

Irena walked over to the sofa and sat. The fake skull still watched us from the low table next to Irena's purse. She inched it to the side to make room for the album and looked up at me. "What did he tell you?"

"He seems to be doing well for himself. Not at all the picture of the destitute, desperate man you painted."

"Your tone, Grace," she said with an inquisitive air, "has changed. Are you doubting what I told you?"

Bennett touched me on the elbow. "What's going on, Gracie?"

Addressing Irena, I said, "Your brother tells me he wants nothing more than to see your father again. He was very convincing. Maybe if you told me your side, I'd be able to connect the dots."

"It is a long, ugly story."

I sat next to her. "I have time."

"I do as well," Bennett said. "Perhaps it would be best if you started at the beginning." He came around to the other side of Irena as she pulled the album onto her lap. The three of us sat there, Irena like the mom preparing to read a story to her two eager kids.

Her purse chirped. Looking grateful for the delay, she reached in and pulled out her cell phone. "My flight," she said by way of explanation. "Excuse me."

She checked her text, replied, then returned the device to her purse. "Everything is set. They're ready whenever I am."

I placed my hand on the album. "Before you go, please: We'd like to know why you told us Gerard refused to talk to your father, when the opposite is true."

She shook her head and took time to make eye contact with both of us before she sat back and sighed. "My brother is a compulsive liar. He's very good at it. Very practiced. I'll bet he told you about his wife and children, too."

"He did," I said.

Bennett exclaimed, "What is this? He has a family? Does Nico know?"

"There is no family," she said with profound sadness. "He lies. Believe me when I tell you that every time I have attempted to facilitate discussion between the two men it has resulted in disappointment for my father. I now refuse to try anymore."

I'd believed Gerard. I'd been so certain. My heart heaved.

"What I don't understand . . ." I began, but was interrupted by familiar voice down the hall.

"Yoo-hoo," Hillary called. "Are you up here, Papa Bennett?"

"In here." Bennett stood. I followed. Irena fumbled with the album, but then got to her feet, too.

Hillary came around the corner all smiles, wearing a tight skirt and stiletto heels that had to be murder to walk in. In her arms, she carried what looked like a giant photo album. "I brought my client here to see the rooms for himself." Her high-pitched voice evidenced her eagerness to impress as she tiptoed into the room. "He was so enraptured by my portfolio." She patted the book in her arms for emphasis. "I know you won't mind."

Bennett thundered his disapproval. "My rooms are not a showplace."

He'd barely gotten the words out before Hillary's companion followed through the doorway after her.

I gasped. "Rudy."

Chapter 33

I TURNED TO FACE BENNETT. "CALL SECURITY,"
I said. "It's Rudy."

From behind Hillary, the would-be flight attendant
smiled. "Why are you so afraid of me, Miss Grace? Didn't
I save you from that terrible fanatic on the airplane?"

Hillary's head twisted back and forth between us. "You
know each other?"

Bennett hadn't hesitated when I sent him to the phone,
but Irena had grabbed his arm and was holding tight. "Rudolfo," she said. "There must be some mistake."

"No mistake," I said. There wasn't time to explain about
how Rudy had killed Pinky on the flight over. There was no
longer any doubt in my mind that the two of them had
started out working in collusion, but when Pinky wavered
and looked ready to spill her secrets, Rudy had taken
her out.

I started for the phone myself.

To my surprise, Rudy didn't stop me. Instead he gripped

Hillary's upper arm and pushed her farther into the room. "Go ahead," he said to me. "But you may want to reconsider before you pick up that phone . . ." Using two fingers of his free hand to resemble a gun, he pointed to Irena.

I spun. She held a hypodermic needle to Bennett's neck.

"If only you hadn't meddled on the flight, Grace," she said, shaking her head. "What were you thinking?"

Hillary was making little squeaking noises, sounding like a teenage girl who'd spotted a hairy spider. The logical part of my brain wanted her to shut up. The rest of me went into immediate shock. Irena was almost as tall as Bennett, and she held him in a powerful hold. The needle running alongside his neck made a sick indentation.

Irena's eyes were bright. "You're going to follow my instructions now. Do you understand?"

"What's in the needle?" I asked.

"Thorazine. Same drug Pinky tried, but in a different form. This dosage should take your boss out permanently. This time, I'm making sure it gets done correctly."

"What good will it do you?" I asked. "I'm here. Hillary's here. You'll never get away with it."

"Don't worry. We came prepared for contingencies." She guided Bennett backward around the sofa and gestured toward the low table with her chin. "Pick up the album and give it to Rudolfo."

"They're not in there," I said.

"What's not in there?"

"The pictures of the skull. The originals." I thanked my lucky stars that I'd pulled them out. It bought us time. To do what? I didn't have a clue.

I moved to the table, reached over the skull and picked up the album. I paged through. "See?" I said when I got to the page with the missing photographs. "This is where they belong. They're not here."

Irena's teeth came together in irritation. I watched her

knuckles go white around Bennett's bicep. Could he take her down without getting injected? I didn't know. I read the question in his eyes: He didn't know, either. She was younger, lithe, strong.

Behind me, Rudy held a similar grip on Hillary, whose squeaking had morphed into low whimpers.

Rudy whispered next to her ear, but I was close enough to make out his words. "There's nothing to fear. This is but a minor inconvenience. Have faith."

I faced Irena, sensing that she was the leader of this outrageous coup. "Don't do this, okay? You don't really want to hurt anyone. I know it. I'll go get you the originals, and Bennett and I will promise never to speak of the skull, to anyone."

I chanced a look at him. Lips tight, his eyes blazed. He'd never agree to keep a conspiracy quiet. I stared, willing him not to voice such a sentiment aloud. We needed to buy time.

"It's too late," Irena said. "Thanks to you, my father already believes that the original has been stolen. He's initiated a more intense inventory, one that will uncover all the other forgeries. If he discovers that I'm behind this, he'll kick me out."

Their faces inches apart, Bennett turned to her, contempt in his eyes. "Your father would give his life for you. When he hears about this, your betrayal will kill him."

Irena's expression was animated, filled with spirited fury. "That is why he must never find out. As long as he's alive, I have access to his possessions. The moment he dies, everything goes to the town." She spat on the floor. "Wasted."

"How long have you been stealing from your father?" I asked.

"We need the originals," she said, not answering me. Addressing Rudy but indicating Hillary, she asked, "Can we trust that one? Send her for them."

"She doesn't know where they are," I said. "I do."

Rudy's whispered words had had an effect on Bennett's stepdaughter. Although she remained in his grip, she'd quieted. Holding tight to her portfolio the way a drowning person might clutch a life preserver, she sent quick glances back and forth across the room as though trying to understand what was going on.

Irena pushed Bennett around and forced him to sit on the sofa. She remained standing next to him, cupping his upward-tilted chin in one hand and keeping the needle tight against his neck with the other. "I don't believe in stalemates," she said. "I believe in winning."

"You can't win. Not without those originals."

"Sure about that, are you?" she asked. Shifting her attention to Rudy, she said, "Sit the stepdaughter here, where I can keep an eye on her."

Rudy complied, speaking in low tones. As he guided Hillary onto the cushion next to Bennett, I heard him say, "I will take care of you. Trust me."

Irena must have heard him, too. Her eyes widened ever so slightly, but then a smile played across her lips as though she was privy to an inside joke. "Rudolfo," she said in an ultra-feminine coo, "is this the woman you told me about? The one you intend to marry and share your wealth with?"

For her part, Hillary remained stoic. She stared up at Irena. "He didn't tell me about you."

Deception curled behind Irena's eyes. "Rudolfo and I go way back. We're friends. Dear friends." She locked eyes with him. An undercurrent passed between them, something deep and dark. Hillary missed it.

"He's not going to marry you, Hillary," I said as pieces of the puzzle plopped into place—much too late for my tastes. I turned to Rudy. "That was the line you fed Pinky, wasn't it?"

"Pinky?" Hillary said the name with a combination of surprise and disdain. "Who's Pinky?"

"The woman Rudy killed on the flight over from Italy," I said. "Or didn't he tell you about that?" Taking a chance, I fabricated, "For what it's worth, I think he was truly in love with the woman. You should have seen the looks that passed between them. A lot like the way Irena is gazing at him now. If he wasn't so afraid of her," I pointed, "I'll bet he and Pinky would have run off."

Rudy glared. "Shut up."

"Stop." Irena's face was puffed and reddening. "We will have to leave the originals here." She shook her head like a dog shaking off water. "There is no other way. My father will be so stunned and saddened to learn of his friend's death that he will put aside the matter of the skull for a while." She fixed her attention on Rudy. "That will be long enough for you to make the necessary adjustments to that skull to fool my father, yes?"

"Of course," Rudy said.

Irena was to my far left. Bennett next to her on the sofa. Hillary next to him. Rudy stood to my far right. All of them glanced at the low table, where the skull sat before me.

I picked it up and turned it over, pointing to the spot where the *P*-shaped blemish should have been. "There's no way he'll fall for that. He's seen this one, hasn't he?"

Irena's eyes lit up. "He asked me to check for him. At that point, I knew better than to lie. You two have truly spoiled what was a perfectly wonderful plan." Her tone changed, and I got the impression she was deciding her next moves aloud. "I'll tell him I misunderstood the mark he described, and that just before the honorable Bennett Marshfield died, he verified that this skull was genuine."

"He won't find it suspicious that I'm dead, too?"

Frankly perplexed, she said, "How would he ever find

out?" She looked up at Rudy. "It's time to go. Is she coming with us?"

Hillary, sitting below and between the two, looked like a child waiting for approval from her parents. "You can't kill Papa Bennett," she said in a small voice.

Irena shot her a quick, indulgent look. "Not only can we kill him, we've taken steps to pin the deed on you. You can either come with us voluntarily or stay here and try to beat an accusation of murder." Wiggling her perfectly trimmed brows, she returned her attention to me. "Double murder, I mean."

This was all too much for Hillary. "But I'm not guilty of anything," she protested. "Rudolfo told me he wanted to hire me. That's all." Scooting forward on the cushion, she instinctively faced Irena. "You can't do this."

Irena's attention shifted at Hillary's outburst. It could very well be the only chance I'd get.

With one word—*please*—screaming in my brain, I hefted the skull at Irena, aiming for her head. She caught the movement out of the corner of her eye a split second too late to react. Either my aim was off, or the skull's weight factored in more than I'd anticipated. The noggin caught her center mass, knocking her backward. The hypodermic needle somersaulted in front of Bennett, who tried to catch it midair. He missed.

I didn't hear or see it land because I was in motion, tackling Irena, as she, Hillary, and Rudy shouted and cursed in surprise. "Get the needle," I yelled to Bennett.

He ignored me, jumping to his feet to go after Rudy.

Irena was strong, but I was bigger and younger. She bared her teeth as I used my body to keep her down on the floor. Arms flailing, she kicked and bucked, doing her utmost to throw me off. I felt as though I was on one of those fake bulls in a country bar. "You're done, Irena," I shouted over her panting breaths. We needed help and we needed it fast. "You're done."

Her jaw clenched and she pushed upward again. "I. Will. Not." With a surge of force, she hit my back with her knees, my face with the heels of her hands. Sweat poured down my face, into my eyes. My left arm jammed against her neck, I hauled back with my right fist and slammed it into her cheek. She cried out.

She wasn't knocked unconscious, but at least I'd slowed her down.

I glanced up, past the sofa next to us, to see that Bennett was losing ground with Rudy. Bennett was on the floor, doing his best to scuttle away. Rudy drew back his right foot as though to land a vicious kick. "Hillary," I screamed. "Get the needle. Hurry."

Bennett stared up at Rudy, no longer crab-walking backward. I watched stern determination, coupled with fury, take over his patrician features. Just as Rudy went in for the cruel strike, Bennett swept a foot out and whacked Rudy's stationary leg. The younger man went down—a tumble of bones banging against the wood floor.

"Yes!" I shouted.

Irena continued to fight, and although I strained to keep her down, Bennett's move had emboldened me. "Hillary, the needle!"

Still looking as though she didn't completely understand, she at least heard me that time. She crouched for a moment then stood, holding the needle upright, like a wild-eyed nurse ready to give a shot to a screaming toddler. The liquid inside hadn't been released yet.

Rudy was on his feet in a moment, but his spill had given Bennett enough time to crawl across the floor and retrieve the skull. He stood now, holding it, looking like a shot-putter ready to wing it at Rudy's head. I'd bet Bennett's aim was better than mine. From the look in his eyes, Rudy thought so too. They stared at one another, breaths coming in wheezed gasps.

Irena fought me, but we both knew she was down for good.

"Hillary, go call for help," I said.

She turned her blonde head toward Rudy. "Was this all planned? You weren't interested in my designs? You weren't interested in me?"

Irena's voice was strangled but still strong. "Of course he is. He plans to marry you. He told me. He loves you and he's rich. Very rich. Who do you think has been able to sell all the goods I've taken from my father? Rudolfo is wealthy beyond your wildest dreams."

Bennett and Rudy were frozen at one end of the room. Irena and I entangled on the floor at the other. Hillary stood between us, alone, gazing at Rudy with puzzled, hopeful eyes.

"Don't believe them, Hillary," I said. "I don't know what their game is, but don't be foolish. They're lying to you."

Beneath me, Irena ceased her struggle. She coughed, using whatever she had left to inject authority into her voice. "I'm not the liar here. Grace and Bennett have been lying to you. Or wait, didn't you know?"

Chapter 34

HILLARY TWISTED TOWARD IRENA.

"They haven't told you, have they?" Irena asked. For being held hostage on the floor, her eyes were bright with triumph.

"Told me what?"

A growl rose in my chest, crawling from my throat as I tightened my grip on Irena. "It isn't true."

Hillary's brows came together, her voice high. "What isn't true?"

Irena took as deep a breath as she could, considering I was sitting on her chest. "You want to know why your step-father favors this woman," she said, indicating me with a derisive glance.

Despite herself it seemed, Hillary asked, "Why?"

With her back on the floor, Irena still behaved as though holding court. I wanted to punch her in the face again. I wanted to shut her mouth. I couldn't do it. She was down.

To beat her senseless would have been wrong. No matter how much I dreaded her next words.

"Grace is his niece." Irena waited a moment for that to sink in. "She's his blood relative. His heir."

"What?" Hillary asked, looking ready to laugh for a half second before allowing for the possibility. She looked at me, at Bennett, at me again. "What?"

"He's planning to change his will," Irena said. "He told my father. You'll be cut out completely. So too, the city of Emberstowne. Grace will get it all."

"That's not true," I said.

"But it is." Irena was utterly calm now. "That's your future, Hillary. Nothing for you. Everything for her. Unless . . ."

Hillary took a step closer. "Unless?"

"There's enough Thorazine in there for both of them. We inject them both, and Rudolfo and I leave." The glimmer in her eyes was back as she regarded Rudy. "You stay, collect whatever inheritance you still have, and Rudolfo comes back for you when things settle down."

"Hillary, they're using you."

"Ha!" Beneath me, Irena's chest rose and fell with her barked laugh. "It is they who have been using you."

"What about all that evidence?" Hillary asked, staring at the needle she still held vertically in her hand. "You said you would pin the murders on me."

"Yes," Bennett said. "Good girl. You're thinking for yourself. Don't be pulled in by their nonsense."

"Why would we try to frame you if you're our friend?" Irena asked.

Rudy took a step away from Bennett. "I promised I would take care of you. You are my life. I will not go back on this promise. Hand me the needle, sweetheart."

She took a step away from him. I guessed it to be involuntary because the look on her face was one of doe-eyed puzzlement. She bit her lower lip and looked ready to cry.

Bright eyes lasered in on Bennett. "Is this true?" she asked. "Is Grace your niece?"

When he took a deep breath and let it out, Hillary's eyes shimmered with tears.

"We don't know, Hillary," he said. "That's the truth. But if you're asking if it's possible, then yes, it is."

She stomped a foot. "Why didn't you tell me?"

Bennett never let his attention waver from Rudy. "We can talk about this later. Right now, you need to call security. Please, Hillary."

"Don't do it," Irena shouted. "Look at the two of them together. You can see what your future holds. They'll shut you out. They'll call you family to your face, but snicker behind your back."

"Hillary," Rudy said, drawing out the syllables. "You are my love. Please don't disappoint me. Not now when we are so close."

Hillary stared at the hypodermic needle.

"It won't hurt them," Irena coaxed. "They won't suffer. It will be over quickly. So quick, and your life will be forever changed. For the good."

"You can't," I said. "Hillary, you can't—"

"Don't tell me what I can and can't do," she snapped.

I couldn't read her expression. With her teeth firmly clamped on her lower lip, she turned wide, sad eyes to Rudy. "Look at me and tell me how much you love me," she said.

Rudy swallowed, worked up a smile and made eye contact. I could see how Hillary had been pulled in by the sincerity in that lying face. He had it down. Expressive, dark eyes gazed at Hillary as though she were the only person in the world who meant anything to him. Maybe because in this moment, it was true. She held his fate as firmly as she held his stare.

Bennett launched the skull. It hit the man like one

linebacker head-butting another. Rudy went down, flat as a board.

Hillary screamed. Openmouthed, she stared at Bennett, who walked slowly toward her, reaching with both hands. "Give me the needle, Hillary. Let's put an end to this."

Hillary shook her head, stepping away. "Wait." Tears streaked down her reddening cheeks. She stared with child-like woe, her voice plaintive. "You're all the family I have. You were going to forget me and give everything to her?" She indicated me with a sideways gesture of her head.

Irena singsonged, "That's right, Hillary."

Bennett didn't waver. "I would never have cut you out. You know that. Look deep in your heart, child. Have I ever forsaken you?" He took a step closer. "You know I care about you."

"But, she—"

"Grace is part of the family now, whether or not she ever agrees to the test to prove it. That's the truth I believe and the truth you will learn to accept. We are family. The three of us. Do you understand?"

"Don't be fooled," Irena shouted. "He'll say anything right now. It's not too late. Come away with us."

Hillary straightened her shoulders.

A door banged open down the hall. "Mister Marshfield," Frances called. "Where are you? Grace?"

"In here," I shouted. "Call security."

She rounded the corner, surveying the room with one sweep. "Already done," she said as three of our guards swarmed in behind her. Hillary dropped the hypodermic needle onto the table, backing away as soon as it left her hands. She made eye contact with Bennett and mouthed, "I would never have hurt you."

He leaned down and picked it up. "Call the police," he said to one of the guards. To Hillary, he said, "I know you wouldn't have."

Frances came over to us on the floor. She folded her arms across her ample chest and stared down. "Well, well, well," she said to me. "Let me guess. You've solved another murder for the Mister, haven't you?"

With the three men taking charge of Irena and Rudy, I scrambled to my feet. "Thanks, Frances. Impeccable timing." Hillary looked away. "How did you know to come up here?" I asked my assistant. "How did you know to bring reinforcements?"

"I didn't," she said. "It was a hunch. You're teaching me some very bad habits. Next thing you know I'll be fighting killers in hand-to-hand combat."

"Let's hope not," Bennett said.

She frowned at him. "Why should she have all the fun?"

Chapter 35

WHEN BENNETT INKED THE FINAL DOCU-
ments to close his agreement with Vandeen Deinhart, I
breathed a sigh of relief that that chapter was now closed.
Two days later, Detective Williamson arrived at Marshfield. It had been almost a week since Irena and Rudy's
skirmish in Bennett's study above, and the detective had
offered to bring us all up to speed on what had happened
since then. I'd insisted on bringing in Ronny Tooney for the
discussion because his undercover work—though it had
given him more grief than he needed—had helped us a
great deal.

Just before Williamson called the meeting to order, I
pulled Hillary to the side. "For what it's worth," I said, "I
know what you're going through."

Her eyes narrowed, gauging my sincerity.

It was painful to admit, but I had to let her know she
wasn't alone. "Not that long ago, a man played on *my* emotions to try to harm Bennett."

She gave the barest of nods.

"All I want to say, Hillary, is that I get it. It hurts. And I'm sorry you had to go through it."

"You mean that?"

"Yeah," I said. "The one good thing that came out of it is that I'm stronger now. I'll bet you'll feel the same way soon. You deserve better." I patted her on the shoulder. "Give yourself time, though. It's still too raw right now, isn't it?"

The tip of her nose went pink. She looked ready to respond, but at that moment Williamson called for our attention and we settled ourselves. As the hazy, late afternoon sun moved low in the sky, casting my office in a cool glow, the detective walked back and forth in front of my desk while Bennett, Hillary, Frances, Tooney, and I sat in chairs like students waiting for a lecture we were actually interested in.

"Now that we have key players in custody, we're able to put the story together," Williamson said. "Irena and Rudolfo had been working together for years. Together they engineered a falling-out between her brother and father. She worked hard to make both believe she was on their side against the other. Truth is, she lied to both." Pointing to me, he said, "Your guess about Pinky, aka Diane Waters, was right on. She was pulled into cooperation with promises of a fabulous future with the handsome Rudolfo. We unearthed one of Diane's best friends, who was happy to tell us about the handsome man Diane thought would whisk her away from her unhappy life. Truth was . . ."

Here it comes. I slid a sideways glance at Hillary.

"Rudolfo was Irena's second husband. Seems they met while he was employed at her father's villa. To keep their relationship secret, they divorced but maintained a clandestine affair."

Hillary's shoulders dropped almost imperceptibly. Her chin came up, though. I thought that was a good sign.

"Let me get everything straight," I said. "Gerard Pezzati never stole from his father."

"Correct."

"What about Angelo, Signor Pezzati's assistant? Or Cesare, his art-collecting expert? Were either of them in on it?"

Williamson had stopped walking back and forth across the room. He stood now with his arms folded. "Both completely clean. As is the former cook, Antoinette. In order to cover her tracks, Irena needed to maintain the illusion that Gerard had connections to someone inside the house. That's where our friend Pinky comes in. Working as a maid there, she set up bogus e-mail accounts and made sure they were found when the accountant noticed that money was missing. Irena masterminded the whole thing, but Rudy ensured Pinky's cooperation."

"What about that Adam fellow?" Frances asked. "I can't believe that his band, SlickBlade"—she said it with dripping disdain—"*happened* to run into Pinky and *happened* to invite her on their flight. That's too much coincidence for me."

"That's where Gerard Pezzati comes in," Williamson said. "Remember, he trusted his sister. They talked and e-mailed quite often. Irena knew that her brother had a group heading back to the States. She and Rudy made a lot of promises to Pinky. All they asked her to do was poison Bennett's food." He set his mouth in a thin line.

"And our original pilot, who was arrested for assault?" I asked. "Was that all part of the plan?"

Williamson nodded, again like a teacher. I felt like the star student who'd figured out the answer to a trick question. "Irena arranged for that," he said. "Trumped-up charges held long enough to get you onto that fateful flight. If the option for the SlickBlade charter hadn't been available to her, I have no doubt she would have come up with another plan. She's wily. A tough cookie. I've encountered that type before. Like cats, they always land on their feet." He smiled. "But not this time."

"If Gerard Pezzati hadn't come to visit me, I don't know that I would have had as many doubts about Irena's story as I did," I said. "Gerard's appearance made me start to question what I thought I knew."

Williamson pointed at Tooney. "Good thing you came out to New York. While I can't advocate your methods, I will admit that you got things started in the right direction. Irena's story held up as long as no one heard her brother's side. Once the truth came out, she had to scramble."

"I did my best," Tooney said shyly.

I leaned over and patted him on the knee. "You've never let us down."

Tooney smiled, a transformative look for his homely face.

"Why did Rudy leave the note on my car?" I asked Williamson.

Williamson shrugged. "Our best guess is that he knew you'd spotted him. Or that he believed you might find out about him working with Hillary."

She squirmed.

"Lies are more effective when based in truth. In the same way, actions are less suspicious when the guilty party calls attention to them." He looked at us all, but his gaze came to rest on Hillary. "They were masters of deceit. There's no shame in having fallen for their lies."

"I wasn't going to do it," Hillary said to the group. She turned to Bennett. "Remember? I made Rudolfo look at me at just the right moment." She turned to me. "I did, didn't I?"

"What is she talking about?" Williamson asked.

Bennett and I exchanged a look. We hadn't shared the specifics of those last moments in Bennett's study before Frances's arrival. Not with anyone, even Frances.

"Hillary means she wasn't going to allow anyone to hurt me or Grace," Bennett said smoothly. "Like she said, if she hadn't been there to distract Rudy, I don't know that Grace and I could have gotten away safely. Isn't that right, Grace?"

"Absolutely," I said.

Hillary sat up a little straighter. She stared up at Williamson. "Yes, that's exactly what I was saying. I would never let anything happen to my *family*."

Frances jabbed me in the ribs with her elbow. I ignored her.

THAT NIGHT, AFTER AMETHYST CELLARS closed for the evening, Bruce, Scott, and I sat at a tall table in Hugo's bar area to celebrate the fact that Bennett and I were still alive and that all was right in Emberstowne once again.

"What about Signor Pezzati?" Bruce asked, taking a swig from his beer bottle. "What does he think about all this?"

I kept my hands wrapped around the base of my wineglass. "I'm getting all of it secondhand from Bennett, you understand, but Signor Pezzati is quite healthy. He had a little cold, that's all. He hasn't been fighting pneumonia. Irena made that up, too. All these revelations have come as a bit of shock to him, as you might imagine, but Gerard and his family are traveling there now. Signor Pezzati will meet his daughter-in-law and his grandchildren for the first time. I understand he got quite choked up to discover that his son made such a success of himself."

"I love a story with a happy ending," Bruce said.

"What about that bodyguard guy—Angelo?" Scott asked. "The one you didn't like?"

"Turns out he didn't like Irena, but knew better than to disparage her in front of her father. He didn't trust her. He tried, apparently without much luck, to institute controls on Pezzati's treasures. That's probably one of the things they were arguing about when we saw them." I swirled the red wine in my glass. "I wish them all the best, but I don't think I want to go back."

"You brought a family together again," Bruce said. "Not for the first time."

I thought about that. "Why does bringing people together always seem to also involve tearing them apart?"

"You aren't responsible for that," Scott said. "People make their own choices and have to live with the consequences."

I nodded but didn't want to answer. Instead, I took a sip of wine.

My two roommates looked up at once, focusing over the top of my head.

I turned, stifling a little gasp of surprise.

"Adam," I said. "What are you doing here?"

His smile was tentative, shy. "I don't really know," he said. "It's not like fireworks go off for you whenever I show up. At least not the good kind." He shrugged. "But now that you know I'm no villain, I thought maybe we could try being friends." He gestured toward Bruce and Scott. "If I'm intruding, though, I'll leave you alone."

I turned to my roommates, who looked as surprised as I felt. Bruce gripped his beer bottle, frozen in place. Scott rested his chin in his hand, watching me. All three men were engaged, observant, waiting for me to make the next move. I looked at Adam. He raised those expressive brows, asking a silent question.

For the first time since we'd met, I felt a flicker of possibility.

I scooched my chair over to make room. "Pull up a seat."

NEW FROM ANTHONY AND BARRY AWARDS WINNER

JULIE HYZY

GRACE UNDER PRESSURE

Everyone wants a piece of millionaire Bennett Marshfield, owner of Marshfield Manor, but now it's up to the new curator, Grace Wheaton, and handsome groundskeeper Jack Embers to protect their dear old Marshfield. But to do this, they'll have to investigate a botched Ponzi scheme, some torrid Wheaton family secrets—and sour grapes out for revenge.

penguin.com

M762T0511